# *Guardians*
## Carter's Story Pt. 1
By
M. J. Brown

This book is dedicated with love and eternal gratitude to my grandparents, Harry and Hilda Brown. Him for teaching me how to tell a good story and her for showing me how to write it.

I love you both. xx

# CONTENTS

# I

Squinting through the gloom, Carter tried penetrating the inky depths of the undergrowth before him with his eyes, without success; even if there was a child in there – or ten of them for that matter – he couldn't see anything, it was too dark. High above, the silvery crescent of the moon hung in the sky, its light too weak to be of any use.

With a sigh he straightened, his breath pluming out in front of him as he did so, a reminder – as if the numbing of the tops of his ears and fingertips weren't enough – just how bitterly cold it was out here. Suddenly, feeling wetness seep into one of his shoes, he realised he was standing on the edge of a puddle and, with a loud curse, stepped back, irritated, despite the gravity of the situation.

Clamping his teeth together to stop them chattering, he angled his head and listened for the sound of movement, but there was nothing. Beginning to wonder if he'd made a mistake and it wasn't even in there, somewhere behind him he heard a rustle; probably some woodland creature going about its nightly foraging he thought, glancing round. Addressing the bush again, his voice echoed through the trees, sounding shockingly loud. "Is anyone in there?"

*Nothing.*

Clearly, the child had no intention of answering. Or maybe it couldn't. Maybe it was injured or in shock or just plain scared. Not that he blamed it he thought; down here in the dark, eerie didn't even begin to cover it. With his bravado evaporating fast, turning his head, he saw the reassuring glow of his headlights higher up on the road, through the trees. Not sure what to do for the best, he didn't like the idea of leaving it down here on its own while he went to get help – clearly, something terrible must have happened for it to be tearing through the countryside in the middle of the night; on the other hand, he was getting nowhere fast and might not have any choice.

At last, having decided to return to the car and call the police on his mobile, he suddenly heard the sound of twigs snapping out among the trees. As he did so, he felt his heart skip a beat as he realised it was too purposeful, too deliberate to be an animal. Trying not to slip on the icy mud he turned and swept the darkness with his eyes, trying to see everywhere at once. "Who's there?"

*silence*

As loud as the crack of a rifle in the deathly silence, somewhere off to the right, he heard another snap.

*"I know you're there!"* he shouted, hoping he sounded braver than he felt.

Suddenly, as if on cue, all around him, rustling sounds began springing up, alarm stealing over him as he realised he was surrounded. Bending, he snatched a stout-looking stick from the ground before standing stiffly with it in his hand, all the sounds fading away again as he did so.

*what the*

And then, unbelievably, he heard something else – something so strange he wasn't sure if it was real or just his mind playing tricks on him – a chorus of soft voices whispering his name in his head.

2

*Carter*

Before he had time to think about it however, chillingly, he heard movement behind him – this time from the shrubbery – the sound of someone pushing their way through and, swinging round, he narrowed his eyes at it, able to make out a pale shape deep within it now. With his heart pounding, he took a few steps back, watching wide-eyed as it pushed its way closer. *"Who are you? What do you want?"* he shouted.

At the sound of his voice, for a moment it paused before moving forward again until, at last, with unseen hands it parted the branches and stepped out into the open. At the sight of it shock hit Carter with all the force of a speeding train and, crying out he recoiled, staring at it wide-eyed with horror, the stick falling uselessly to the ground. As it stepped towards him, a child-like scream pierced his mind

*what is it dad*

and, turning, he bolted before bouncing from tree to tree like a pinball, oblivious to the thorns and brambles that snagged his clothes and skin as he shot through them.

*you know what it is*

Suddenly, he realised the headlights were no longer in sight and, in panic he spun, raking the darkness with his eyes before seeing them off to the right. Filled with relief, on legs that felt like lumbering pieces of timber, he propelled himself forward, making a beeline for them, determined not to lose sight of them again. With gravity working against him he toiled up the slope towards the road, suddenly freezing as he heard the sound of running feet behind him, realising he was being chased!

3

*OH-GOD-NO*

Feeling his knees buckle, all of a sudden, he heard another voice – his dad's this time – screaming at him

*RUN*

and, with a reserve of strength he'd never believed possible, staggered forward again, heading for the bank, expecting to be jumped at any moment. Clambering up the slope, with the trees above him illuminated by the headlights, at last he reached the top and charged for the road, only too late remembering the gulley he'd leapt over when he'd first entered the woods. With his arms pin-wheeling wildly in mid-air he lurched headlong into it, frantically clawing his way up the other side even before he'd stopped rolling. At last, cresting the ridge, he streaked out from the tree line and, unable to stop, crashed into the side of the car, knocking the breath from his lungs as he did so. Crying out, with his ribs singing, he fumbled the door open and, throwing himself inside, hit the lock. As stars exploded in his vision, he clutched the steering wheel and, dropping his head, sucked in vanilla and mango scented air, at the same time willing himself not to black out.

Raising his head once more, he gaped in horror at the sight of a large, bulbous head rising up from the gulley, its eyes the thing of nightmares, insectile and as black as night. Aided by stick-thin arms, it

*you know what it is*

pulled its spindly body upwards quickly followed by another right behind it, the pair of them straightening before turning to stare at him. Shaking his head he made a strange inhuman sound in his throat, as more began to appear,

4

*three-four-five*

all of them pulling themselves upright before standing in a row and staring at him, starkly illuminated in the headlights against the backdrop of trees.

*Caarter*

Not daring to take his eyes off them for a second, in panic he fumbled for the keys in the ignition, accidentally plunging the car into darkness. With a cry he twisted them again and, as the headlights blazed, saw there were even more of them now.

*you know what they are*

Tearing his eyes from the gulley he released the handbrake and, stomping on the accelerator, with a squeal of brakes, quickly shot forward, the strange chorus of voices in his mind dwindling as he did so. Clasping the steering wheel in a white-knuckled death-grip he fought the urge to look back, instead trying to concentrate on the road ahead, the thought of crashing out here with those things, terrifying. Following the road through the wood, a few minutes later he shot out from the canopy of semi-naked trees, the sky yawning high above him, stars appearing every now and then between the ragged clouds.

Suddenly, without warning the road veered sharply to the left and, going way too fast, he skidded into the bend leaving rubber behind before hurtling towards the hedgerow on the opposite side of the road. With his heart in his mouth, somehow, he managed to straighten the car just in the nick of time and, on the legal side of the road once more, forced himself to slow down. A few minutes later, cresting the hill, below, the village was an oasis of light in the darkness and, going as fast as he dared, he descended towards it, seeing a sign on the side of the road as he did so.

*Welcome to Brentwood Down*
*Please drive carefully*

Torn between relief and hysteria, he snorted loudly, the irony not lost on him. A few minutes later on the edge of the village, the Red Lion public house loomed up, ablaze with light and, needing nothing more than to be near other people right now, on impulse, he swerved over the empty road and, pulling into the car park, jerked to a stop.

As he did so, suddenly the car began to spin and, convinced he was about to throw up, with his throat working, he quickly shoved the door open. After a moment or two however, after breathing in the cold night air the nausea began to pass and, leaning back against the seat, with hands that shook, he covered his face. *What had just happened – what he'd seen – it wasn't possible was it?*

## II

*Three weeks before*

*Inside a lab at the Research Centre for Medical Genetics, deserted at this time of night, in one of the labs, the only illumination came from a single light above a workstation at which three men stood, two in white coats, the other in a dark suit.*

*Bending, the suit peered down the lens of a microscope on the bench before him, the two lab technicians standing either side of him, waiting. Adjusting the focus, as the sample swum into sharp relief, the suit's heart leapt. Raising his head, he blinked before lowering it again, adjusting the focus once more with fingers that trembled. Noticing it, the technicians, exchanged nervous glances over his hunched back. At last, the suit straightened and released his breath, his eyes bright with barely concealed excitement, belying his calm exterior. "When did this come in?"*

*"A few days ago – a week at the most." The elder of the two replied. "The university has been conducting an anonymous genetic survey and it came here because they don't have the facilities to test it properly. I didn't get around to it until a few hours ago, but as soon as I saw it, I knew there was something wrong with it."*

*"You don't know what it is?" The suit asked, raking his face for any sign of duplicity. Shaking his head, the technician met his gaze levelly. "No, I've never seen anything like it before, that's why I made the phone call in the first place..."*

*"What about you?" the suit asked the other.*

*Under his scrutiny, the younger man shifted awkwardly. "No."*

*"Where's the rest of it?" The suit asked, addressing the first one again.*

*"That's it – that's all there was. They only took a cheek swab."*

*"Has anyone else seen it?"*

*"No, no one."*

*"You sure?"*

*"Positive."*

*"You haven't told anyone else about this?"*

*Again, the technicians exchanged glances. "No – why would we?"*

*With a satisfied grunt, the suit turned back to the microscope and, removing the slide, slipped it into a small, plastic container he'd taken from his pocket.*

*"Thank you, gentlemen, you've been most helpful." He said, turning. At the door where two more men waited, the suit gave them an almost imperceptible nod.*

*"Kill them."*

\* \* \* \* \*

With the chase playing over and over again as if on some kind of unstoppable loop, Carter closed his eyes, images of the creatures

*you know what they were*

vivid in his mind; creatures' sanity and logic dictated couldn't possibly exist, but which did all the same,

*just standing there*

as real as the trees he'd smashed against in his attempt to escape them. With a shudder, he thought how that

8

thing had stepped out of the shrubbery the way it had, nothing but a few feet between them, filled with horror at the memory of how he'd stood there talking to it, urging it to come out.

*CHRIST*

Had he known what had really been caught in his headlights, he'd never have stopped, not for anything! Closing his eyes he swore quietly, still unable to believe any of it had actually happened. And what about the strange voices he'd heard in his mind? Had it been them and if so, how had they known his name – *how was that possible?* And then his dad's voice, as clear as if he'd been standing right behind him, urging him onwards and giving him the strength to escape – surely, he hadn't imagined that, had he?

Hearing laughter, he stared owlishly at a couple as they left the pub before watching them cross the car park, heading for a high-end silver Mercedes. Parked next to it was a battered blue pick-up truck resplendent with rust and dents, the contrast which, ordinarily, he'd have found amusing.

Exiting the car park, the Mercedes disappeared round the corner and, knowing he couldn't stay here all night and that he should follow their cue, with what felt like a monumental effort, he straightened in his seat.

Desperately thirsty, he licked his lips, his tongue as dry as sandpaper, wincing as he realised his bottom lip was cut, something he hadn't even been aware of until now; hardly surprising he thought, given the circumstances. Reaching for the rear-view mirror, he suddenly stopped, his hand hanging in mid-air, staring at the mess of deep scratches and clotting blood crisscrossing it before dazedly looking down at himself, realising how dishevelled he was, his front caked with drying mud and his shoes ruined. Angling the mirror, hardly able to recognise himself, he stared into the eyes of a stranger.

Already pale and gaunt with grief, he looked even worse now, his eyes glassy with shock in his ashen face, his lips bloodless. And that wasn't all. For some reason he was struggling to think straight, having to plan every action in his head before doing it as if his mind was out of sync with his body. Not sure he should be driving at all, starting the engine, he drove through the car park like a drunk, slowly and overcautiously, everything seeming to have a strange, nightmarish quality about it, as if he were dreaming.

Thankfully, at this time of night the main road cutting through the village was empty, his being the only car about. After passing Pretty's the bakers and the post-office, he turned onto Bear Hill Road driving upwards, the village behind him now. Up here it was darker, modern lamp posts few and far between and looking oddly out of place against the backdrop of old, black and white beamed houses. Glancing at them, he thought about the people inside, watching telly or going about their nightly routines, completely unaware of the terrifying reality underlying everything, a deeper, darker world where monsters

*you knew what they were*

lurked and where anything could happen, no matter how unthinkable.

At the top of the hill, he turned right onto Tanyard Lane. Built in the nineteen-forties, most of the houses here were set back from the pavement, screened by high, well-kept hedges which shielded them from public view. Halfway along the lane he slowed before pulling up outside a detached house open to the road, the front garden having been turned into a driveway years ago. Staring at it he thought about the last time he'd seen his uncle, pale and gaunt at his parent's funeral, Elizabeth by his side. Glancing at the house next door he saw her bedroom window was filled with soft light.

With a crunch of tyres, he pulled onto the gravel drive and, getting out, quickly glanced round at the darkness, suddenly feeling incredibly vulnerable and exposed. Looking over the road he saw most of the houses were in darkness, only faint glimmers of porch lights visible through their hedges. As he took his bag from the back seat he looked up at the house, wishing he'd booked into to a hotel now, the thought of staying here alone after what had just happened, filling him with dread.

Opening the front door, he flicked the light switch on and flooded the hallway with light, taking in the black and white runner on the polished wooden floor and the framed diplomas adorning the walls. Wondering how everything could still look the same when so much had changed, going inside, silence enveloped him like a blanket.

Going to the telephone table he put his bag down and picked up a silver framed photograph. Taken on the day he'd graduated from Oxford, it had been one of happiest days of his life, his eyes twinkling beneath his mortarboard as he clutched his diploma, his mom and dad on his left, his uncle to the right, all of them grinning manically, together and happy, back when the world had

11

been sane. Narrowing his eyes, he stared down at it, waiting to feel something

*anything*

but all he felt was numb. Putting it down, all of a sudden from the corner of his eye he saw movement, whirling as he did so before realising it was his own reflection the mirror on the wall. Rolling his eyes, with a curse he picked his bag up and took it upstairs with him, his nerves shot. Over the road, in one of the darkened houses, a curtain twitched.

\* \* \* \* \*

*Ever since he could talk, Geshe Thrupen Chophel had been full of questions, eager to learn all he could about the world he'd been born into. Deeply curious about everything and with an intellect far in excess of his age, he positively craved knowledge, often driving his parents and his three elder brothers – and anyone else who would listen – to distraction.*

*Sometimes the questions were simple such as 'what's that?' and 'what's would happen if...?'. As he got older however they became more obscure such as 'why is the sky blue?' and 'why is grass green?' impossible questions they couldn't answer.*

*Undaunted, nevertheless, Thrupen continued with his relentless quest for* knowledge, *all the time pondering what he had learned so far. Because of this he was often the brunt of his brothers teasing, but instead of responding with anger – being exceptionally mature for his age – he understood why they treated him the way they did.*

*Most of the time he felt a lot older and wiser than his family – not just his siblings but his parents and grandparents too – something his brothers were maybe able to sense and which, because they couldn't understand it, frightened them, in turn, leading to anger.*

*Instead of playing with other children he could often be found sitting quietly beneath a tree or by a stream or on one of the many hills surrounding the village with the Tipitaka, the sacred book of Buddhism, alternatively reading and thinking.*

*As a Buddhist, he'd been brought up to believe that all life, whether it was animal or human, plant, fish or insect was Samsara, a cycle of life, death and reincarnation, a cycle which one had to try and escape from by Karma or 'intentional action.' Although believing in reincarnation, Buddhists didn't believe in a soul, instead believing it to be energy being reborn instead. He'd read Buddha taught that human beings were each born an infinite number of times unless they reached Nirvana, the ultimate goal of religious practice, breaking free of Samsara, a state which, once achieved, would rid them of the need to be reborn.*

*Fascinated by the whole concept, he often wondered if he – or rather the energy that was him – had lived before, thus explaining his feeling of having experienced a great number of things despite his young age. It was on a day such as this that he decided to become a monk. At last, his parents took him to the local monastery at Dhankar.*

*By that time Thrupen was eight.*

# *III*

In the shower, consumed with pain, Carter planted his
hands against the tiles, the sting of a thousand cuts and
scratches flaring as the hot water pelted over him,
cleansing them. Once the fiery burn had died down to a
mild sting, he washed and shampooed his hair, the
bottom of the shower awash with mud, sticks and leaves
by the time he'd finished. Towelling off, he wiped the
steam off the mirror before turning one way then the
other, assessing his injuries, surprised at how many there
actually were.

Finding a tube of antiseptic cream in the medicine
cabinet above the sink, he dabbed it on the worst of the
damage and, leaning on the basin, stared at himself in the
mirror. Even with his face flushed a healthier-looking
pink from the shower he still looked haunted, the strange
sensation of having become un-tethered from reality
lingering. Leaving his soiled clothes in a heap on the
floor he dressed and went downstairs before padding
down the hallway towards the kitchen. As he did so
however, he paused before a door.

*The sitting room.*

Not sure it was a good idea after what had just
happened, he paused. A few moments later however, he
took a deep breath, and, with the air of a condemned man
going to the gas chamber, pushed it open and went in, his
eyes going straight to the armchair as he did so, picturing
his uncle sitting there.

*Heart-failure.*

Going over he stood before it and, staring down at it,
waited to feel something

14

*anything*

but, clearly still in shock, all he felt was numb. Turning, behind him, the patio doors were a solid wall of black, the room and his own, solitary figure reflected in them. As images from the wood began filling his mind again, he felt panic soar, suddenly wondering if those things

*you know what they are*

were out there somewhere, watching from the darkness, maybe having followed him here somehow. With his heart hammering he turned, and, giving the armchair one last glance, hurried from the room.

In the kitchen on top of the white shaker units topped with grey marble, files and papers lay about everywhere, evidence of an academic in residence if ever there was one, he thought, and no different from his own flat back home. Suddenly, seeing the moon through the window above the sink, he quickly pulled the blind down over it, blocking it out.

Going through the cupboards, at last he found a bottle of his uncles favourite Red Stag whisky and, with a hand that shook, sloshed a couple of inches into a glass, coughing for a moment as it burned its way down his throat to his chest. Clearing a space on the table he put both bottle and glass down and, feeling as if he'd run a marathon, dropped heavily onto a chair.

With George and Rebecca Stanbrook, the renowned archaeologists as parents and the ground-breaking molecular biologist Robert Sterling for an uncle, from the word go he'd been steeped in academia. Not falling far from the tree, he'd been a somewhat serious, studious child, fascinated by the wonders of the world around

15

him, eager to learn all he could about it. As an avid bookworm, he'd spent most of his childhood with his head in one book or another, usually on science, on loan from his uncle. Much to his parent's chagrin. For as long as he could remember they'd tried to get him hooked on archaeology like them but it had never happened. As soon as his uncle had begun talking science he'd listened with rapt attention, spellbound as he described how everything was constructed of lattices, made up of neutrons and protons creating atoms, all held together by the electro-magnetic force. Showing him the true nature of things, he'd transformed the world about him, elevating the most mundane objects to nothing short of scientific miracles, in doing so, sowing the seeds of his own life-long obsession with science, leading to his career in Astrophysics.

Six years older than his mom, his uncle had always been overly protective of her, especially after their parents had died within a few years of each other, despite them being adults by then. Apart from his own, her opinion had been the only one he'd had time for and the only person he'd actually listen to.

Right from the start, his dad and uncle Rob had never got on, the gauntlet having been well and truly thrown down when they'd first met, his uncle apparently having called his dad a 'confounded ninny' for having the tenacity to question one of his theories. After that a heated discussion had then ensued resulting in his uncle storming out of the house after telling his mom she could do a hell of a lot better than *that* blithering idiot! Racing to the door his dad had shouted after him that he'd rather be a blithering idiot than a self-opinionated ego-maniac with all the personality of a dead houseplant, that story, which, to this day, still made him smile. Needless to say, after that, things between them had remained decidedly frosty, each one tolerating the other with barely disguised contempt, their encounters more often than not ending with his mom threatening to bang their heads together. Just your ordinary, dysfunctional, run-of-the-mill family.

*Before everything changed.*

One night, three months ago, his uncle had rung him, and, breaking it to him as gently as he could, had told him about the accident, saying his parents had been killed in a cave-in. Afterwards, numb with shock, he'd sat at the kitchen table in the gathering darkness trying to process it. Only when the first streaks of dawn had begun to appear in the sky had he gone to bed.

The day of the funeral – the worst day of his life and the last time he'd see his uncle alive – had been hell, neither of them knowing what to say or having the faintest idea how to begin comforting the other. Just trying to get through the day any way he could, afterwards, Elizabeth had suggested it might be better if he came and stayed at Brentwood Down for a while, but at the time he hadn't been able to face it and had gone home alone. Throwing himself into work, every now and then Elizabeth had called to check up on him, telling him his uncle was doing the same. Unable to accept what had happened and even more reluctant to talk to each other about it, a distance he'd never have believed possible had opened up between them and they'd ceased contact.

And then, last week, as he'd been opening a bag of Chinese take-away in his kitchen, Elizabeth had rung him

17

in tears, to tell him his uncle had passed away a few hours ago at home. Heart failure the doctor had said.

Lost for words, for a moment he'd stood there, clutching the phone, his hand like a block of ice, once more filled with the same mind-deadening disbelief as the night his uncle had told him about the cave-in.

Afterwards he'd stared out of the kitchen window at the darkness, seeing nothing but his uncle's face, filled with churning regret, realising they'd left it too late, the chance to reconnect with each other having irrevocably passed. Bereft, he couldn't believe that in the space of a few short months his entire family had been wiped out.

And then, tonight, on the road cutting through the woods less than two miles from Brentwood Down, caught in his headlights, he'd seen what he'd believed at the time to be a naked child dash across the road, before disappearing into the darkness. Shocked, he'd pulled to the side of the road and hurried down into the wood after it, able to hear it tearing through the darkness seeing it disappear into thick shrubbery. Clearly something terrible had happened and, in an attempt to reassure it, had called out to it.

*hello*

*do you need help*

But, looking back he needn't have bothered, because, as it turned out, it hadn't been a child down there in the shrubbery after all, far from it. Filled with horror, he saw himself making his way down the slope, descending deeper into the woods, a lone figure in an ocean of darkness, miles from anywhere.

The rest, as they say, was history.

Raising his head, he reached for the glass and, picking it up, drained the contents in one go.

*Had it really happened?*

Had he really been chased through the woods by aliens or was he losing his mind, he wondered? Or, maybe he'd crashed the car and, in reality was lying in a hospital bed somewhere in a coma, tonight's events being nothing more than a brain-damaged hallucination.

Flexing his hands, pain flared.

*It had happened.*

As an astrophysicist, he had little choice but look at things with an open mind having learned long ago that despite what humanity fooled itself into believing, it actually knew very little about anything – hadn't quantum physics proved that? However, no matter how open-minded he'd believed himself to be, tonight, those boundaries had been pushed to breaking point and he'd fallen

*been chased*

down the rabbit hole, reality as he'd known it, disappearing in an instant. And so, that being the case, where did the hell did that leave him, he wondered?

\* \* \* \* \*

*May 1970*

*Roused from the dream he'd been having, blinking, Tenzin sat up and stared around him in confusion, a deep rumble travelling up from the floor through the legs of the wooden bed on which he lay making it shake, becoming louder, more intense, as if the very air itself in the hot, darkened room was vibrating.*

19

*Next to him, his wife, Dolkar cried out while on the other side of the room on his own bed, his four-year old grandson Dawa bolted sat upright, his eyes wide with fear. "Po-la – what's happening?" he cried, leaping off the cot towards them.*

*On his feet, Tenzin caught Dawa up in his arms and held him tightly, the three of them with their arms about each other, the rumbling sound all around them intensifying.*

*"What is it? What's happening?"*

*"I don't know!"*

*Clinging to him tightly, Dawa buried his face in his shoulder, trembling with fear, Dolkar wide-eyed and terrified. Suddenly, the rumbling began to fade before disappearing completely, as inextricably as it had begun. Hurrying to the door, Dolkar pulled it open and, going outside, saw their neighbours spilling out from their own houses, the sound of their voices filling the still night air.*

# IV

*Feeling something rough against his cheek Carter blinked, realising he was lying on the ground under a tree. In panic he leapt to his feet, his heart pounding, staring at the darkened trees around him.*

*WHERE WERE THEY?*

*Suddenly he felt something run into one of his eyes and, touching it, saw blood on his fingers, realising he must've knocked himself out on the tree during the chase. All of a sudden, from the darkness, someone called his name.*

*Caarter*

Crying out Carter bolted upright, instantly regretting it as whisky-induced pain pierced his head like an arrow. Realising he'd been dreaming, with images flooding into his mind, the horror of the night before washed over him, once more filling him with terror. All of a sudden, hearing a sound in the kitchen he froze.

With his heart pounding, he slipped off the sofa and slowly made his way to the kitchen before pausing in the doorway, his eyes wide. As he did so a small, vivacious-looking woman of about sixty with light brown hair and twinkling blue eyes turned to look at him.

"Carter!"

"Elizabeth!" he gasped, his shoulders sagging.

"Did I wake you?"

"I didn't know who was in here…"

"I'm sorry." She said, coming to him. "I saw the car and thought you might be hungry."

"You didn't have to do that." He replied, shaking his head.

"Come here." She said giving him a hug. "Carter, I don't know what to say. I can't believe this has happened especially coming so soon after…well, you know." As her eyes filled with tears, she magically plucked a hanky from her sleeve. "I'm sorry. I promised myself I wouldn't do this."

"Please Elizabeth, don't apologise." he said, shaking his head, putting an arm round her shoulders. "You're the one that found him – how are you holding up?"

"As well as I can be, I suppose." She sniffed. "If it's all the same with you I'd rather not talk about it though."

Suddenly, noticing his hands, her eyes widened.

"What on earth – *what happened?*"

"Brambles." He said quickly, thinking on his feet. "I was doing a bit of gardening."

"With no gloves?" she gasped, looking at him askance. "Carter!"

"I'm fine, really." He said.

"You don't look it." She replied staring up at him. "You look awful. When was the last time you ate?"

"I'm not sure." He said, shaking his head. "I don't really feel like eating at the moment."

"Listen to me." She said quietly. "I know it must feel like the end of the world at the moment and I can't even begin to image what you're going through but you've got to keep your strength up. Why don't I make you a bit of breakfast and see how you feel? If you don't want it you don't have to have it, but at least you'll have tried, okay?"

Knowing she wasn't going to take no for an answer, he nodded. "Whatever you say, Elizabeth."

"Now, sit down before you fall down and I'll make you a coffee."

Pinching the bridge of his nose with his fingers, he closed his eyes, all of a sudden filled with the urge to unburden himself about what had happened in the woods the night before. "Elizabeth." He began. "About last night…you're not going to believe what happened."

Lifting the kettle, she poured water into two mugs. "I already know."

"You do?" Carter gasped, his eyes wide. *"How?"*

Bringing the mugs over she put one down in front of him and sat down. "I saw the bottle. Not that I blame you under the circumstances, mind. Years ago, I had a friend who died. At the time we'd had an argument and we never got the chance to make up. I've regretted it ever since." Covering his hand with her own, she shook her head. "One of the things I've learned over the years is, grief either brings people together or it drives them apart; it's no one's fault, it's just the way it is that's all. Carter, it wasn't your fault. He didn't get in touch with you either did he?"

Staring at her, he suddenly realised how his story of being chased through the woods by aliens would sound; she'd think he was crazy – *who wouldn't?* Realising he'd just dodged a bullet he shook his head. "I hadn't seen him since the funeral."

"I know."

"How was he after I left you?"

"Honestly? Not good. Losing your mom almost killed him. He couldn't accept she'd gone and he went to

23

pieces; I've never seen him like that before and I must admit, I was worried about him. I tried to be there for him as much as I could but he threw himself into work and shut himself off from everyone, me included. I think that's why he didn't get in touch with you, because he couldn't face talking about it."

Clearing his throat, Carter nodded. "For as long as I can remember, we always had this special bond, sometimes even more than I had with my parents. I always felt he understood me in ways they couldn't and seemed to know exactly how I was feeling. God Elizabeth, I don't know what I'm going to do without him."

"You and me both." She replied quietly.

For a moment they fell silent, each with their own thoughts before she suddenly got to her feet. "Right." She said briskly. "Let's get this breakfast going and then I'll take you to see him."

\* \* \* \* \*

*Shocked out of the dream he'd been having by the shrill ringing of the telephone, George turned over and, blinking sleepily, picked it up, Rebecca stirring next to him.*

*"Stanbrook." he muttered thickly.*

*Sitting up, he stiffened, instantly alert, his eyes wide. Lifting her head Rebecca looked at the alarm clock, groaning quietly as George spoke again, the excitement in his voice evident. "How unusual?"*

*Not an emergency then.*

24

*Once again, the voice squeaked in his ear and he nodded enthusiastically. "Yeah of course – as soon as we get sorted this end! We'll let you know when we arrive and we'll come and pick you up. Oh, and Tenzin – thanks."*

*Putting the phone down he looked at her staring at him questioningly, her interest piqued. At the sight of her still half-asleep with her hair so ruffled, looking so bloody beautiful, he felt a tug at his heart, once more thinking how she'd suffered. Still, it was over now and they had no choice but to put the past behind them and look to the future – it was all they could do.*

*"Well? What was all that about?" she asked.*

*Planting a kiss on her forehead, turning, George got out of bed. "That, my sweet, was Tenzin." he explained unnecessarily, disappearing into the bathroom. "I gathered that!" she said, rolling her eyes. "But what did he want?"*

*At sixty-two, Tenzin was as a guide in the foothills of the revered Mount Kailash in Tibet. And only the foothills because no one but religious pilgrims were allowed on the mountain, and even then, only with a special permit. Knowing the area like the back of his hand, nevertheless, he got parties of tourists as near to it as he possibly could. Having been their first and only guide, over the years they'd become firm friends with Tenzin becoming their eyes and ears, keeping them in the loop about digs in the area and who was digging up what and where. Re-appearing in the doorway with a mouth full of toothbrush, George's eyes twinkled with excitement.*

"He shed..." Taking it out, he pointed it at her. "He said, they'd had a large tremor in the area – shook up their village pretty badly apparently. Looking decidedly rabid, he spoke round a mouthful of foam. "And then, this morning while he was with a party of tourists, he noticed a crevice in a shelf of rock which he was sure hadn't been there before. While they were having lunch, he went to have a look at it and to his surprise, found it opened up into a cave with stuff in it."

"Stuff?" Rebecca asked, sitting up. "What kind of stuff?"

"Pots and stuff..."

"What kind of pots?"

"I don't know – he didn't say but the pots aren't important..."

"They're not?"

"No because..." George began before disappearing back into the bathroom. Hugging her knees, she rolled her eyes again, impatiently listening to the sound of the tap. "Because there's something else in there – something strange." George said reappearing again, his twinkling with excitement, Rebecca realising she hadn't seen him like that for a while.

"What do you mean strange?" she asked, leaning forward, hugging her knees, his excitement contagious.

"I don't know, some kind of tablet with symbols on it." He said opening the wardrobe. "He said he didn't know what it was and that he'd never seen anything like it before."

Having gleaned archaeological experience through not just them, but the other digs in the area over the years, Tenzin, like most other seasoned guides in Tibet,

26

*knew more about archaeology than most. Perfectly capable of recognising artefacts and knowing what he was looking at, logic dictated if he'd seen something and didn't know what it was, then it must be something special.*

*"But that's not all." George went on, wielding a coat hanger. "He reckons it's made of glass."*

*"What?" Rebecca gasped, her eyes widening. "How could it be made of glass?"*

*"Exactly!"*

# V

At first Carter had been horrified when Elizabeth had suggested taking him to the Chapel of Rest so he could pay his last respects to his uncle; never having seen anyone dead before, especially not a member of his own family, frankly, he couldn't think of anything worse.

*you sure about that*

After meeting the funeral director, they were shown into the small chapel where his uncle's body lay in a plain pine coffin on a trestle – no frills – just as his uncle had wanted. "Go on." Elizabeth urged gently. "It'll help, believe me."

Taking a deep breath, he went down the aisle, his shoes whispering on the carpet before stopping in front of the coffin. Dressed in his favourite black suit his uncle looked as if he were sleeping, his face gaunter than before, the weight having dropped from him since the accident; thinner though he might be, even in death he still looked powerful.

Feeling he should say something, but not having the first idea what, instead he placed a hand over one of his uncles, shocked at how cold it was. Just about to withdraw it again, all of a sudden, he felt it twitch. Shocked, he quickly pulled away from it but, as he did so, all of a sudden it darted upwards, feeling long, bony fingers enclose his wrist, holding him firm. Looking up, Carter gaped at what, a few seconds ago had been his uncle's head, replaced now by a hairless, grey dome crushing the dainty satin pillow beneath it. Filled with terror he balked as the eyes suddenly snapped open, huge, black, bug-like eyes, *blacker than anything*

his own terrified face reflected in them, once more hearing his own voice as a child screaming hysterically.

*what is it dad*

At last, in panic he somehow managed to wrench himself free of the vice-like grip before staggering backwards down the shallow steps, his eyes bulging, unable to tear his eyes from the inky black gaze. And then, just when he thought it couldn't get any worse, with a loud creak of the trestle, the creature sat up in the coffin, its huge head swivelling round to look at him as it did so.

*RUN FOR GOD'S SAKE*

With a strangled cry, Carter backed down the aisle, hearing the strange chorus of voices in his mind once more.

*Caarter*

As it began climbing out of the coffin, spinning, Carter tore down the aisle. Sitting on a chair at the back, Elizabeth looked up from the prayer book she was leafing through in surprise as he shot by. Out in the hallway, in the full throes of panic Carter spun on the spot and, seeing a fire-exit at the end of the corridor, bolted towards it, his feet pounding over the soft, noise-deadening carpet.

*Caarter*

As he burst through the doors into bright winter sunshine an alarm began to wail. Charging down the alleyway he shot out onto the pavement, almost colliding with a couple, the woman crying out, the man's eyes wide with shock. Skidding to a halt, with his lungs on fire, he leaned back against the wall, sucking in huge gulps of air, still able to feel the icy grip round his wrist.

Bursting from the alleyway, Elizabeth stared at him in horror. Trembling from head to toe he remained where he was, unable to speak had he wanted to.

Behind them the alarm fell silent.

*"Carter – what happened?"*

"I'm okay." He gasped. "I just need a minute that's all." Half an hour later, with panic having receded to a safe distance and Elizabeth clucking over him like a mother hen, in a café down the road Carter clutched a mug of hot tea, unable to stop thinking about what had just happened. *What the hell was wrong with him – was he going insane?*

Feeling he needed to give her some kind of explanation – preferably one that wouldn't make him sound like a lunatic – he cleared his throat. "I don't know what happened, I just saw him and panicked."

Covering his hand with her own, mortified, Elizabeth shook her head. "I'm so sorry Carter, it's all my fault – I should never have made you go there after everything that's happened. I don't know what I was thinking!"

"I feel like I'm losing my mind." He said quietly.

"I know it might feel like that right now, but things will get better, I promise."

Shaking his head, he wondered what she'd say if he told her what he thought he'd seen back there in the Chapel of Rest, clearly some horrific hallucination, probably after what had happened last night. After another mug of tea, once his colour had returned and the trembling had all but stopped, Elizabeth glanced at her watch. "Carter, I feel awful saying this after what's happened but I promised my sister Millie I'd help her out at the café lunch time – the chef's off sick and she's on her own in the kitchen."

"No, you go." Carter said, giving her what he hoped was a reassuring smile. "I'm ok, really."

*"Are you sure?"* she asked, looking at him doubtfully.

"Of course. It was just the shock of seeing him there…like that, that's all, I'm fine now." He lied, feeling just about as far from fine as he could get.

"Alright but come over to mine for dinner later on then – it's the least I can do after what's happened."

Shaking his head, he managed a weak smile. "There's no need, Elizabeth, really. Listen, why don't we go out for dinner tonight, my treat."

"Are you sure?"

"Of course. It'll be a pleasure."

"Well, so long as you're sure." She said, getting to her feet. "I know just the place – I'll book us a table. Carter…I really am sorry."

Standing up he held her coat for her as she shrugged into it. "Don't worry about it, no harm done."

Turning, with her head to one side, she studied him.

"What are you going to do now?"

"I might take a walk down memory lane, you know, have a look round and see what's going on."

"Not a fat lot I should imagine." She snorted quietly. "Nothing ever happens around here." Raising his eyebrows, Carter thought that had to be the understatement of the year. "Just take it easy, okay?"

After she'd left, alone with his thoughts, he frowned, his mind racing. Still reeling after what had happened

31

last night, one of the most disturbing aspects of it had been that when that thing that thing

*you knew what it was*

had emerged from the shrubbery, unbelievably, for a split second he'd been filled with the strangest notion that he'd seen it somewhere before – *that he knew it.* All of a sudden, sensing he was on the brink of some life-changing revelation, something he might be better off not knowing, filled with fear, he quickly closed his mind on it – *whatever it was, he didn't want to know.*

# VI

*Pausing to get her breath, Rebecca stared at Mount
Kailash in all its splendour in the distance, it's white,
snow-covered, almost pyramidal shape standing out in
sharp relief against the vivid blue sky looking – so she'd
always thought anyway – not like a natural formation so
much as carved from the rock it stood on, the scene
breath-taking.*

*Not just a mountain, but the sacred peak of far west of
Tibet – Kang Ripoche or Precious Snow Mountain as the
Tibetans called it – was referred to in ancient texts as the
centre of the world, probably due to the source of the of
the mighty Indus River to the north, the Sutlej in the west,
the Brahmaputra or Yarlung Tsang-po to the east and
the Kamali, the largest tributary to the Ganges in the
south, all within a thirty-mile radius. A great holy site,
Tibetan Buddhists believed it to be a national Mandela
representing the Buddhist cosmology on earth, while
Hindus worshipped it, regarding it as Shivas or Symbolic
Lingam, the very name Mount Kailash being a Sanskrit
name for Earth. The Bonpos believed it was the site
where the founder of the bon religion had landed when
he descended from the sky whereas the Jains claimed it
to be where their religions founder had been spiritually
awakened.*

*At its base was Darchen, the starting point for Kitora,
a religious pilgrimage where, depending on their
religion, pilgrims either walked the base of the mountain
clock-wise or anti-clockwise up to a hundred and forty-
nine times, considering the act of doing so a religious
necessity. Dotted around it were five temples, most of*

*them derelict now, to her, the very idea of them being abandoned to the elements abhorrent. According to legend, no one had ever seen the mountain without it's icy cap, not Tenzin and certainly not them. Below it on the scorched-looking foothills, Kasturi Kamal grew, a native plant with narrow leaves and small, white, furry flowers which the yaks, sheep and cows fed on, the sparse patches of it beginning to yellow now, it's season in the sun coming to an end. With its ethereal beauty, there was, she thought, something decidedly mystical about this place and could perfectly understand why religion had sprung up here. Further ahead, George glanced over his shoulder and, seeing she'd stopped, turned to look at her, concerned. "Sorry. Were we leaving you behind?"*

*Knowing he was worried but trying his best to hide it because only yesterday she'd yelled at him for smothering her, Rebecca shook her head, giving him a reassuring smile. "No, I was just enjoying the view, that's all."*

*Looking relieved, nevertheless she knew he wouldn't go on without her and so, with a sigh, started up the slight incline towards them, both of them knowing that, under normal circumstances it would've been her waiting for him. However, the last couple of months had left her feeling weak and depleted and even the little things she'd done so easily before, quickly wore her out now, her body taking longer to heal itself this time, the mental and emotional scarring deeper than ever.*

*At last, the trail narrowed out, and, coming to a long cliff of rock they began making their way along its base steeped in shadow, the mountain out of sight behind it now. After a few minutes Tenzin rounded an outcrop of rock jutting out from the base. Joining him, they stared at a narrow crevice in the cliff face, tucked out of sight behind it. "Just here." Tenzin said, nodding his head.*

*"Lead the way." George replied him and Rebecca exchanging excited glances, impatient to see for themselves the strange tablet Tenzin had described in such detail, lying in wait in the darkness.*

*Taking his torch from his belt he stepped forwards and, turning sideways, deftly slipped through the gap. Following suit, they found themselves in a long, narrow cavern, the ceiling only thirty feet or so above them. Playing their torches over the rough walls they glinted with streaks of what looked like quartz. All around them the floor was littered with shards of rock and small stones, the cavern tapering to a point ending in rough-hewn rock at the back.*

*"Where's the tablet?" Rebecca said sweeping the beam of her torch round the small space.*

*"This way." Tenzin said, turning before carefully picking his way over the littered floor. Reaching the back, stooping now, he disappeared through a narrow gap, all but invisible among the shadows.*

*"No wonder he wasn't worried about anyone else finding it." George muttered quietly, glancing at Rebecca. "No one would know it was there."*

*Training their beams over the floor, they followed the cavern to the end and, just as Tenzin had done, slipped through the narrow opening. On the other side, they found themselves in a slightly larger space, the air almost chilly in here. Steeped in silence it had a crypt-like feel about it, all of them sensing it was old – really*

*old – and that they were the first people to have stood
inside here since God-knows-when, an odd sensation
both she and George had experienced before at certain
ancient sites. Sometimes simply by entering them, they
felt they'd crossed some kind of threshold, in effect,
leaving the modern world behind into one long gone,
crumbling foundations, statues, cracked pots and dusty
jewellery the only things remaining of the people that
once populated it. Sometimes she was sure she could
hear faint whisperings of their voices coming to her
down through the eons or see shadowy movements of
their ghosts in darkened corners or in the faint stirrings
of the sand, like echoes from the past. Suddenly, startling
her out of her reverie, Tenzin said "Over there – see?"*

*Next to her George gasped. "My god!"*

*Against the far wall, in the beams of their torches they
saw a slew of pottery, most of it faded, broken and
covered in dust while some larger urns remained intact,
covered in what appeared to be early Brahmi.*

*"They have to be two thousand years old." Rebecca
breathed, staring at them with narrowed eyes.*

*"But here, look." Tenzin said excitedly, drawing their
attention to the other side of the space. Leaning against
the wall was a tablet of what looked like stone, about the
size of A4 paper. As they shone their torches on it
however, they saw a clear patch on the surface where
Tenzin had cleaned the thick, ream of dust from it.*

*"That's it." Tenzin said quietly following behind them
as they crossed the small space towards them. "Exactly
where I found it."*

*Wide-eyed with excitement, carefully George picked
his way around the slew of pottery before going down on*

36

one knee before it, staring at the exposed spot, able to
see quite clearly an opaque, glass-like surface beneath.

Putting the torch on the ground he unslung his canvas
bag and, taking out a small horsehair brush, began
removing the thick dust which had accumulated over the
eons, a small circle of eight indentations at the top
becoming clearer, below which were line upon line of
what looked like tiny, stylised, symbols. Staring at them
he frowned. With mounting excitement, he removed more
dust, counting sixteen lines in all, like the indents above
them, they looked as if they'd been impressed upon the
surface, rather than carved.

Raising his hand to touch them, without warning a
deep sense of foreboding and irrational fear washed over
him and he shivered involuntarily, as if the temperature
had suddenly dropped. Confused, he paused, the brush
hovering in mid-air, an inch or so away from it now.
Behind him Rebecca and Tenzin exchanged glances.

"George?" Rebecca asked quietly, her voice low
almost as if it were expected of her in this shrine-like
place. "What is it?"

For a moment the silence seemed to deepen all
around them and, feeling watched, turning, George
swept the cavern with his eyes. With a shiver he decided
he didn't like this place much, there being something
strange about it, something he couldn't put his finger on.

"George, what's wrong?" Rebecca asked again with
a frown.

"Nothing." He said replied quickly, giving his head a
quick shake. "I was just trying to think if I'd seen
anything like this before, that's all."

"Oh."

*Making her way through the debris Rebecca squatted down next to him, her eyes twinkling with excitement. Tilting her head, she studied the strange symbols intently. "And have you?"*

*"Have I what?"*

*"Seen anything like it before?"*

*Shaking his head again, George frowned. "I'm not sure, although they do remind me of something."*

*"Yeah, I know what you mean – they do look sort of familiar don't they?"*

*"You've seen something like this before?"*

*"Maybe. But, for the life of me, I can't think where."*

*Behind them, moving nervously from foot to foot, silently, Tenzin watched them.*

# VII

With no real plan in mind, Carter made his way along the high street. Suddenly, almost as if compelled to do so, he turned and stared at the gently undulating hills to the north of the village seeing the woods not far away, a thin mist clinging to the tops of the trees. Quickly turning his back on them, he went on his way, once more finding himself outside the Red Lion.

Narrowing his eyes, he stared at the spot where he'd parked last night

*after the chase*

thinking about his panic-fuelled flight from the woods, the whole thing, the stuff of nightmares amazed he hadn't ended up wrapping the car round a tree.

Going towards the tinted glass door the couple had come out of last night he stared at his reflection, wondering why he'd come back here. Deciding to go in, he was greeted by a subtle blend of furniture polish and freshly-brewed coffee. On the walls framed pictures of the original pub in bygone days hung while horse-brasses dotted the beams. In the large, red-brick fireplace a fire crackled, long tongues of flame licking around newly sawn logs giving the place a welcoming, homely feel just like he remembered, the only difference being slim-line tv screen attached to wall above the mantlepiece, the newsreader's voice little more than a whisper. Next to the fire at a table, two old men were playing cards, one large and florid in a check shirt, the other in a grey cardigan and flat cap, his sinewy neck and heavy-lidded eyes reminding Carter of a tortoise. Raising their heads, they looked at him curiously, giving him the once over.

Giving them a brief nod, he went to the bar, its ruddy patina of burnished wood glowing warmly under the small spotlights fixed above it, while behind it, large mirrors lent the whole place a feeling of spaciousness which otherwise, it would've lacked. Next to him on the end of the bar, a vase of freshly-cut flowers rested, their heady aroma filling the air, transporting him back to the Chapel of Rest. With his nerves jangling, he took a deep breath, refusing to think about it. After a few minutes when no one appeared, he glanced over at the two men, questioningly.

"Probably in the back." Check shirt muttered thickly before clearing his throat. *"Rick!"*

Nodding his thanks, Carter slid onto a stool and a moment later a head belonging to a man of around his own age appeared around a door behind the bar.

"What now?" he asked resignedly looking over at them.

"Customer." Check shirt said, nodding at Carter.

Drying his hands on a tea-towel, the man came towards him, shaking his head as he did so. "Sorry." he said staring at Carter curiously. "I didn't hear you."

"Heard me, though. didn't you?" Check shirt said plonking a card down.

"Hard not to."

"I can hear, you know!" Check shirt muttered. "I might be old but I'm not deaf!"

"What can I get you?" Rick asked, ignoring him.

"A coffee please." Carter replied. "And a whisky."

Not being much of a drinker, the Red Stag had effectively kicked his ass last night and he still felt groggy. Putting a cup of coffee on the bar before him,

40

Rick turned towards the optics. "Haven't seen you in here before – you just passing through?"

"Not exactly." Carter said stirring his coffee. "My uncle lives here – lived here – but he's passed away. I've come for the funeral and to sort things out."

"Sorry." Rick said, bringing the glass over. "Me and my big mouth."

"Don't worry about it." Carter replied, shaking his head. "You weren't to know."

"Would I know him?"

"I expect so." Carter replied. "Robert Sterling?"

"What, the scientist guy?" Rick said raising his eyebrows.

"That's him." Carter nodded.

"I didn't know him personally but I knew of him." Rick said giving his head a quick shake. "Apparently, he was a bit of a whizz in his field, wasn't he?"

"You could say that." Carter snorted, amused, wondering what his uncle would've thought about that.

"My condolences." Rick said extending his hand over the bar. "Rick Morley."

"Nice to meet you. Rick." Carter said shaking his hand. "Carter Stanbrook."

"When's the funeral?"

"Three days." Glad of the distraction from his own, horrific thoughts, he took a sip of his coffee before asking: "This your place?"

"I wish!" Rick snorted, leaning on the bar, his arms folded. "No, I just do the bar and help out in the kitchen when it's busy – a bit of everything really – and I look after place when the owners are away which is a lot lately."

41

"Tony and Patsy Cornell are the licensees." Check shirt piped up behind Carter. "Been here about eight years now. Moved here from London to be nearer to their daughter Jackie when she had a baby, didn't they Wilf?"

Next to him the tortoise nodded.

Turning his head, Rick addressed him over his shoulder. "Yeah, thanks Reg – but we're trying to have a private conversation here."

"No such thing in a pub." Check-shirt snorted. "You should know that by now."

Looking as if he were about to say something before deciding against it, Rick looked back at Carter. "So, when did your uncle...you know...pass?"

"Last week. I've just been to the Chapel of Rest to him."

Shaking his head, Rick clicked his tongue. "Not nice."

Once again, the events of the morning flashed into Carter's mind in vivid clarity and, aware they were all looking at him, he tried to remain calm. With a hand that shook he raised the glass to his lips, the burn of the whisky on the back of his throat taking his breath away.

"You okay?" Rick asked, staring at him in concern, misinterpreting his panic for grief.

"Yeah."

Picking the glass up Rick returned to the optics and refilled it before placing it in front of him again. "On the house."

"Thanks." Carter said. "But there's really no need..."

"Don't worry about it. You know, as soon as I saw you, I knew something bad had happened to you – it's written all over your face; in this game reading people becomes second nature. Before this I worked at a place in

42

London and as soon as people came through the door I knew if they'd come in to party or fight, and it was that second lot – the ones that came in all wound up after a row with the missus or if someone had pissed them off – you had to keep your eye on. It was rough at the best of times that place and there were plenty of them like that came in, believe me. Trouble with a capital T, that lot. But the others, well, they were the ones who came in looking poleaxed, the ones who'd just been fired or found out their partners had been cheating on them. Top shelf people I used to call them because nine times out of ten they'd have something off the top shelf, something to take the edge off before it hit them for real, and most of them looked exactly like you do right now – intuition, see?"

Considering his haggard appearance, Carter thought a blind man would've been able to tell something was up. As if reading his mind, Check-shirt snorted. "Intuition my ass!" Laying his cards on the table he leaned back in his seat, tipping his head to the side, his eyes narrowed, staring at Carter thoughtfully. "You know son, the last time I saw anyone looking like you do right now was when Harry Bennett came through that door looking as if he'd seen a ghost. And he doesn't scare easy, believe me."

"Carter." Rick sighed, resignedly. "These are two of our regulars – Reg Tarney and Wilf Robson." On his stool Carter gave them a nod and a tight-lipped smile.

"Nice to meet you son." Reg, in the check shirt said jovially. In his early sixties, shrewd blue eyes twinkled out from his florid face. The type that wouldn't miss much, Carter guessed. Next to him, the tortoise – Wilf – studied him with rheumy eyes.

"I remember it as if it was yesterday." Reg went on folding his arms over his chest. "Round about the time we had that big power cut and all that business over Durston, you remember that Wilf?"

Wordlessly Wilf nodded.

"Right to-do that was!" Reg went on shaking his head. "One night half the transformers in the substation blew out for no reason and none of them could work out why. My son-in-law was one of the engineers sent up there to fix it and he told me they'd never seen anything like it. You remember Maurice, Wilf?"

Once again Wilf silently nodded, accompanied by a slow, long blink as if it were an effort to keep his heavily-lidded eyes open.

"Over there working on it day and night they were and it still took them a week to get it up and running again, isn't that right Wilf?"

*Nod.*

"Anyway, like I say, since then I've never seen anyone looking like Harry did that day, not until you came in today, anyway."

Not quite sure how to respond to that Carter remained silent.

"You know, years ago, there was this family living right on the outskirts of the village – one of those bad families every place has – the Beasley's – each and every one of them trouble…"

"Here we go." Rick muttered quietly at Carter from the side of his mouth. "Once he gets going there's no stopping him."

"Like I said before sonny." Reg said shooting him a look, his voice hardening. *"I'm old, not deaf!"*

With a ghost of a smile, Carter looked at Rick who rolled his eyes. Undeterred, Reg went on. "One of the sons – Colin it was and only eighteen at that – got killed on his motorcycle, you remember that Wilf?"

*Nod.*

"The other brother, Billy's banged up for armed robbery so I don't think we'll be seeing him around these parts for a while yet, and a good job too! Now, around the time Colin died – what, fifteen years ago it must be now – Ernie Baker and his misses had this place and he used to let them get away with murder cos he was too much of a wimp to stand up to them; gutless wonder, he was. Not that he was the only one mind, because no one would say boo to them, not unless they wanted their face smashed in that is. Anyway, one day in here, Old Marvin Beasley – the dad – was two sheets to the wind just like he usually was on a Saturday afternoon when all of a sudden right here at the bar in front of everyone, he gave his wife Sarah a slap for back-chatting him and I can tell you this now it wasn't too light either, was it Wilf?"

Blinking his moist-looking eyes, Wilf shook his head in agreement.

"Now we all saw what happened." Reg went on his eyes distant now as he stared back down through the years, remembering. "And no-one liked it, but none of us said anything – no one but Harry, that was. Back then he was a lot beefier than he is now. Even so, he was nowhere as big as Old Marvin and I don't think any of us could believe what happened next. He put his pint down on the bar – right where you're sitting now Carter – and went up to him and told him if he ever saw him lay a finger on her again, he'd be waking up in the middle of next week."

Looking round, Reg paused for dramatic effect.

"Well, you should have seen Old Marvin's face change – as black as thunder it went – and he looked at Harry as if his eyes were about to fall out of his head. He couldn't believe anyone had had the guts to speak to him like that. And then, Harry told him to apologise to her. Well of course by then Sarah was crying her eyes out all upset like, begging Harry to leave it alone, saying it didn't matter, but he ignored her and stood his ground, staring up at Old Marvin towering over him looking as if he was about to tear his head off, that's right, isn't it, Wilf?"

*Nod.*

Animated, Reg sat up straighter, his eyes twinkling now. "Anyway, Old Marvin put his pint down on the bar as well then, dead slow and deliberate like, and he pulled himself up – and believe me there was a lot of him to pull up wasn't there Wilf?"

*Nod.*

"By then the whole pub had gone quiet, so quiet you could hear a pin drop, all of us just standing there holding our breath wondering just how many times Old Marvin was going to have to hit Harry before he went down. At the time he was a member of the Barnt Green Boxing Club and he wasn't half bad either, remember that Wilf?"

*Nod.*

"As quick as lightening, he grabbed Harry by the lapels and stared down at him, his face all puckered up in

46

an angry snarl the way he did – like a dog baring its teeth – and we all thought Harry was a goner, but then the strangest thing happened, you remember Wilf?"

*Nod.*

Wide-eyed Reg spread his hands. "And then Harry leaned forward and whispered something in his ear and he froze. White as a sheet, looking as if his eyes were about to fall out of his head and a few seconds later he shoved Harry away from him so hard he almost went flying. And then, without another word, he turned and stormed out. Almost yanked the door off its hinges didn't he Wilf?"

*Nod.*

"And then Sarah dashed out after him and we all stood there, gob-smacked because none of us could believe he'd simply walked out like the way he had without there being a punch-up. A lot of people bought Harry a drink that afternoon, whether he wanted one or not and the whole place was buzzing with what happened. But you know what, even though we begged him to tell us what he'd said to Old Marvin that had put the wind up him like he had, he wouldn't say, would he Wilf?"

*Shake.*

"To this day no-one knows. But the strangest thing about it was every time Old Marvin and Harry saw each other it was just like nothing happened and that wasn't like Old Marvin because he could carry a grudge like no one else I've ever known, believe me! So far as anyone knew he never raised a hand to Sarah again – not in public anyway – but that doesn't mean he never did and it might've been a different matter behind closed doors. In my experience a leopard never changes its spots and

47

Old Marvin being the way he was, I couldn't imagine him trying too hard either. So, you see, when Harry came in here that night looking as white as a sheet with the same look on his face you had earlier, I knew it had to be something really bad."

"So, what was wrong with him then?" Rick asked, intrigued despite himself. "Harry. I mean."

Looking up at him, Reg shook his head in surprise. "What, you telling me you don't know?"

"No." Rick said frowning slightly, shrugging a shoulder.

"You haven't heard the stories?"

"No."

"Bloody hell!" Reg muttered shaking his head, appalled at the inefficiency of the local grapevine. "Can you believe that Wilf?"

*Shake.*

"So, come on, what was it then?"

Pausing, Reg stared at them all in turn before answering, his voice low. "He said he saw something when he was out in the truck – something he couldn't explain."

"What?" Rick asked, with a frown.

As if still unable to believe it, Reg shook his head solemnly. "He said he saw something strange in the sky – *one of those flying saucer things!"*

On his stool, Carter started as if someone had just thrown a bucket of ice water in his face. Behind the bar, Rick snorted cynically. "You're joking, right?"

Looking at them, pleased by the reaction he'd elicited, with a smug smile of satisfaction, Reg crossed his arms over his chest. "Wilf?"

48

*Nod.*

"What, you're saying he just walked in and told you he'd seen a UFO?" Rick snorted. *"Harry?"*

"Yeah," Reg replied matter-of-factly, nodding. "And not just me either – Big Danny and Steve Fisher as well."

"What, they actually heard him say it?"

"We all did!" Reg replied. "I'm not a liar."

"I wasn't saying that, was I..."

"And that wasn't all, either – there was something else."

With his heart pounding in his ears, Carter waited, unable to believe Reg had brought this up, coming so soon on the heels of his own terrifying experiences, wanting nothing more than to

*run*

get the hell out of there.

"Not only did he say he saw it, but he said he saw it land!"

At those words Carter went cold.

*"I don't believe it!"* Rick snorted loudly. *"You're pulling my leg!"*

"I swear to God..." Reg ejaculated. As he did so his hand caught the coffee cup, knocking it over, the contents spreading across the table in a dark, sweet-smelling puddle before dribbling over the edge onto the floor.

*"Bloody hell Reg!"* Rick muttered impatiently flipping the hatch up and grabbing the tea-towel from his shoulder as he did so before striding to the table and mopping up the spill. Seizing the opportunity Carter slipped off the stool and on legs that felt like rubber,

followed the sign to the toilets, Reg's voice behind him now. "Anyway, like I was saying about Harry..."

"Forget it." He heard Rick say. "That's enough for one day. "I don't believe it anyway."

"Well maybe he did and maybe he didn't, but I suppose we'll never know, because that was the last time he ever talked about it, wasn't it Wilf?"

Leaning on one of the basins, Carter's heart pounded, his reflection in the mirror looking how he felt – *scared shitless*. Turning the tap on, he sloshed cold water over his face, Reg's words booming in his mind.

*said he saw it land*

Taking a deep breath, he straightened. What the hell was going on here? It was almost as if something had made him come here so Reg could tell him that story. Or maybe it was nothing more than sheer coincidence and he was losing his mind after all.

Returning to the bar he made his excuses and after thanking Rick, gave the others a curt nod before hurrying for the door, just wanting to get out of there as quickly as he could before Reg started speaking again. "Come back anytime." Rick said, raising a hand in farewell. "You know where we are."

Giving him a quick nod, Carter pushed the door open and escaped. Behind him, Rick stared at his receding back through the glass door intently, his eyes bright with excitement.

# VIII

*Sitting Cross-legged on the bed, Rebecca ran a finger over the tablet, her head tilted, studying it.*

*As soon as they'd seen it, she and George had known it was something special and that leaving it in the cavern wasn't an option and so they'd done something they'd never done before – taken it with them. In all their years, as archaeologists (or, treasure hunters as George liked to say), never before had they removed an artefact from a site without first going through the proper channels and by doing what they'd done, had compromised not only their own careers but the reputation of the Carnaby Museum to boot.*

*When they'd got it back to the hotel, they'd cleaned it with water and cotton wool revealing a slab of crystal or glass in pristine condition, startlingly perfect and unblemished, not so much a mark on it. Afterwards George had tried to take a small scraping of it from the back of it with his pen-knife in order to try and determine what it was made of exactly but, to their astonishment it had been impossible, the blade skittering off it every time without so much as a scratch, the obvious conclusion being it must be made of toughened glass. Except it wasn't heavy like a glass tablet would be, it was light like plastic, making them wonder if it was an ancient artefact at all. It certainly didn't look old. On the other hand, if it was made from some kind of modern material, that in itself raised more questions than it answered.*

*"Damn it."* she whispered quietly.

*At the dressing table, George got to his feet, a piece of paper and a stick of charcoal in his hands. "Annoying, isn't it?"*

*"You can say again."*

*Dropping to his knees he pulled the tablet towards him.*

*"You're taking a rubbing?"*

*"I can't write every character down individually – I'd be here all night."*

*"No, what I mean is, why?"*

*"Well, there's that chap at Oxford who specialises in ancient languages. He might know what they are."*

*"What if it turns out to be from a factory in Taiwan?"*

*Glancing up at her he grinned, pleased to hear her sounding more like her usual self. Maybe this trip was exactly what she'd needed. When Tenzin had rung, he hadn't been sure she'd be up to an overseas trek into the wilderness but, knowing her as well as he did, had he suggested coming out here alone he'd never have heard the end of it. "Then we're going to look like idiots, aren't we?" he said.*

*"I think they look a bit like scientific equations." She mused quietly. "Maybe we should show it to Rob first."*

\* \* \* \* \*

Still reeling from not only what had happened in the Chapel of Rest earlier but now Reg Tarneys' almost too-coincidental story of Harry Bennett's UFO sighting to boot, rattled, Carter made his way back along the High Street. On impulse he went into a place called Sam's

Café but, despite two cups of steaming hot coffee he couldn't dispel the chill inside him.

Back at the house, he went into the sitting room again and drawn to it like a magnet, went to the armchair before gently laying a hand on one of the arms wondering what his uncle would've made of all this.

Would he have believed him?

Probably not.

A staunch critic of anything that couldn't be explained by science, no doubt he'd have put it down to some kind of hallucinatory episode; either that or the possibility he was losing his mind. Going to the patio doors for a moment he stood with his hands in his pockets, staring out at the garden, remembering hot summer days as a child with the paddling pool out there. At last, giving the chair one last, lingering look he left the room, closing the door quietly, almost reverently, behind him.

Outside in the hall, not knowing what to do, in an attempt to distract himself from thinking, he decided to take a look around. Upstairs were three good-sized bedrooms, the first the one he always used when he visited. Next to it in the spare room piles of books and files were stacked on almost every surface. At the front, his uncle's bedroom was dominated by a large, king-size bed, books and sheafs of paper everywhere as usual. On the bedside cabinet his uncle's reading glasses sat on top of a couple of books. Picking them up he held them in his hands, once more feeling nothing. Picking the up he held them in his hands for a moment, waiting to feel something,

*anything*

feeling nothing. Picking the books up he read the titles, 'X and Y' by H. D. Winger and 'Filling in the blanks, an in-depth investigation into the chromosome and genetic mapping' by George Heinemann. Exactly the kind of thing he'd expect him to have as light reading.

Going to the window he parted the net curtain and stared at the house directly opposite, its curtains closed giving it a closeted, almost secretive, look. With nothing but a rake leaning against the wall and no car on the drive, there were no clues as to what the people who lived there were like.

On the landing he stared up at a short flight of stairs leading to the room at the top of the house – the study – the one room he'd never been in due to the fact it had always been strictly out of bounds to everyone and which his uncle had kept locked. As a child, he'd often wondered what was in there, only too easily imagining some kind of secret laboratory swathed in cob-webs with potions and concoctions bubbling away in huge, globe-shaped flasks and wizard-like tomes containing descriptions of unimaginable, magical experiments. Sometimes, filled with unbearable curiosity, the sight of the door had been too much and he'd crept up the stairs and pressed his ear to the door. Unable to hear anything however, he'd remained in the dark at what lay beyond it although he knew where his uncle kept the key.

Suddenly filled with curiosity, he went up the stairs, unable to help feeling guilty at what he was about to do, before reminding himself his uncle was no longer here and that he had no choice now. Reaching up he took the key down from the ledge above the door and pushed it into the lock, glancing quickly over his shoulder as he did so, imagining his uncle's discarnate spirit hovering close by, shaking his head and cursing, unable to do anything other than watch as he breached his inner sanctum. Muttering a quick apology, he opened the door and went in seeing a computer on a modern, utilitarian-looking desk in front of the window amid a slew of papers, folders and notebooks. Pushed to the side was a black leather swivel chair, a hefty-looking tome on it. Sparsely decorated, other than a white board fixed to the back wall covered in with his uncle's distinctive spidery handwriting in bright blue felt tip pen, the cream walls were bare.

Filled with a sense of anti-climax, he went to the desk, gently moving the paperwork with his hand, a letter of request from Nottingham University for his uncle to be a guest speaker, three copies of Science Forum monthly, and an electric bill, just some of them. Picking up a black, ring-bound notebook he opened it curiously, the pages covered with spidery writing, obviously having been scribbled down quickly, most of it illegible. Putting it back where he found it, behind the door was a bookcase, its shelves bowed under the weight of books on them, seeing everything from the Big Bang to Unified String Theory and quantum mechanics. All of a sudden, his heart skipped a beat.

'UFO's – the true reality of our world.'

Going towards it, once more filled with the strange sensation of having become un-tethered from reality, he shook his head in disbelief; not only that his uncle would have a book on this subject in the first place but the fact he was being confronted by it yet *again*. Almost, he thought as if he were being forced to think about it whether he wanted to or not. Reaching up he took it down, chilled at the picture on the cover, a brightly lit saucer-shaped craft hovering low over a car on a darkened road.

*said he saw it land*

As images from last night flooded into his mind like an unstoppable torrent,

*oh god, those eyes*

filled with fear, with a hand that trembled he quickly shoved it back onto the shelf and, turning, hurried from the room, the door slamming loudly behind him.

* * * * *

*"I know it sounds crazy." Rebecca said down the line, her excitement evident. "But that's what they remind me of – scientific equations."*

*On the other end of the line, her brother raised his eyebrows, taken by surprise not only by the fact they'd taken the artefact from the site in the first place, going against their usually rigid code of ethics but had then casually packed it in their suitcase before bringing it home with them.*

*"I want you to come and take a look at it." She went on. "Why don't you come over for dinner one night this week – it's been ages since I've seen you and we can have a catch up."*

*"That'd be nice." He replied, the prospect of spending a whole evening making polite conversation with his insipid brother-in-law, tedious to say the least. Still, he thought, it would be good to see her and make sure she really was alright again now.*

"Rob – what have I told you?" she asked warningly.

"Yes, I know. Don't worry, I'll be polite."

"And nice."

"Yeah, and nice." He sighed, rolling his eyes.

# IX

That night, following Elizabeth's directions, Carter drove them to The Mooring Place, a former boat repair shop on the bank of the canal, now a restaurant. Designed like the prow of a boat, inside, large windows looked out over the sluggish-moving water beyond, lit by strategically placed spotlights dotted around the base of the building. In sight of the boat-yard itself, it was a regular haunt for narrow-boat travellers and locals alike and even now in the middle of the week, was half full.

Inside, soft lighting illuminated the wood panelled walls, the warm ambience of the place furthered by tea lights in red votive holders on each table. On arrival they were greeted by a waiter who escorted them to a table next to one of the windows.

As promised, the food was excellent and they took their time over it, reminiscing about happier times while they did so. Whether it was the slow-moving water beyond the window or the restful atmosphere Carter couldn't be sure, but, for the first time since he'd arrived last night, this was about as normal as he'd felt.

"Have you always lived here?" he asked.

"More or less." Elizabeth nodded. "My parents owned Beckett's Farm a few miles from the village. Good old English farming stock, I am."

"Really?" Carter breathed, surprised.

Shaking her head, Elizabeth smiled. "Why does everyone react the same when I tell them that?"

"Sorry." He said, smiling too. "I just never imagined you as the farming type."

"Me and Millie follow our mother in that way; she was petite like us – but as strong as an ox. She owns Sam's café in the village. It was Sam Hurst's before she married him but he keeled over one night right in the middle of a card game, God bless him. Mind you he was getting on a bit, fifteen years older than her in fact. I remember when they first started seeing each other our parents kicked up a right fuss but Millie didn't care, just carried on seeing him anyway. When she came home one night and told them he'd asked her to marry him and that she'd accepted, our dad went up the wall! Caused a hell of a lot of trouble that did but she said she was going to marry him with or without their blessing and that was all there was to it. She always was headstrong our Millie – not spoiled mind, but as stubborn as a mule. If she wanted something, nine times out of ten she'd end up getting it. Of course, when our dad realised she meant it, he had no choice but to come round and everything turned out alright in the end. Two kids they had, David and Suzanna. Suzanna's a nurse down in Dawlish and David married a girl from New Zealand and became a solicitor – a lawyer as they call them there. He pays for her to go over there and see them every so often but it's expensive. I've been over with her a couple of times but we're both getting on a bit now, especially Millie, and she can't do as much as she used to."

"So, what about you, Elizabeth?" Carter asked, realising he hardly knew anything at all about her background. "What's your story?"

Leaning back in her chair, Elizabeth gave him a quick shake of her head. "There's not a lot to tell really. I was twenty-one when I married my Frank. We'd known each other all our lives and grew up together, went to the same school and everything. His family had a farm a couple of miles away from ours. Once we were married, I moved in with him over there. When my father died, we did our best to help my mother run the farm as well but it was hard work and we couldn't afford to pay for extra help. And then she got ill with Emphysema and that was a real struggle I can tell you; it's a horrible illness and she spent the last few months in hospital. After she died me and Millie sold the farm and divided the money between us. I churned all mine back into our farm and we ran it for a good twenty years after that. But when Frank died, my heart wasn't in it anymore and I was completely isolated out there on my own. In the end, it all got too much for me, so I sold it and bought the house and the rest as they say, is history."

"You never wanted to move away?"

"Me and Millie used to talk about moving to New Zealand but it never came to anything. Brentwood's always been our home, our roots are here and it would be too much of an upheaval, you know? Sometimes I regret not going when I had the chance though and I wonder what life would be like for me now if I had. Brentwood's lovely but it can be a little dull sometimes. Nothing exciting happens around here much."

Raising his eyebrows, Carter thought that that had to be the understatement of the year. "What about children?"

"We did try." She replied quietly. "But it wasn't meant to be. I've had a good life with a good man and that's enough for me. You can't have everything, can you?"

"I suppose not." Carter replied, suddenly thinking of Miranda. "My mom used to worry about Uncle Rob not having anyone and being lonely."

Leaning forward on the table, Elizabeth met his eyes levelly. "He was happy enough, believe me. His work was everything to him and wasn't interested in that kind of thing."

"You got on with him alright, though, didn't you?"

"I suppose so." She sighed, inclining her head. "But only because he knew I wouldn't put up with any nonsense. If I thought he was wrong about something I'd tell him and I he wasn't used to that and I think it amused him. Most of the time he was okay but sometimes he was a pain in the ass."

About to take a sip of water, Carter spluttered.

Having been accused of exactly the same thing by former girlfriends, Carter nodded non-committedly.

"Just before the accident he'd seemed as if he were constantly on edge, distracted as if he was worrying about something."

"Really?" Carter frowned. "Like, what?"

"I don't know." Elizabeth replied, spreading her hands. "I used to ask him what was bothering him but all he'd say was it was work – that's all I ever got out of him." Tilting her head, she studied him, her eyes narrowed. "You know, you don't look anything like your dad, although I can see a lot of Robert in you. You've got the same nose and the same shape face. Your parents were good people Carter, a rare thing these days, I'm afraid."

"Thanks." Carter said, giving her a tight-lipped smile.

"My dad used to rave about your chocolate cakes. My mom tried making one when she was in the mood but they were never as good as yours."

Smiling, Elizabeth nodded. "When I knew he was coming down for one of his visits, I'd make one especially."

"You mean when we came down?"

"Yes." She nodded. "Of course, but I'd sometimes make him one specially to take back with him when he came down here on his own."

"What do you mean when he came down here on his own?" Carter asked, confused. "Where was my mom?"

Shrugging a shoulder, Elizabeth shook her head. "I don't know, I didn't ask."

Straightening, Carter stared at her. "Hang on, my dad used to come down here on his own, *without my mom?*"

"Yeah, quite a lot at one time. He used to stay at Mrs. Burns' B and B in the village."

"Did my mom know?"

"I suppose…" Elizabeth said spreading her hands, arching her eyebrows at him.

"When was this?" Carter asked, leaning forward, staring at her intently.

"Oh god – at least three, four years ago…"

*"Why?"* Carter asked, gobsmacked, unable to think of anything less likely. "My dad and Uncle Rob couldn't stand the sight of each other!"

"I don't think it was your uncle he came down here to see so much as Harry."

"Harry?" Carter asked, narrowing his eyes. "Harry who?"

"Harry Bennett."

Harry Bennett who Reg Tarney had been telling him and Rick about earlier in the Red Lion, the one that had stood up to Old Marvin when he'd slapped his wife in the pub that day. Harry Bennett who'd burst through the door as white as a sheet because he'd seen something strange,

*said he saw it land*

a UFO!

"My dad knew Harry Bennett?" Carter gasped, once more filled with the sensation of having fallen down the rabbit hole.

"Oh course." Elizabeth nodded. "Harry's a good friend of mine. We used to go to school together. He lives just outside the village."

"And he and my dad were friends?" Carter pressed.

Taking a sip of wine, Elizabeth shook her head. "Not at first, not until your uncle introduced them to each other. I must've mentioned Harry to him sometime because one day Rob started asking me questions about him, you know, what was he like and all that stuff. When I asked him why he wanted to know, he said he'd heard some interesting things about him. Then he asked if I could bring him to the house so he could meet him and I said I'd speak to him. Well, when I told Harry Rob wanted me to take him round, at first, he thought it was because he needed something doing to his car."

"What?"

"Harry's always been fascinated with cars, you know, buying old bangers, doing them up and selling them and even now, people still take their cars to him because it saves them having to pay top prices at the garage. It's always been a bone of contention between him and

Benny Critcher who owns it, so much so they nearly came to blows over it in the Swan one night."

"And was it?"

"Was it what?"

"Something to do with his car?"

"No, I don't think so."

"So, what was it all about then?" Carter asked.

"I don't know."

"I thought you were there?"

"I was for a bit but then they went off into the living room and closed the door. A little while later Harry came out and said he had to get going."

"He didn't tell you what it was about?"

"No."

"You didn't ask him?"

Shaking her head, Elizabeth spread her hands.

"Harry's a very private person, always has been. If he wanted to tell me he would've."

"Didn't Uncle Rob tell you?"

"Why would he tell me? I was his cleaner-slash-friend, not his confidante."

"It didn't strike you as strange?"

"A bit, at the time. And then one day when I was cleaning, I heard Rob on the phone asking Harry if he could come round on such-and-such a day because he wanted to introduce him to someone. A few days later your dad arrived on his own and then a little while later Harry turned up and they all went down to the Red Lion for lunch."

*"What?"* Carter gasped, reeling, simply unable to picture his dad and his uncle popping down to the local for a good old jolly together. *"Are you sure?"*

64

"Of course, I'm sure! A lot of the time it was just your dad and Harry but every now and then Rob would join them."

Floundering, Carter's head spun. Why had his uncle been having a drink with not only Harry Bennett, who for the life of him he couldn't imagine him having anything in common with, but also his dad, who he couldn't stand the sight of at the best of times? Why had his dad come here to see Harry and more to the point – why had his uncle wanted them to meet in the first place, the whole thing being frankly, beyond comprehension, both his uncle and dad acting completely out of character. Deeply disturbed for reasons he couldn't explain, he stared through the window, his mind racing.

* * * * *

*In the room George and Rebecca used as an office, Robert stared down at the tablet lying on a piece of black felt. About the size of a piece of A4 paper, it was a lot smaller than he'd imagined it would be.*

*Flawless with a slightly blue tint, he thought it might be some kind of crystal or glass. At the top was a circle of eight perfectly round indents while below, sixteen lines of symbols covered the rest of it, so small and uniform it was almost as if they'd been etched with machine-like precision. Bending, he thought Becca had been right about them resembling scientific equations because the way they were laid out, that's exactly what they looked like. Intrigued, he took his reading glasses from his pocket and put them on, the intricate body of text sharpening, familiar symbols leaping off the surface up at him. Freezing, his heart skipped a beat.*

*can't be*

*Glancing up, he cleared his throat. "Do you have a magnifying glass?" Opening a drawer George silently handed him one. Training it over the symbols Robert's eyes widened, simply unable to believe what he was seeing.*

*how in god's name*

*In an effort to buy himself some time and regain his composure, he tipped his head first one way then the other, pretending to study it further. After a few moments however, straightening, he took his glasses off and turned towards them, hoping they couldn't hear his heart thumping.*

*"Well?" Rebecca asked, staring at him intently, her arms folded.*

*"It's modern." He replied nonchalantly. "Somebody's idea of a joke I expect."*

*"What?" Rebecca gasped, crestfallen. "It can't be!"*

*"Are you sure?" George asked, stepping forward with a frown. Because there's definitely something strange about it."*

*"What do you mean strange?" Rob whispered, tersely, his eyes narrowed.*

*"Show him Georgie."*

*Going behind the desk, George picked up an electric drill resting on a chair. Raising his eyebrows, Robert stared at him.*

*"Watch!" Rebecca said, glancing up at him.*

*Turning the tablet over, face down on the piece of velvet, George ducked behind the desk and plugged the* drill into a socket. Realising what he was about to do, Robert lunged forward. "No!"

"It's okay!" Rebecca said, grabbing his arm, pulling him back. "Watch."

With one hand on the tablet to keep it in place, George put the tip of the drill bit on it, a shrill high-pitched shriek filling the room as he pressed the button, deafeningly loud in the enclosed space. Helpless to do anything other than watch, inwardly Robert groaned. Instead of shattering however, the tablet however remained intact, the drill bit skittering over its flawlessly smooth surface, unable to secure a grip, no matter how hard George tried. After the drill had fallen silent, George picked the tablet up before wordlessly handing it to him, the crystal-clear surface, as flawless as it had been before, not so much as a scratch on it. Astounded, he turned it over in his hands, staring at it in disbelief.

"At first, we thought it must be some kind of toughened glass." George shrugged but we've tried everything on it, fire, acid, the lot and nothing touches it. Which of course begs the question – how was it created in the first place? Frankly, it's beyond us.!

For the first time in his life Robert found himself completely lost for words. With technology moving forward in leaps and bounds scientists were forever creating newer and stronger materials, but, so far as he was aware, nothing like this. Lying the tablet back down on the velvet he assumed a nonchalant stance. "Well, it's certainly strange I'll give you that." He said inclining his head, his eyes meeting his sister's levelly now. "But nevertheless, still modern."

"Are you sure?" Rebecca asked, the disappointment in her eyes evident.

"Yeah." Robert nodded, lying through his teeth. "Probably some high resistance resin or something, but definitely modern, no doubt about it."

# X

*what is it dad*

Jerking awake, as the last vestiges of the dream faded, images from the wood jostled for attention on the periphery of Carter's consciousness. Refusing to acknowledge them he got out of bed and headed for the bathroom, a futile act tantamount to plastering over the cracks, he knew. Hardly sleeping at all now, he was a nervous wreck and there was no getting away from the fact that sooner or later he'd have to confront what had happened in the woods head on.

*But not today.*

Just needing to be doing something, he walked the short distance down to the village and went into Sam's Café, and, even though he had no appetite, ordered a cheese omelette. While he waited, he looked at the two women behind the counter neither of them fitting Elizabeth's description of her sister Millie.

Staring through the window unseeingly, he thought about what Elizabeth had said last night. Why had his uncle asked Elizabeth to bring Harry Bennett to the house in order to meet him and why had he then gone on to introduce him to his dad? Clearly, it had been discussed beforehand but if so, when? And why? After being at loggerheads for years, why had his dad and uncle suddenly decided to bury the hatchet – what had been the incentive? What had his mom made of it and why had his dad come here her without her? The more he thought about it, the more bizarre it all seemed. What had been going on?

After half-heartedly picking at his omelette for a while, after, he returned to the house and, in an attempt to distract himself, began going through some of his uncle's paperwork. Later on, Elizabeth called round and offered to cook him dinner, an invitation he was more than happy to accept, the silence of the house magnifying the fear inside him.

* * * * *

Confident he couldn't be seen behind the nets in the bedroom, holding a pair of binoculars to his eyes, Agent Mark Stevenson stared at the house opposite, looking for any sign of activity. Seeing none, he trained them on a red Skoda, following its progress down the lane before it disappeared from sight round the bend – the first car he'd seen in half an hour. Making his way up the lane an old man carried a string bag of groceries, his progress watched by a tabby cat perched on a fence not far away.

"How can anyone live here and not go crazy?" he muttered. Lowering the binoculars, he set them down on a table beneath the window next to a Long-Range Laser Surveillance Device. Like most agents, he hated surveillance, hour upon hour of mind-bending boredom, waiting for something to happen. Up till now most of his stake-outs had been conducted in the U.S. in one city or another centred around abandoned warehouses on dockyards, factories or ships, and, even though tedious, there were at least things going on to watch to stop him going completely nuts. But out here – buried deep in the English countryside – nothing ever seemed to happen and time crawled by at an excruciatingly slow pace. Not, that his mom would have any complaints he thought; she'd be more than happy for him to be stuck out here out of danger, without risk of being shot or blown up.

Still classed as a novice – even after three years with the elite branch known only as the Bureau – when he'd been given this assignment and learned who the senior agent was he'd be working with, he couldn't have been happier, his hard work obviously not having gone unnoticed. In intelligence circles, Andy Rieker was legendary, the opportunity of working with him not just a privilege he knew, but also a test of his mettle, Rieker's final report on how he conducted himself throughout the operation having the power to make or break him at the Bureau. Right now, the legend was sprawled out on the bed, an arm thrown over his eyes, snoring quietly.

Smiling to himself, Stevenson returned to his chair and, leaning forward, stared at the monitor on the coffee table before him, an image of the empty kitchen filling the screen. Knowing the mark was out, bored, he pressed a button on the keypad, the screen splitting, one half showing the hallway with the stairs leading upwards, the other, the landing. About to return to the main screen, all of a sudden, he paused, having just seen movement through one of the half-open bedroom doors.

Leaning forward he narrowed his eyes, waiting to see if it would happen again. After seeing nothing more however, just to make sure, he pressed another button. Instantly, at the top right of the screen an inset box appeared, showing the non-contact MEMS thermal sensor wasn't picking anything up, the whole house devoid of anything larger than a spider.

Deciding it had been nothing more than a trick of the light, he got to his feet and, picking his mug up, took it downstairs with him to make a coffee. On the screen, slowly, the bedroom door began to close.

\* \* \* \* \*

*In the study at the top of the house, bathed in the glow of the lamp on the desk, Robert stared at the piece of paper in his hand – the last page of his interpretation of the symbols from the rubbing he'd made, hardly able to believe what he was seeing.*

*Last night after Rebecca and George had shown him the tablet, he'd been forced to sit through dinner making idle conversation with them, unable to think about anything other than the table in the other room. While they'd been in the kitchen washing up and making coffee, he'd sneaked in and taken a rubbing of it. Not long after, he'd thanked them for dinner, made his excuses and left.*

*Gripping the steering wheel, his mind had raced as fast as the car, the darkened countryside flashing by him unnoticed in his haste to get home and examine it properly.*

*And now he had.*

*Lowering the piece of paper, he stared at his reflection in the darkened window. With no time to waste, he had to do something. And fast.*

# XI

Leaning against a post on the veranda, Harry Bennett raised a half-smoked cigarette to his lips, nervously sweeping the darkening wall of trees with his eyes. Bathed in purple tones of twilight, their depths were nothing more than impenetrable shadows in which anything could be lurking, unseen.

Below, Bess, a black and white Collie, lay in the doorway of the kennel he'd built for her after he'd first got her and she'd started chewing through the furniture, the chain on her collar attached to a small metal clasp on the front. As if sensing him watching her, she raised her head and looked at him with soft, brown eyes, her tail thumping gently on the wooden floor in the dark recess behind her. Silently man and dog regarded each other before she decided nothing of interest was about to happen after all, and, after stretching her maw in a wide yawn, dropped her head back down on her paws with a deep sigh, as if in exasperation at the follies of human nature.

Pulling smoke deep into his lungs, Harry flicked the nub end over the rails where it fell to the ground a few feet away, a tiny red glow in the gathering darkness, thinking about that strange afternoon not so long ago when Robert Sterling had turned up here out of the blue, the last person he'd have expected a visit from.

At the time, he'd been watching the Saturday afternoon footie – Chelsea at home against Newcastle – eating a cheese and ham doorstop in his armchair when suddenly, above the blare of the telly, Bess had started barking. Aiming the remote control at the tv he'd muted it, hearing the sound of a car approaching. With a curse he'd reached for his stick and come out here, surprised at the sight of Sterling's black Jag pulling up in the yard.

Amid a crescendo of frenzied barking the door had opened and Sterling's head had appeared, looking round the cluttered yard with an expression of disgust on his face. Already annoyed at being disturbed, that look had filled him with indignation and, instead of silencing Bess as he usually would, he'd let her carry on. As yet unnoticed, he'd watched with wry amusement as Sterling eyed her, the chain on her collar pulled taut as she strained against it, barking echoing around the yard, deafening in its intensity.

No doubt weighing up his chances of being mauled to death should she suddenly become loose, Sterling had cautiously remained behind the car door. Having obviously decided not to risk it, he'd just reached back inside the car to blow the horn when all of a sudden, he'd noticed him standing here.

*"Harry!"* he'd shouted, the relief in his voice evident. "I need your help!"

Surprised, he'd stared at Sterling, knowing under ordinary circumstances Sterling wouldn't have had anything to do with him, not for shit. A low-life with no class or education, that's how Sterling saw him and if it hadn't been for Liz, he wouldn't have bothered going to see him at all.

"I need to speak with you about something!" Sterling said. *"Will you please shut that bloody dog up?"*

Raising his eyebrows, he'd been tempted to turn and go back into the house but Sterling's sudden appearance in his yard had aroused his curiosity.

74

*"Bess!"*

Instantly, the dog had fallen silent, dropping back onto her haunches with a whine. "Well?"

"Not out here."

Intrigued, he'd nodded. "You'd better come in."

Closing the car door, Sterling had hurried towards him, before following him through the house into the living room. As he did so, Sterling had glanced nervously through the window, sweeping the yard with his eyes for a moment before turning to face him, his next words taking him by surprise. "Harry – I'm in trouble."

"What kind of trouble?" he'd asked, taken by surprise, his curiosity deepening.

*"Really deep shit Harry, believe me."*

"What kind of shit?"

Thrusting his hands into his great-coat pocket, Sterling had paused then, choosing his words carefully.

"I can't go into details – it's too risky, suffice it to say I desperately need your help."

With the tension in the room palpable, they'd stood stiffly, facing each other.

"How?" he'd asked, at last.

"I need you to look after something for me." Sterling had replied, his voice quiet now as if afraid of being overheard. "A box."

All of a sudden, suspicious, he'd frowned. "A box of what?"

"Just some papers, files and stuff, nothing to worry about." Thinking Sterling couldn't have looked more worried if he'd tried, he'd narrowed his eyes.

"What, secret stuff?"

Surprised, a ghost of a smile had appeared on
Sterling's face. "No flies on you, is there, Harry?"

"What happens if I get caught with it?"

"Nothing." Sterling had replied, spreading his long,
bony hands. "If – and that's a big if mind – anyone did
find it here, all you'd have to say is I asked you to look
after it for me but you didn't know what was in it."

Snorting loudly, he'd shaken his head. "Like they'd
believe that!" Suddenly, out in the yard Bess had barked
a single bark before falling silent again, Sterling freezing
as she did so before turning his head as if listening for
something. "I'm sorry Harry, I don't have time for this –
can you help me or not? I'll pay you of course..."

"I don't want your money." He'd muttered. "I just
don't want to end up inside that's all..."

*"You won't!"* Sterling had hissed then, his eyes
flaring with anger before taking step closer, the urgency
in his voice unmistakable. "You have my word on that, I
promise."

Taken aback by the strength of the fury he'd
momentarily been privy to he was just beginning to
wonder if he'd made a mistake inviting him in here at all
when Sterling had spoken again.

*"I'm begging you – please!"*

Despite what he'd thought of him, seeing how
desperate he was, he'd felt himself weaken. With a sigh,
he'd nodded. "Yeah, okay."

"Thank you." Sterling said, turning. "I'll just go and
get it." After a few minutes, he'd reappeared and dropped
an ordinary-looking cardboard box on the floor, before
taking a folded piece of paper from his pocket. Passing it
to him he said: "One more thing Harry. If anything

76

should happen to me, you need to send it to that address straightaway, understand?"

On it was a name and address in scrawling handwriting and at first, he hadn't been able to make it out the writing had been so spidery, his eyes widening with surprise as he realised it was a name he was already familiar with. One which George had mentioned a couple of times.

"What do you mean if anything should happen to you?" he'd gasped then, his eyes wide. "Just what the hell have you gone and got yourself into, exactly?"

With the air of having to explain to a child who was finding it hard to understand, Sterling had stiffened. "It's best you don't know Harry. All you've got to do is look after it, that's all! I'm sorry but I don't have time for this – I've got to go!"

"Hang on a minute." He'd said. "What I anyone comes here and starts asking questions…"

From the doorway, Sterling had fixed him with a look.

"They won't – this would be the last place they'd ever think of looking, believe me!" he'd muttered, his voice clipped.

"Who?" he'd gasped, then. "Who are they?"

"I can't tell you that."

"But what if they do?" he'd insisted, angrily.

*"Then guard it with your life!"* Sterling had hissed disappearing from the doorway.

And that had been that.

Alone in the living room

*just him and the box*

he'd heard the creak of the front door

*nothing to worry about*

followed Sterling's feet thudding down the wooden steps to the yard, accompanied by Bess's frenzied barking. Halfway down the hall the car door had slammed followed by the throaty sound of the engine purring into life. Bursting through the front door onto the veranda he'd limped to the rail, watching Sterling as he sped off, his words

*guard it with your life*

echoing through his mind like the deep tolling of a bell, wondering if he'd meant them literally or if it had just been a throw-away remark. With a sigh, he'd turned and gone back into the house, Bess falling silent again behind him. And then, a few days later Liz had rung him in floods of tears, in such a state he'd hardly been able to make out what she'd been saying at first but then he had,

*Rob's dead*

Sterling's words

*if anything should happen to me*

returning to him. Had something happened to him because of the box? Except the doctor had said his death had been heart failure

*natural causes*

and although he desperately wanted to believe it, nevertheless, he couldn't help wondering. Unwilling to take it from its hiding place for fear of what might happen, he'd left it where it was. And then Liz told him Sterling's nephew was coming to Brentwood Down and he'd decided to just give it him instead – at least that way it would be out of his hands and he could rest easy. That was the plan.

\* \* \* \* \*

*"And this morning when we went into the office, the window had been forced!" Rebecca gasped. "They must've broken in even though we were right there, upstairs in bed! The police said it was a good job we hadn't heard anything and gone down and confronted them because we could've been in real danger but I wish we had because they'd have had a fight on their hands – bloody cheek!"*

*On the other end of the line, Robert closed his eyes.*
*"What did they say, the police?"*
*"Not a lot. They've dusted for fingerprints and had a look round but they didn't seem to think there was much chance of getting any of it back, especially the money."*
*"What money?" Robert asked, surprised.*
*"Oh, just two hundred quid George kept in the desk drawer for emergencies. I didn't even know it was there but George says we'll be able to claim it back off the insurance." Raising his eyebrows, Robert thought maybe his brother-in-law wasn't that much of an idiot after all.*

*"The strange thing is, apart from the money and the tablet – the chopping board if that's what it was – nothing else was taken, even though that rare pot was right there on the mantlepiece. It's a shame though because I'd have liked to have found out more about it and how it was made. I suppose we should be grateful they didn't take the telly or the stereo either. But it's not just that – someone was in our home while we were there and the thought of it…well it's horrible!"*

*Christ.*

"I'm sorry Becca." He muttered, hating himself. "I don't know what to say..."

"Rob, I've got to go." She interjected. "The burglar alarm man's pulling up on the drive. How's that for closing the stable door after the horse has bolted?"

Hanging up, for a moment he remained where he was, his hands to his face, reminding himself he'd had no choice. Going up to his study he took a key from his trouser pocket and, bending, unlocked the top drawer of the desk before sliding it out, the tablet nestled in newspaper, resting inside it.

# XII

After they'd finished eating, Carter helped Elizabeth wash up. "I'm dreading tomorrow." She sighed. "I'll be glad when it's over."

"Why?" he asked with a frown. "What's happening?"

Turning, Elizabeth looked at him, aghast. *"The funeral?"*

"What?" he replied. "The funeral's not till Thursday."

"It's Thursday tomorrow!"

"No, it's not, it's Wednesday tomorrow."

"Today's Wednesday."

"It's Tuesday today." he replied with a snort.

"That's not funny." She said cocking an eyebrow at him. "And I don't think it's in very good taste…"

"What?" he asked, halfway through drying a plate. "Why would I joke about something like that?"

Taking the tea-towel from him she stood before him, holding his eyes levelly with her own. "You really think today's Tuesday?"

"No." he replied quietly, giving his head a quick shake. "I *know* it is."

"No, it's not." Frowned, wondering if the past few months had affected him more than she'd thought.

"Okay." He said planting one hand on the worktop and the other on his hip, looking at her. "When did you cook me breakfast?"

"Yesterday – Tuesday."

"No…it wasn't – I got here Sunday, remember?"

"No, you didn't." Elizabeth corrected. "You got here Monday night and I cooked you breakfast yesterday morning – Tuesday."

81

"Elizabeth..." he said quietly. "I know finding Uncle Rob must've been a terrible shock and..."

*"Don't patronise me!"* she gasped hotly, bristling.

"All I meant was..."

"I know what you meant!" she grated, her eyes sparking. "Are you seriously trying to tell me you don't know what day it is?"

"Me?" Carter faltered. "Elizabeth, I hate to say it but I think..." Thrusting the tea towel at him she turned on her heel and disappeared through the doorway. Aware he'd offended her, nevertheless, convinced he was right, he followed her into the living room. Pointing the remote control at the television, she thumbed a couple of buttons, and, with a flick, the twenty-four-hour news channel appeared. Turning her head, she looked at him defiantly, her eyebrows raised. *"Well?"*

Speechless, Carter stared at the telly.

*October the ninth – Wednesday.*

"I suppose you're going to tell me the telly people don't know what day it is either!" she asked.

"I don't believe it." he breathed, aghast, staring at the screen. "I was *sure* it was Tuesday! What happened to Monday then..."

Coming to him, she looked up at him in concern.

"Carter, you've been through a lot the last few months...you're bound to be a bit..."

"No." he cut in quickly, giving his head a quick shake, his mind racing. "You don't understand – I *know* it was Sunday when I left home!"

"Perhaps you were mistaken."

"I'm not." He insisted, turning to look at her. "I *know* it was Sunday because on the way here I was listening to

82

a science lecture on the radio – a live lecture – and that was Sunday!"

"It must've been recorded."

"*It wasn't!*" Carter replied hotly, adamant.

"So, what are you saying?" she asked, narrowing her eyes in confusion, her head on one side now.

"I don't know." Carter breathed, his heart racing, feeling adrift. "Unless..."

"Unless what?"

"Unless when I got here, I got so drunk I completely missed a day..."

"God Carter, how much do you think you had?" she gasped, looking at him askance. "It's nothing to do with that, I know that for a fact."

"How?"

"Because Monday morning I looked to see if your car was outside but it wasn't so I thought you might've put it in the garage, but when I went over, there was no one there."

"I wasn't on the sofa?"

"No, of course not – I'd have seen you, wouldn't I?" she replied, spreading her hands. "How could I not have?"

"So where was I Monday then?" he breathed. Filled with fear he got to his feet, a memory of something that had happened when he'd been a small child suddenly surfacing in his mind – something he'd forgotten about until now.

"Carter?" Elizabeth gasped. "What is it – what's wrong?"

As the room melted away, he was

*eight years old again, sitting under the tree in the
back garden, reading, when he saw something out of the
corner of his eye – a flash in the sky. Looking up
however, there was nothing to be seen except the clear
blue sky. Thinking he must've been mistaken he dropped
his eyes again when all of a sudden it happened again,
only brighter this time. Looking up, he swept the sky with
his eyes once more, unable to see anything until – there –
a quick white flash of white against blue, something
moving slowly through the sky, heading toward him in a
zig-zag motion.*

*Putting the book down he got to his feet, and, shading
his eyes with his hands, stared at it intently, trying to
make out what it was, his eyes smarting with the effort
wondering if it was some kind of aircraft – a light plane
maybe – in trouble.*

*flash*

*And then, all of a sudden, as if someone had flicked a
switch, the bright, mid-morning sunshine was no more,
inexplicably bathed in the mellow tones of afternoon, the
sun hanging just above the trees in the distance now, the
shadows all about him in the garden longer. Shocked,
gasped and took a step back, unable to believe it,
wondering how so much time could've passed in the
blink of an eye without him being aware of it, all the time
knowing he hadn't fallen asleep because he'd been
standing in the exact same place as he had been before...*

*And then he remembered the flash in the sky.*

*With his heart racing he raised his head again,
searching the sky for it with his eyes but it was nowhere
to be seen. Turning, he tore through the garden into the
house, skidding to a halt in the kitchen at how quiet*

*everything was, the thought occurring to him that he was alone there, the house feeling empty about him. But then, all of a sudden something changed and he heard a sound in the living room, filled with relief at the sight of his dad waking up on the sofa, for a moment looking as if he didn't know where he was.*

*Running to him, Carter clung to him, bawling his eyes out without knowing why, his dad's arms trembling as his held him, clinging to him just as tightly. And they stayed there for ages, him crying, his dad right there on the sofa not saying a word, just clinging to each other...*

*"Carter!"* Elizabeth gasped, bringing him back with a bump. "Are you alright?"

Shocked at the memory of what had happened that day and wanting nothing more than to be alone to think about it, knowing Elizabeth was no fool, he dropped his shoulders. "I've been better." He said simply.

\* \* \* \* \*

*Narrowing his eyes, Robert stared down at the tablet. While he'd managed to decipher most of the symbols completely out of his depth, there were parts he couldn't make head or tail of. This wasn't his field, it was Helys – but could he trust him? Taking his glasses off he tapped them against his teeth, thinking. Deciding to sleep on it before he made a decision, he got to his feet, and, snapping the light off was just closing the door behind him when, all of a sudden, he stopped.*

*The tablet was glowing.*

*Crossing the room in two easy strides he stared down at it, the lines of script bright with blue-white light like the numbers on a luminous watch now.*

*what the*

*With his mind racing he wondered how it was possible before suddenly looking up, realising the tablet had been on the desk in direct sunlight for most of the day, which could only mean one thing – the tablet must be solar-powered!*

*Was it possible?*

*With his heart pounding he gently ran a finger over the script, accidentally brushing one of the still-dark indents. As he did so, the glowing lines flickered out, replaced by another set below it for a moment before disappearing again. Wide-eyed, he touched one of the indents again, this time more text appearing at the bottom. Hardly breathing, one by one he touched all eight indents, in turn revealing more pages embedded within the tablet, all of them glowing with the same eerie luminosity as the first. Hardly able to believe it, he shot down the stairs two at a time and, bursting into the living room, snatched a marble ball from the solitaire game on the side-board.*

*Back upstairs, he placed it in the first indent, then one after the other, page after page appearing one after the other as he did so, all on different levels and at different angles within the tablet, his face bathed in the light. Hardly able to believe it, weak-kneed he dropped onto the chair and, picking up a pen, with a hand that shook, began to write.*

# XIII

As the sound of the alarm clock permeated his dream, leaning over, Carter silenced it and lay back against the pillows thinking about what had happened at Elizabeth's last night. Had that day all those years ago really happened how he remembered it or had it been nothing more than a dream? Surely it had to be didn't it, after all how could a whole day pass in a matter of seconds?

*what about Sunday*

What indeed. Somewhere between leaving the flat and arriving at Brentwood Down, apart from being chased through the woods by aliens, something else must have happened, something he didn't remember. Not wanting to think about that, all of a sudden, filled with panic he threw the covers off and shot out of bed.

\* \* \* \* \*

*"Have you completely lost your mind?" Hely gasped. Spooning sugar into his coffee, he still couldn't believe Rob had come all the way out here in the middle of the night and woken him up.*

*At thirty-eight, Hely Walberg was an Irish-American New Yorker who, after being relentlessly head-hunted by the Biochem Institute, had joined him on a secret research programme for the military but, despite their efforts, after eight years of intensive research, they weren't much further along than when they'd started, frustration and despair being the order of the day.*

*"Believe me, I know how it sounds but if it's what I think it is, it's unbelievable." Robert said quietly, unfazed.*

*Leaning on the breakfast bar, Hely stared at the buff-coloured folder lying on the counter between them, his eyebrows raised. After hearing what Rob had to say, he couldn't help but wonder if he'd really lost it this time, there always having been something of the 'mad scientist' about him.*

*"All I'm asking you to do is have a look at it and tell me what you think." Robert urged, pushing the folder towards him. "Humour me."*

*Over the counter, they locked eyes for a moment. "Please."*

*Raising his hands in submission, Hely pulled the folder towards him, shaking his head at himself as he did so. "I don't believe I'm doing this." He muttered. "I must be as crazy as you are right now."*

\* \* \* \* \*

Perched majestically on a hill overlooking the village, constructed from grey stone, St. Laurence's was a typical Norman church. On the square tower was a gold latticework clock whose subtle chimes had rung out on the hour, every hour, ever since Benjamin Finchley a rich land-owner had had it commissioned, way back in the eighteenth century. Getting out of the car Carter stared at a large crowd in front of the church. "I didn't expect this many to turn up."

"Who are they?" Elizabeth asked, joining him.

"Scientists, mainly, I expect." He replied.

88

"And half the village as well, by the looks of it."
Elizabeth said. "I wonder where the boys are." Turning
her head, she looked around before nodding. "There they
are."

Following her gaze Carter saw two old men standing
in front of a bench, a third man sitting, a black Stetson
partly covering his face. Hearing voices he turned to see
three men approaching before introducing themselves as
scientists from the Biochem Institute. After offering their
condolences, turning, they all headed for the church,
others coming up to him as they did so, their names
forgotten even before he'd finished shaking hands with
them, some he knew, most he didn't, all wanting to say
farewell to his uncle.

As he joined the pall-bearers, with the coffin resting
on his shoulder, the organ boomed in the vaulted space,
and, with the heady scent of flowers in the air, he
couldn't help but think of the incident in the Chapel of
Rest. Feeling panic flutter, he saw the thing
*you know what it was*
climbing out of the coffin again, imagining he could
feel it moving around inside right now. Telling himself to
get a grip, taking a deep breath, he concentrated on
keeping in step with the others, just wanting to get it
safely to the alter without mishap. With the mellow lights
hanging from the ceiling reflected in the wood and a
large wreath of white lily's resting atop the lid, it was his
uncle down to a tee he thought; respectful with no fuss.

Joining Elizabeth in the front pew, he shivered and,
mistaking his fear for grief, gave his hand a reassuring
squeeze. After the service, outside, Elizabeth introduced

him to the two old men they'd seen earlier, Jack Solomon and Seth Calloway.

"My condolences." Jack said shaking his hand, staring at him curiously with faded blue eyes, his suit two sizes too large for him.

"Nice to meet you, Carter." The other one said from beneath a black trilby, looking dapper in a black suit and grey silk shirt. "Although I feel as if I know you already."

"You do?" Carter asked.

"Of course! Liz has told us all about you."

"All good I hope." He replied, glancing at her quickly, hoping she hadn't told them about him passing out drunk on the sofa.

"Of course." Seth nodded.

Looking past them, Elizabeth beckoned. "Harry, come and meet Carter – George's son."

Turning his head Carter saw a tall man dressed in a somewhat shabby-looking suit – the man in the black Stetson. Dropping his cigarette, he ground it out with his foot before coming towards them with a slight limp, aided by a walking stick.

"Carter, this is Harry Bennett, another good friend of mine." Elizabeth said. Feeling his heart miss a beat, Carter stared at the man Reg had told them about, the man who his dad had so mysteriously come down here to meet see after Uncle Rob had introduced them and who'd claimed to have seen a UFO.

*said he saw it land*

As soon as Harry lifted his head, seeing his face Carter was suddenly sure he'd seen him somewhere before, all of a sudden filled with a deep, resonating fear.

At the same time, staring at Carter as if he couldn't believe his eyes, Harry froze, his face bleaching.

Speechless, they stared at each other.

"Carter? Harry?" Elizabeth asked, staring from one to the other, wondering what was happening.

At that, realising everyone was staring at them, giving his head a quick shake, Carter stepped forward, offering his hand as he did so. "Nice to meet you, Harry."

Looking down at it as if it was a shit-covered stick, for a moment Harry remained where he was, unmoving. Looking up at him Elizabeth narrowed her eyes.

"Harry?"

Before he had a chance to reply however, all of a sudden, the vicar appeared and the tension broke. Sliding her arm through Carter's, the others following close behind, looking up at him, Elizabeth whispered: "What was all that about?"

"I have no idea." Carter replied, still unnerved by the encounter.

"Do you know each other?"

Shrugging Carter shook his head. "Not so far as I know although I'm sure I recognise him from somewhere."

"Maybe you met him when you were down here with your dad." Elizabeth suggested.

"Maybe." He replied, wondering if that was it.

After the burial during which Elizabeth went to bits, sobbing into a handkerchief, in a reversal of roles, Carter took her arm and led her back towards the church, the others trailing after them. After offering their condolences again with most of them politely declining Elizabeth's invitation to join them back at the house, people began making their way towards their cars, Carter secretly relieved, having to make small talk with a bunch of strangers, the last thing he felt like doing. As they made their way through the car park, behind them, Harry cleared his throat. "If no-one minds, I'm going to clear off."

"Why?" Elizabeth asked, turning to look at him.

Dropping his eyes, Harry shook his head.

"Somethings come up and I've got to go."

"But Harry..."

"I'm sorry, I can't!" He muttered, turning.

"What the hell?" Jack gasped, staring at him, incredulously.

"Do you want a lift?" Seth called after him.

Without answering, head down, Harry disappeared through the gate.

"I take it that's a no then." Seth muttered.

"I'm so sorry Carter, I don't know what's got into him!" Elizabeth muttered, shaking her head angrily.

"I don't know why you're surprised." Seth said quietly, putting a hand on her shoulder. "You know what he's like."

Following them to an old, slate-coloured Renault, Carter got in the back with Jack. In the driver's seat, Seth looked at them in the rear-view mirror. "You okay back there? I've put the heater on."

"Fat lot of good that'll do." Jack replied, rolling his eyes. "By the time it gets going, we'll be there!"

"You'll be able to meet Millie when we get back. She's at the house sorting the food out – or at least I hope she is." Elizabeth told Carter her shoulder, her indignation at Harry having all but disappeared now.

"Fine woman!" Seth said quietly, meeting Carters eyes in the mirror.

"Jesus Christ!" Jack muttered gruffly beside Carter. "Show some respect will you today of all days!"

As they drove through the car park, back in the churchyard, from behind a tree, a figure watched them.

\* \* \* \* \*

*With the only sound, the low hum of the refrigerator, pacing, Robert stared at Walberg's bent head with narrowed eyes, waiting for some kind of reaction. At last, Hely raised his head, his eyes bright with excitement.*

*"Where did you get this?"*

*"I'd rather not say, suffice to say I have the original source." Robert replied, his heart racing. "Was I right? Is it what I think it is?"*

*"Oh yeah, it's that alright – and so much more!" Hely snorted, getting to his feet. "Christ – I need a drink."*

*Sloshing a couple of inches of Bourbon into a glass, he raised it tremblingly to his lips, still unable to believe what he'd just read, it being nothing short of a scientific miracle, more information than he could ever possibly hope to learn in a lifetime, effectively changing their research beyond all recognition. Watching him quietly, Robert waited, giving it time to sink in, knowing only too well how he must be feeling right now. Staring owlishly at Robert, his eyes wide behind his glasses, Hely spoke again, his voice barely above a whisper.*

*"It's not ours, is it?"*

*"No."*

*"It's theirs?"*

93

"Has to be. We're not even close to anything like that yet."

"How did you even…"

"You know what kind of people we work for – the less you know the better. We're the only ones who know about this and I intend to keep it that way. I suggest we work on this privately – just us."

"You can't be serious!" Hely gasped coming round the counter towards him now, his face pale. "We'd never get away with it…"

"If I disclose it, it'll disappear never to be seen again – is that what you want?"

"No, of course not, but it's insane to think we'd ever be able to work on it ourselves without anyone finding out."

"As insane as letting an opportunity like this pass us by?"

"Have you even considered the repercussions, the risks we'd be taking?"

"Of course." Robert replied almost flippantly. "And I think we should do it anyway."

"Goddammit Rob, you can't just spring this on me and ask me to come in on something like this at the drop of a hat…" Hely hissed, his face pale.

"That's exactly what I'm doing." Sterling replied, his eyes boring into his, refusing to let them drop. "We don't have time to waste – now, are you in or out?"

# XIV

As promised, when they arrived at the house, Millie was already there, fussing around in the kitchen. A small bird-like woman with blonde hair neatly pinned up in a coiffure and nothing like he'd been expecting, nevertheless, a blind man could see she and Elizabeth were close. Greeting him warmly, she stared up at him, her eyes filled with curiosity. "I used to see you around the village with your uncle when you were a kid but I don't expect you remember, do you?"

"I'm sorry. he replied apologetically.

"No need to apologise." She replied, flapping her hand at him. "It was a long time ago."

Later on, after everyone had left, with the evening being an unseasonably mild one, Carter and Elizabeth sat on Elizabeth's patio in her back garden. "I suppose you'll be leaving soon." She asked with a touch of sadness in her voice.

"I'm afraid so."

"I think the boys wanted you to have a drink with them before you left."

"They did? He asked. "Why?"

"They were quite fond of Rob. Sometimes he'd go down to the park and play chess with them."

"Really?" Carter asked, surprised.

Smiling sadly, Elizabeth nodded. "Yeah. I think he enjoyed it because they were so down to earth. I think he felt he could be himself around them. They took to you straightaway."

"They seem nice."

"You don't know the half of it." she said, giving her head a quick shake. "They're like a pair of kids sometimes; mischief on a stick Seth is, always has been, ever since we met him. Me, Harry and Jack, we all grew up together but we only got to know Seth when he and Martha his wife moved here. She was lovely – really beautiful – and they adored each other. Four years after they moved here, she became ill. There was nothing anyone could do and when he lost her a few months later he was devastated."

Nodding, Carter thought of the way Seth had joked about Millie in the car. Maybe humour had been his way of dealing with the funeral, it all being too close to the bone, even after all this time. Let on at the wake he'd been the life and the soul of the party, giving Carter a glimpse of his mischievous side.

"What about Jack?"

"When we were kids, Jack's parents used to have the paper shop in the village – the estate agent's office it is now. His mother, Janice was a tyrant. We used to call her Boadicea because that's what she looked like but his dad, Maurice was a tiny little man and let her walk all over him; not so much a husband as an unpaid servant, up at the crack of dawn doing the papers and still there late at night. Everyone thought he'd snap and do her in but it never happened because one day his heart packed up and everyone said she'd worked him to death. At the time Jack was only ten so she sold up and bought the house, the one he's in now. As soon as he was old enough, she started treating him the same way she'd treated his dad, making him to the shopping, the cooking, the cleaning, everything while she sat about on her backside eating and drinking, squandering their savings and getting meaner and fatter every day. Thankfully though, Jack was made of sterner stuff than his dad and the day he turned eighteen, without her knowing he signed up for the army, just upped and left. None of us heard anything from him for years until she died and he came back. Everything was okay again then until Seth and Martha moved here and then everything changed."

"Why, what happened?"

"You may well ask." Elizabeth said clicking her tongue. "Jack used to like a flutter on the horses every now and then but when Seth started work at the Palace dog-track over in Broughton, he was always there. They became good friends – inseparable – and after seeing him and Martha so happy, well, I think it made Jack realise how lonely he was. He had us of course, but no amount of friends make up for having that special somebody in your life, do they?"

Nodding, Carter thought of Miranda.

"Anyway, one day Seth told him about this chap he knew that had met his wife at the conservative club in Durston on a solo night – a special night for single people – so, one night, Seth and Martha took him so he could see what it was like. After that, he went on his own a few times and met Connie Bishop as she was back then, a hairdresser. Fifteen years younger than he was and the minute I set eyes on her I knew she was going to be trouble."

"Why, what was she like?"

"A big girl, cheap-looking with dyed auburn hair, and her cleavage on show. When me and Martha were talking to her, we tried to find out more about her but it was like trying to get blood out of a stone and Jack wasn't saying anything either and that was strange in itself because he usually told Seth everything."

Behind his hand Carter couldn't help but smile, only too easily able to imagine the flamboyant Connie sweeping into the village like a whirl-wind, and, in a backwater like this the news would've spread like wildfire. Thwarted, unable to discover who exactly was in their midst, who Connie was and where she'd come from must've driven the gossip-mongers crazy.

"And then, before we knew it, she'd moved in with him, lock, stock and barrel! We warned him about rushing into things and it being too soon but he was smitten and it was like water off a duck's back. Six months later they got married in Hadley at the registry office and even though we were all invited and we all went, none of us were particularly happy about it but what could we do? Afterwards we all went out to dinner in town and in all honesty, we'd never seen him happier, so for his sake, me and Martha decided to give her a chance. Not that it was appreciated. She stand-offish and wasn't interested in village life and unless she was out and about in the village, we never saw her. Coming from Bristol, I think she was a city girl at heart. Me and Millie we love being in the countryside but then it's not to everyone's taste, is it?"

Nodding, Carter thought he couldn't agree more.

"I don't think she realised how quiet it was going to be out here and I think she was bored stiff. Sometimes I'd see her and she'd have this sort of restless look on her face as if she were waiting for something exciting to happen. Maybe if she'd have had a couple of little ones to keep her occupied, things might've been different, but Jack told us she wasn't interested in having kids, something she never told him until after they were married. Needless to say, he was far from happy about it and it they used to row about it, and that wasn't the only thing. She did didn't like him spending so much time with Seth saying he was a bad influence on him, especially as he worked at the dog track. Mind you, she wasn't wrong there because Seth was always getting him to put a fiver on a dog here or a tenner on a horse there. At the time, Jack was only working part time in the printers in Hadley and Connie wasn't doing anything really, a bit of hairdressing now and then and so what little money they did have left over at the end of the month, she didn't want him frittering away. One day though Jack had a big win at the dog track and told Connie she could trade her old car in for a new one, something she'd been wanting to do for ages. Well of course she was over the moon and the next day she went over to Hadley to find a car and that's where she met Danny Hanson at Nova Motors. Two years younger than her he was, handsome and on good money, living life to the full and I think it made her realise how dull her own life had become. They ended up having an affair and then one day about six months later they upped and left."

"No!" Carter breathed.

Elizabeth nodded sombrely. "Yeah. I think if it had been a one-off or a quick fling, he might've been able to forgive her, but the fact they'd been sneaking about so long behind his back really got to him. He realised what kind of woman she was then and why we'd warned him about her in the first place. Apart from signing the

99

divorce papers, I don't think he ever heard from her again. He's got us, his friends and that's all that matters."

"He's lucky to have you all, you're a great bunch."

"What, even Harry?" Elizabeth snorted. "I don't know what got into him earlier. He looked at you like he'd seen a ghost. You said you thought you might've seen him before somewhere?"

Biting his lip, he nodded. "That's what I thought, as if I recognised him from somewhere. On the other hand, I'm sure I'd remember – Harry doesn't seem the type anyone would be able to forget in a hurry."

"He's not. He's always been a bit strange but he's got worse over the years. I don't think it helps being out there in that house, all on his own."

"He never married?"

"What Harry?" she snorted. "Harry's not the marrying kind. When he was younger, he used to say marriage was for suckers and he liked being free to do as he pleased; not that he'd have had any trouble getting anyone to marry him back then."

"Really?" he asked, surprised.

With a faint smile playing around her lips, she nodded. "Oh, I know it's hard to believe now but when he was younger Harry was a catch; not particularly handsome mind but sort of rugged and he could charm the birds out of the trees – all the girls used to fancy him. When he was a truck driver, he used to say he had a woman in every town. I don't know if that was true or not but he never seemed short of female company. He's got a heart of gold and he'd give you his last penny if the thought you needed it but he's no fool and nothing gets past him, believe me."

"I don't doubt it."

As twilight began to creep through the garden Carter couldn't help wondering what the truth was about Harry's UFO sighting. Had he really seen one or was it nothing more than village gossip?

*said he saw it land*

Not wanting to, nevertheless feeling almost compelled to ask, Carter cleared his throat.

"Someone told me he'd seen a UFO."

Shaking her head, Elizabeth tutted. "You'd think they'd have better things to talk about by now!"

"Is it true?" Carter asked. "Did he see one?"

"I don't know but one thing I will say, Harry's no liar. If Harry said he saw a UFO, then that's exactly what he did see. Unfortunately, I can't say the same about everyone else, and, let's face it if there were as many flying saucers around here as everyone says there is, the streets would be full of little green men."

"What, other people have seen them around here as well then?" Carter gasped, staring at her wide-eyed, the shadows all about them seeming suddenly deeper.

"If it's all the same with you I'd rather not talk about it, it's been a hard enough day as it is. Let's go in, shall we?"

Only too happy to oblige, Carter got to his feet and followed her into the house. As he did so he paused for a moment in the doorway, sweeping the darkening sky with his eyes before closing door firmly behind him.

\* \* \* \* \*

In his cluttered kitchen, Harry sat at the table, his brows drawn together in a deep frown, his eyes dark, the box of papers all but forgotten now.

Ever since he'd remembered what had really happened up on Bowers Hill, he'd thought nothing could ever bring him to his knees again like that day, but now he realised he'd been wrong – *so very, very wrong.* Because as soon as he'd seen Carter outside the church earlier,

*OH-MY-GOD*

shock had exploded through him, unable to do anything other than simply stand there gawping at him, his mouth hanging open like an imbecile.

*IT CAN'T BE*

Rendered speechless, looking back, that had probably been a good thing otherwise he might've screamed simply because, standing right there in front of him was the man who, up till then he'd never even been sure existed. A man whose face had haunted him for years; a face he'd never forget till the day he died. Closing his eyes he trembled with fear, remembering the first time he'd set eyes on him, Carter's bloodied face vividly imprinted upon his mind.

\* \* \* \* \*

*Behind the desk Doctor Kirby looked at the couple nervously sitting side by side, looking at him expectantly. With a sinking feeling, this, he thought, was the downside to being a doctor because it never got any easier breaking bad news to good people; especially people who'd become friends rather than patients over the years.*

*Leaning forward he cleared his throat in an attempt to buy himself some more time, choosing his words carefully. Sensing they weren't going to be hearing anything positive the couple exchanged glances, the man's hand quickly enclosing hers.*

*"I've had the test results back." Dr. Kirby began quietly, looking from one to the other.*

*Next to him the man felt his wife stiffen and glancing at her quickly, squeezed her hand a little tighter, both of them staring at him intently now, waiting with bated breath, their hearts racing. Getting to his feet the doctor came around the desk and, perching on a corner of it, folded his hands in his lap, silent for a moment or two before raising his head and looking at the woman.*

*"It's not good news, I'm afraid. You have a tilted uterus which explains the reason for the miscarriages."*

*Sighing deeply, the woman shook her head – at least now they knew what had been causing them. Glancing at her husband she saw that he was already looking at her, waiting for her reaction. Giving his hand a reassuring squeeze, she looked at the doctor again.*

*"So now you know what's causing them, what can we do?"*

*Knowing there was no easy way to break it to her, the doctor slowly shook his head. "With this condition, I'm afraid there's nothing we can do."*

*Next to her the man groaned and dropped his head.*

*"What?" the woman gasped her eyes wide in her pale face. "There's got to be something you can do…"*

"I'm sorry." He said quietly, shaking his head. "I know how devastating this must be, especially after everything you've been through but..."

"But what?" The woman demanded shrilly. "That we can never have children?"

"I don't know what to say. I'm so sorry. I know how much you wanted them."

Devastated, the woman dropped her head into her hands and wept.

# XV

Leaving Elizabeth's, Carter went back to the house flicking lights on as he did so, his childhood fear of the dark apparently having returned with a vengeance since the night in the wood. Rubbing his hands over his face, he yawned, mentally and physically exhausted, the day all but having drained him. Looking at the empty bottle of Red Stag on the draining board he decided to heat some milk in a saucepan for a cup of cocoa.

While he waited, he thought about Harry's unnerving reaction to him when they'd met earlier, the look of shock on his face unmistakable. Rattled, it had bothered him more than he'd cared to admit. And then Harry had left, clearly something the others hadn't been expecting, the nagging feeling it was somehow his fault had staying with him although for the life of him, he couldn't imagine why. Frowning, he heard Elizabeth's words again,

*if there were as many flying saucers around here as everyone says there is, the streets would be full of little green men* the implication being that others had seen them as well, besides Harry, in which case, maybe his own terrifying encounter the other night wasn't the isolated incident he imagined it to be. Once again, images from the wood began pouring into his mind and, once more engaging in a mental battle to drive them out again, wondered when the world had gone insane, and what he'd been doing at the time. *Being chased through the woods,* his inner voice reminded him.

* * * * *

*Norman Kepple was the caretaker at the Biochem Institute; although not a caretaker so much as a bloody dogsbody, he thought. When he'd taken this job, he'd understood the upkeep of the building was his sole responsibility, ensuring lightbulbs were replaced, squeaky doors silenced and that everything was kept in good working order; in short, making sure everything ran smoothly on a day- to- day basis. Which most of the time he did. Except days like this when he ended up fetching and carrying things from one department to another, something he was far from happy about because he wasn't a removal man.*

*And now someone had spilt something in one of the corridors and he'd been asked to clean it up and surely that was a job for the cleaners, he thought sourly. Except the cleaners didn't start till eight. Deciding the sooner he got it sorted the better, he collected the keys from the security office in reception and took the service lift down to the basement heading for a passageway lined with* pipes, dimly lit by evenly spaced wall lights covered with wire brackets.

Making his way down it he glanced nervously over his shoulder every now chilled, despite the fact that down here amid the labyrinth of hot water pipes and boilers it was stiflingly hot. Despite having been down here more times than he cared to remember, the place gave him the creeps; the kind of place he'd seen in horror films where anything could be lurking in the shadows. And even though there were hundreds of white-coated scientists and lab technicians on the five levels above him, it made no difference because down here in the gloom with nothing but the hum of generators and the occasional rattle of old pipes, to all intents and purposes he was completely alone.

Hunching his shoulders, he quickened his pace, heading for the cupboard, just wanting to get the hell out of there. After filling the bucket from the clanky tap over the ancient sink, carrying the mop in his other hand, he was just heading back the way he'd come when he heard a strange sound that seemed to come from all around him.

what the hell

Spinning, his heart leapt.

And then, just as suddenly as it started, it stopped.

A moment later it started again, louder than before, rebounding off the walls and the ceiling, filling the air around him. Freezing he stared back along the darkened passageway lined with pipes snaking away into the darkness behind him, wondering what the hell was down there with him. Suddenly the pitch changed and, rolling his eyes he recognised the sound for what it was, *amplified by one of the ventilation shafts somewhere above. Shaking his head at himself he made his way back along the passageway before getting in the lift and pulling the metal gate closed behind him once more.*

*After clearing up the remains of what turned out to be a broken flask of urine of all things, he once more descended into to the basement. After emptying the bucket and rinsing out the mop he locked the door behind him. Idly he thought about the sound he'd heard, wondering what it was doing in a place like this. By the time he'd got back in the lift again he'd forgotten all about it.*

\* \* \* \* \*

Sitting before the dressing table, Elizabeth stared at her reflection, thinking how peaceful Rob had looked in his chair the day she'd found him, her throat tightening.

*Twice she'd loved and twice she'd lost them.*

When Frank had died, with her heart broken, seemingly beyond repair, meeting someone else had been the last thing on her mind. Except she had, her broken heart apparently having mended itself without her even being aware of it. And how was that possible she wondered, after Frank, her soulmate and the love of her life? All she knew was meeting Rob had completely taken her by surprise; with breathless excitement it was as if she'd woken from a deep sleep, realising how lonely she'd been all these years, no-one to look after or care for her in an empty house, going through the motions, day in, day out. Not that she'd ever been truly lonely, she thought, because she'd had Millie and the boys. Having

108

said that, it wasn't the same as having that special someone who made her heart race when she thought of them and filled her with a warm glow; someone special to come home to, to tell the silly little things of the day to. Someone to share the laughter and the tears with.

With a sigh she thought about the first time she'd seen him. She'd just moved in and had been unpacking a box in the living room when she'd heard a car engine next door. Going to the window she'd seen a shadowy figure in a gleaming black Jag reverse off the drive before speeding off down the lane out of sight.

The next day in the village, on her way to have lunch with Millie at the café, it had pulled up at the crossing and, seeing him behind the wheel, her heart had skipped a beat. Not long after, they'd bumped into each other in Pretty's, the bakers and, taking a chance, she'd introduced herself. After that they'd begun talking with her offering to cook him dinner. He'd come round and they'd talked long into the night. Now and then she'd make him a cake or a casserole and take it round and even offered to do some cleaning and a bit of ironing for him. However, despite their friendship growing, romance had never happened.

And then, one day everything changed.

In those dark days after the accident, on his knees emotionally, he'd reached out for her and she'd been only too willing to be there for him, helping him any way she could, making sure he ate, listening, being there for him and they'd grown closer. Or maybe they hadn't and it had all been in her mind, nothing more than simple, wishful thinking. Still overcome with grief, against her advice, he'd gone back to work and she'd hardly seen him.

One day She'd gone over to put a casserole in the fridge in the hope he might eat it if and when he ever decided to come home, to find him sitting in his armchair, a tumbler of whisky in his hand. And as soon as she'd seen him sitting there clutching the glass, she'd known something terrible had happened. Going towards him she'd asked what was wrong and he'd almost jumped out of his skin. When he realised it was her, he'd quickly pulled himself together, muttering something about work but after seeing the look of fear in his eyes, she hadn't believed him. Why had he so fearful and who had he been expecting to see, if not her? Quiet and sullen and clearly in no mood for company, she'd left him to it. After that, she hadn't seen him for almost a week and when she did, he'd looked haunted. Concerned, she'd asked him if he was alright. For a brief moment he'd opened his mouth to speak but then, as if suddenly thinking better of it, closed it again. Clearly, whatever it was he didn't want to talk about it. She hadn't pressed him but looking back now she realised maybe she should've because two days later she'd gone into the sitting room and found him dead.

"What was it, Rob?" she whispered to the empty room, tears filling her eyes now. "What were you so afraid of?"

Soulfully, her reflection stared back at her.

* * * * *

*A few days later, this time heading for the equipment store where old or defunct equipment was kept with a view to one day being repaired, Norman took the lift down to the basement once more, carrying a coffee machine that had packed up.*

*Ducking under a low section of pipes, he entered another, narrower passageway branching off from the main one, running directly beneath some of the more obscure, highly classified labs, a part of the building which he'd only been allowed to enter once or twice before and then only under escort.*

*Unlocking the metal wire gate to the storage space, he went in and, putting the box on the floor, pushed it into a corner with his foot. Relocking the gate, he was just about to head back the way he'd come, when he heard the sound again, louder this time, coming from one of the ventilation shafts above him. About to continue on his way, all of a sudden, he heard a man's voice, sounding far from happy. "Jesus Christ! Can't you shut that thing up – someone's going to hear it!"*

*Pausing, Norman recognised it as belonging to Hely Walberg, an American scientist, realising he must be right beneath his lab. Cocking his head, he grimaced as the sound filled the dimly lit space, once more.*

*"What in here?" Another man's voice replied, one he didn't know. "It's sound-proof remember? What's the matter with you – you're like a cat on hot bricks."*

*"Never mind me – what the hell's wrong with it?" Walberg asked, over the din.*

*"I don't know." The other said. "It could be anything."*

"That's the problem, isn't it?" Walberg replied. "We don't know what it could be!"

Suddenly, silence fell.

"There you go!" The unknown voice said quietly a moment later. "Happy now?"

"Yeah – till next time."

"Do you want to tell me what's going on?"

"Ignore me." Walberg muttered thickly. "I'm fine."

"Obviously not."

Silence.

"If you must know, I haven't been sleeping too well lately – this whole damn thing's creeping me out."

"Why?"

"I don't know it just is, that's all..."

"What we've accomplished here..."

"I know that." Walberg retorted quickly. "But sometimes I can't help thinking we've taken things too far this time."

"We're scientists – isn't that what we do?" The other voice replied tartly. "Just think of it as another experiment, that's all."

"But it's not, though, is it?" Walberg hissed, lowering his voice. "It's not just another experiment is it because no one's ever done anything like this before, have they?"

"I'm sorry, I don't see what..."

"That's just it, Rob!" Walberg gasped. "You don't do you? What we've done...that thing...it's nothing short of playing God!"

In the darkness, Norman froze.

Suddenly, the sound started up again and spinning, Norman hurried back along the passageway as fast as his legs could carry him.

112

# XVI

Somewhere, a phone was ringing.

Opening his eyes, Carter frowned, the words *behind the paper* at the forefront of his mind. Shoving the covers back he swung his legs out of bed and hurried downstairs.

"Mr. Stanbrook?" A woman's voice on the other end of the line asked. "Mr. Carter Stanbrook?"

"Yes?"

Clearing her throat, in a well-to-do voice, she announced herself as Miss Watson, secretary to Mr. Gerard Wallace, his uncle's solicitor. After offering her condolences and saying his uncle had been a valued client and would be sadly missed, she went on to ask when he could attend their offices in Hadley for the reading of his uncles' will.

"Oh, thank God…" Carter gasped, relieved it wasn't bad news for once. Suddenly realising how it sounded, he quickly mumbled something about not having meant it that way before stuttering into silence. After an icy pause, Miss Watson continued. "There are two other beneficiaries as well as yourself and unless you require a private reading, I can arrange for you to be present at the same time."

"No, I don't need a private reading." Carter said, shaking his head. "Can you tell me who the other beneficiaries are?"

"I'm sorry, Mr. Stanbrook." Miss Watson replied snootily. "I'm not at liberty to divulge that."

Irritated by her tone he rolled his eyes.

After arranging an appointment for two o'clock the next day, released from the bonds of conversation, he hung up and went into the kitchen, the words he'd woken up returning to him now like a distant echo,

*behind the paper*

wondering what they meant.

Flicking the kettle on he was just taking the milk from the fridge when all of a sudden, the face emerging from the shrubbery appeared unexpectedly in his mind, startlingly vivid, making him start. Dropping the bottle, it smashed, a puddle of milk spreading out over the floor amid the debris. With a curse he threw a tea towel over it before hunting for a dustpan and brush. With no milk left and nothing but a small cube of cheese and a shrivelled tomato in the dismally empty fridge he decided to go to the café for breakfast.

When he arrived, it was a bustling hive of activity, a tantalising blend of fresh coffee, toast and bacon filling his nostrils as he entered. With no sign of Millie, he took a window seat, hungrily scanning the menu while he waited for a waitress to come and take his order. Afterwards, laying it down, he gazed through the window at a pair of black wrought iron gates on the other side of the road leading to the park, remembering his uncle taking him there when he'd been little. At that moment a young waitress – Phoebe on her name tag – apologised for the wait and took his order on a small pad. After she'd gone, he turned his head back to the window once more, thinking about his conversation with the charming Miss. Watson earlier, wondering who the other beneficiaries of his uncle's will were.

A few minutes later Phoebe brought his coffee over and not long after, his breakfast. Afterwards, leaving Phoebe a generous tip, he crossed the road and went through the tall metal gates into the park.

Bathed in nostalgia he gazed around, the early morning sunshine sparkling on the frosted dew coating the slightly overgrown grass, everything crisp and fresh. To his right was a new tennis court, while to the left a path snaked down an avenue of ancient Horse-chestnut trees leading deeper into the park. Remembering one of the days he and his uncle had come here collecting conkers – conkering, his uncle had called it – he started towards it leaving footprints behind on the frosted grass. As he crunched over the thick carpet of leaves covering the path, high above him in the treetops, a light breeze sprang up, the sound reminding him of the sea and home.

Glancing up at the clear autumn sky, he took a deep breath, filling his lungs with woody fragrance. As a child, he'd delighted in the seasonal changes in the countryside from the spring blossoms to the blazing riot of colours of autumn, more so than most children he supposed, simply because travelling around the world with his parents as he had – exciting though it had been – most of the places they visited had been barren wildernesses with little or no vegetation. On returning home it had always struck him anew how lushly verdant Britain was.

Rounding the bend, the trees began tapering out, the meadow opening up before him. To his right he saw the old cricket pavilion was now a café, the door shuttered and padlocked for the winter. Attached to the side of it a brightly painted board announced: 'The best ice creams in town!' In front of it a dozen or so picnic tables with built-in benches rested in the straggly, overgrown, winter grass. Remembering sun-dappled days and the sound of a cricket ball against willow, he smiled, swept away on a tide of bitter-sweet memories.

Suddenly, on the other side of the meadow, squawking loudly, a cloud of birds took noisily to the air, the sound of their wings carried to him over the expanse of grass. Wondering what had spooked them, all of a suddenly he saw movement, staring in surprise a small bundle of sticks beginning to appear round a tree trunk.

*what the*

Frowning, he narrowed his eyes, staring at them intently before shock hit him, realising they weren't sticks at all but a long-fingered hand! Rooted to the spot he balked as a domed head peered out from behind the tree, it's huge eyes

*blacker than anything*

looking straight at him.

*RUN*

With a strangled cry he spun and tore back along the path as fast as his legs could carry him, his breath coming in short, misty gasps. Skidding round the corner, with the tennis court and gates back in sight, turning, he walked backwards, waiting for it

*you know what it*

to appear. However, the pathway remained empty and, sweeping the park with his eyes and seeing nothing, with his lungs on fire, he sucked in huge gasps of air, once more quaking from head to toe. On legs that felt as weak as water he hurried towards the gates, glancing fearfully over his shoulder every now and then. Behind the fence on the other side of the tennis court, unseen in the shadowy recesses of the tree-line, a man in a dark overcoat stood un-movingly watching his progress. After watching him disappear through the gates, the man broke cover and hurried after him.

* * * * *

*Sixteen now, sitting on a low wall, Geshe Thrupen-Chopel raised his eyes from his prayer book to stare at the snowy peaks of Mount Kylash in the distance, the top as usual invisible, shrouded by clouds, the sight filling him with joy, his body suddenly feeling incredibly light not as if he were sitting on the wall anymore so much as hovering a few inches above it.*

*And something else.*

*Something which had been with him ever since he could remember, a secret wealth of knowledge lying dormant within him as if he were nothing more than a vessel for it, a knowledge not learned but given, waiting for the right time to surface. Taking a deep breath, he closed his eyes, going deep within himself, trying to see it but as usually happened all he sensed was warm light, the gently whispering voice he'd heard before, returning.*

*Be patient.*

*Wait.*

*With a sigh he opened his eyes, and came back up out of himself, the secret knowledge inside him waiting.*

* * * * *

Still reeling from what had just happened, Carter leaned against one of the gateposts. How could one of those things from

*behind the paper*

the other night be right here in the bloody park of all places, in broad daylight – *how was it possible?* At least down there in the woods in the darkness, miles away from anywhere it was understandable – so far as logic dictated – but right there in broad daylight? Was nowhere safe? Chilled, Elizabeth's words returned to him once more.

*if there were as many flying saucers around here as everyone says there is, the streets would be full of little green men*

Crossing the road, he went back into the café. Empty now, except for a scruffy-looking man in the corner reading a newspaper, he retook his seat by the window, determined to keep the gates in sight at all costs. Another waitress – this time named Jo – took his order for a mug of coffee saying nothing about him quaking from head to toe, if she had in fact, even noticed. Like a man obsessed, he narrowed his eyes, unable to tear them from the gates, a section of the tennis court fence visible through them.

Had he really seen what he thought he had or was he losing his mind? Once more terrifying images poured into his mind and, swallowing deeply, he closed his eyes, fighting to stay in control. Not long after, the waitress brought him his coffee, looking slightly nervous as she did so, his strange manner obviously having being noted. A little while later, after the warmth of the cafe the cold air outside hit him like a wall. With a shiver he shoved his hands into his pockets before making his way along the High Street.

Passing the small square lined with shops, he'd just pressed the button at the zebra crossing when, to his surprise he saw Elizabeth in the passenger seat of the battered old truck that had been parked next to the Mercedes in the Red Lion car park the other night, Harry next to her in the driver's seat. Even more surprising was the fact she was facing him, her cheeks flushed with anger, her mouth moving silently while Harry leaned on the steering wheel glaring through the windscreen, his face like thunder. Clearly something had hacked her off and it didn't take a detective to work out that something was Harry.

In an attempt to get a word in, Harry turned towards her but she was having none of it. Shaking his head angrily he slammed his hand against the steering wheel hard. Alarmed, Carter wondered if he should go over and make sure she was alright, not, he thought, that she looked like she needed him to. Besides which, if the strange episode in the churchyard was anything to go by, he would want to see.

As the lights changed, he crossed the road. On the other side he saw Elizabeth open the door of the truck. Climbing out she slammed it noisily behind her, Harry rolling his eyes and gritting his teeth as she did so before watching her storm off through the car park. Starting the engine, he slammed the truck into gear and swung out onto the road with a screech of tyres before speeding off out of sight. Turning his head Carter looked for Elizabeth, but there was no sign of her now.

Back at the house he'd just put the bags on the kitchen counter when the phone rang again.

"Carter Stanbrook."

*"Carter!"* A man's voice said. "It's Seth! We met at the church yesterday. Me and Jack are having a bite to eat and a few beers at mine today and we wondered if you'd join us. We thought you might need cheering up."

With no plan other than moping around the house all day in a never-ending battle to keep panic at bay and the terrifying events of the past few days playing over and over in his mind as if on a loop until he went completely insane, he nodded. "Thanks – I'd love to."

"Great! About one?"

"Fine by me." Carter said, before jotting the address down. "Thanks again."

As he unpacked the groceries Carter thought that despite the solemnity of the occasion yesterday, nevertheless he'd been able to sense Seth's zest for life bubbling away beneath the surface. Under normal circumstances he imagined he'd be the life and soul of the party and it was only too easy to see why Connie had thought he was a bad influence on Jack. As for Jack himself, after life with his mother and the discipline of the army, meeting Seth must've been like a breath air. Stuck out here in a quiet backwater like this, no doubt he'd grabbed the chance for some fun with both hands. With a snort he thought it was a shame Seth's influence hadn't rubbed off onto Harry as well because if anyone looked like they could do with a healthy dose of fun, he was a perfect candidate for sure.

# XVII

*Unable to hear anything but his pounding heart,
Norman hurried along the deserted corridor, the card
burning a hole in his pocket. Even though most of the
scientists had left for the day, nevertheless he glanced
nervously over his shoulder knowing only too well how
much shit he'd be in should he get caught. Turning a
corner, for a moment he paused, feeling his stomach
tighten at the sight of the brushed steel doors at the end
of the corridor.*

*Taking a deep breath, he hurried towards them, taking
the card from his pocket as he did so. Outside the doors
he stared down at it in his hand knowing this was his last
chance to leave, to just turn around and go back the way
he'd come before any real damage was done. However,
no matter how much he wanted to, leaving wasn't an
option. Ever since he'd overheard the conversation the
other day his imagination had been working overtime;
whatever it was in there, he had to know.*

*Before he could change his mind, he ran the card
through the slot in the security panel next to the doors,
the two halves swishing open as he did so. With his heart
in his mouth, he quickly stepped inside, the light from the
hallway disappearing as the doors silently closed behind
him. Wreathed in shadows the lab was silent, he stared at
a sheet-covered tank in the middle, lit from within, wires
snaking out from beneath it. Swallowing, he slowly went
towards it, his eyes widening at the sight of a dark
smudge lying on the bottom.*

*Hardly breathing now, with his heart pounding inside
his chest like a piston, he went forward, and, hardly able*

121

*to believe what he was doing, took hold of the sheet and
lifted it, almost too scared to look.*

*Suddenly, from the darkness behind him he heard a
sound and, jumping like a scalded cat, he whirled,
dragging the sheet with him as he did so, freezing at the
sight of Walberg slumped in a chair only a few feet away,
his glasses tilted slightly to one side of his face, fast
asleep.*

*Christ*

*Clutching the sheet still, he turned back to the tank
realising it wasn't a tank so much as an incubator,
staring wide-eyed at a small figure lying on a foam
mattress, its tiny rib-cage rising and falling rhythmically
as it breathed. Encircling each limb were bands with
wires attached them to it which snaked out through a
small opening and connected to the bank of free-standing
monitors on which numerous lights flashed on and off,
all completely silent.*

*Intrigued, he bent and peered in at it, his face inches
from the glass. As he did so it dawned on him there was
something wrong with it, its head way too large for the
small body. Behind him, Walberg stirred, Norman
glancing quickly behind him as he did so. Turning back
to the incubator, all of a sudden, the figure turned its
head and looked straight at him.*

*OH-GOD-NO*

*Filled with shock he recoiled and staggered
backwards a few steps, his eyes wide. Unable to move,
for a moment he simply stood there gaping at it, hardly
able to believe what he was seeing. And then something
happened, something so terrible and inexplicable, he
almost screamed.*

*After a few moments later spinning, he bolted for the door, knocking a sheaf of paperwork off the top of a unit in his haste as he did so. On the security-panel next to the door a small green light flashed, and he stabbed at it wildly, the two halves instantly parting and flinging himself through it, pelted up the corridor at full speed before disappearing round the corner.*

*Back in the lab, silently the sheet slid off the tank and fell to a heap on the floor.*

\* \* \* \* \*

About to put a bag of rubbish in his wheelie-bin, from the corner of his eye Seth saw a shape streak down the garden before disappearing into the Rhododendrons at the bottom – those bloody kids from up the road again, he thought. Narrowing his eyes, scowled at it.

"You know this is *my* garden, right?"

Cocking his head, he waited for the usual sniggers or cheeky retort but there was nothing. All of a sudden, staring around him in surprise, he realised everything was completely silent, no birds, no distant hum of traffic out on the new by-pass, nothing. Hearing a loud hiss, he turned his head and saw Monty, the next-door-neighbour's cat perched on the fence halfway down the garden.

Only six months old, except for a white streak on his forehead and a front paw, Monty was completely black. A regular visitor in the garden, he could often be seen crouched low to the ground, his emerald green eyes fixed on the birdbath or perched on the fence having a wash. Once or twice he'd even come into the kitchen and had a

123

saucer of milk and, apparently lacking the usual haughty indifference with which most of his brethren seemed to regard humans, was friendly to the core. But, looking at him now, Seth thought he couldn't have looked any different – Monty like he'd never seen him before.

With his back arched high and his head low, in a typical witches-cat-on-a-broomstick' stance his tail stuck out like a bottle-brush and, with his fur standing on end, looked twice his size. Fixated on the Rhododendrons, he looked a force to be reckoned with.

Suddenly, from within the bush there was a series of crackles and, chillingly, in response, Monty hissed again, revealing needle-like teeth in a fiendish snarl before beginning to slowly backing away along the top of the fence, Seth staring at him in amazement as he did so. All of a sudden there was a loud snap and Monty's bottle went and, leaping from the fence he disappeared out of sight. Unnerved, Seth narrowed his eyes, staring at the Rhododendrons once more, wondering what the hell it was in there when, something suddenly touched his shoulder. Crying out he spun, coming face to face with Jack, in turn, making him jump, too. *"Christ almighty, you'll give me a heart attack!"* Jack cried, rolling his eyes at him, putting his hand on his chest.

*"Me?"* Seth gasped, wide-eyed. *"What do you think you're doing sneaking up on me like that?"*

"I wasn't sneaking up on you!" Jack gasped hotly. "I called out but there was no answer." Suddenly, he paused. "What's the matter with you, you look like you've seen a ghost..."

Hearing something reminiscent of a champagne cork popping from a bottle, spinning, Seth stared at the

Rhododendrons again, the sound of birds and the faint hum of traffic returning as he did so.

"What was that?" Jack asked behind him.

Turning his head, Seth stared at the empty spot on the fence where Monty had been only moments before.

*"Seth!"* Jack hissed, impatiently. *"What's going on?"*

"I'm not sure." Seth muttered quietly. "I thought I saw something go into the bush at the bottom of the garden."

"What?"

"I don't know – something though."

"I can't see anything." Jack said narrowing his eyes.

"Whatever it was it terrified the life out of Monty."

"Who's Monty?"

"The cat next door. I've never seen him like that before all puffed up and spitting and stuff."

"Where did it go?"

"Back in his own garden…"

"Not Monty." Jack said impatiently. "The thing in the bush – do you want me to go and have a look?"

Unnerved still, Seth shook his head. "No. Forget it, it was nothing. Come on, it's cold out here."

"You bringing that back in with you?" Jack asked, nodding at the bag of rubbish in Seth's hand. Turning, Seth lifted the lid of the wheelie bin and dropped it in.

"You know, this is how it starts." Jack muttered, turning. "First you start seeing things, then you start forgetting things and the next thing you know you're in Southill stuck in front of a tv all day being fed mush..."

"Shut up." Seth muttered, shaking his head.

Meanwhile, back in the safety of his own garden, wide-eyed, Monty peered round the corner of the shed, his body tensed, trembling with fear.

\* \* \* \* \*

*Opening his eyes Hely straightened and, turning, swept the lab with his eyes, sure he'd just heard something, all of a sudden filled with horror as he realised the sheet had come off the incubator and that the creation was staring straight at him. Jumping to his feet he quickly snatched the sheet from the floor before coving it up again, wondering how long it had been watching him for. Suddenly seeing the paperwork scattered over the floor he stiffened, thinking about the sound he was sure he'd heard, wondering if they were somehow connected...*

# XVIII

Despite everything, Carter found himself looking forward to the afternoon ahead. Jack and Seth were like an old married couple and even after the funeral he hadn't been able to help smile at their banter. Also, as Harry's friends, they might be able to shed some light on his dad's puzzling visits down here.

Leaving the car behind, he set off in good time and, following the directions Seth had given him, found himself outside the park gates once more. Instead of having to go through it however, instead he followed the road round it. At last, finding the house, the front door opened and Seth appeared, smiling broadly.

"Carter!" he cried, coming down the garden path towards him. "You found it alright then?"

"Of course, he did – he's here, isn't he?" Jack muttered from the doorway, shaking his head. "Talk about stating the obvious!"

"Ignore him." Seth said ushering him up the path. "Come in – there's a beer in the fridge with your name on it."

In the doorway Jack enclosed Carter's proffered hand warmly in both of his. "Nice to see you again son." he said, smiling at him. "How are you, after yesterday?"

"As well as can be expected." Carter replied, nodding. Lifting his head, he sniffed the air. "What is that? It smells delicious!"

"That Carter, is my chicken curry." Seth beamed. "I hope you like it."

"If it tastes half as good as it smells I will." Carter said, impressed. "I'm not much of a cook myself."

"Nor's he." Jack sniffed. "You haven't tried it yet."

"I haven't had any complaints." Seth replied, grinning good-naturedly.

Following him into the house Carter found himself pleasantly surprised how neat and tidy it was. With Seth being single he'd expected it to have more of a man-living-on his-own look about it, rather like his uncle's house or his own flat, nothing like this. As he stepped into the sunny south-facing kitchen he saw a large pot simmering on the hob, its lid perched at a jaunty angle and the source of the mouth-watering aroma. Going to the fridge Seth took out three bottles of beer and after opening them, handed them round.

"To Robert." he said solemnly raising his bottle, his face serious again now. "God rest his soul."

"To Robert." Jack said.

"Uncle Rob." Carter added quietly touching his bottle to theirs with a clink.

"We used to play chess sometimes with him down in the park." Jack said pulling a chair out for him.

"I know, Elizabeth told me." Carter replied, sitting down.

"He wasn't a bad player." Seth said. "But not as good as me, mind."

"You wish!" Jack snorted. "He thinks he can beat anyone, Carter."

"And can he?" Carter asked.

"Sometimes." Jack said, shaking his head, smiling now. "Other times, he's crap."

"Do you play, Carter?" Seth asked.

"Now and again." Carter replied.

"Maybe we can have a game or two after lunch." Seth said.

"I'd like that." Carter replied, nodding.

"Now, before we start, we want to ask you something." Seth said, lowering his voice. "And you don't have to tell us not if you don't want to but Jack's been dying to know – what happened with you and Harry the other day outside the church?"

*"What the hell?"* Jack spluttered, lowering his beer, shooting Seth a look.

"As have I." he finished, grinning impishly at Jack. "We didn't know what was going on. Have you and Harry already met?"

"I'm not sure." Carter replied, giving his head a quick shake. "I thought I recognised him from somewhere though."

"He looked like he'd seen a ghost." Jack said. "And that's not like him. Mind you, he can be a funny bugger sometimes. You know, in all the time we've know him, neither of us have ever been to his house, not once. A born loner if ever there was one. Remember how he was with you when you first moved here Seth?"

"Yeah." Seth nodded. "Treated me like I didn't exist."

"He thought Harry was mental but then they got to know each other and they're okay now."

Seizing the chance to find out more, Carter cleared his throat. "He knew my dad."

"Nice chap he was." Jack nodded. "Harry introduced us to him in the Swan one day."

"Apparently, he used to come here to meet up with Harry – do you know why?"

"Liz told me she overheard Rob talking to Harry on the phone, once." Jack said. "Saying your dad wanted to meet up with him again, so they could talk some more and I remember her saying at the time it was a bit odd."

"Odd?" Carter asked. "Why?"

"She thought something was going on."

"Do you have any idea what?"

"Not a clue." Jack replied, shaking his head. "But she was right, there was something strange going on. We saw them in the Red Lion one afternoon and your dad was asking Harry questions and writing in a notebook. They looked pretty serious so we left them to it. When they'd finished, Harry called us over from the bar – Alan Fletcher and that Frank Simmons was there as well – and we had a drink or two."

"A bit more than a few!" Seth grinned, winking at Carter. "We ended up playing cards all night and then after closing time, Danny Sadler, the landlord joined us."

"What questions was he asking him?" Carter frowned, intrigued.

"How should I know?" Jack snorted. "You'll have to ask Harry."

"I don't think that's very likely do you?" Carter muttered.

"Don't worry about yesterday." Jack said, shaking his head again. "He's alright when you get to know him. Me, Harry and Liz, we were at school together. Back then she was the prettiest girl there and there wasn't a boy who wouldn't have given his right arm to take her out, me included, but she only ever had eyes for was Frankie Bell. They ended up getting married and when he died, she was devastated. After that I thought she'd never look at another man again."

"Even though he tried!" Seth beamed giving Carter a knowing wink.

"Ignore him. He doesn't know what he's talking about!"

Seth shook his head, grinning widely now. "He's only saying that 'cos when Connie left, Liz was there for him a lot – we all were mind – but during that time they got quite close. Anyway, he must've misread the signals or something because he asked her out for dinner one night and she told him she'd go but only on the understanding it was just as friends and not a date!"

"She said nothing of the sort and you know it!" Jack bristled. "You're just pissed off 'cos you asked Poppy Sanders out and she rejected you!"

"He's right, she did." Seth chuckled throatily, his eyes dancing. "But only because she was seeing some else, not because she didn't fancy me."

"You're full of shit!" Jack growled shaking his head before taking a long gulp of beer, Carter and Seth exchanging amused glances.

"So, they're good friends then, Elizabeth and Harry?" Carter asked, thinking of the altercation in the truck he'd witnessed earlier.

"Yeah." Jack nodded. "Always have been. Back in middle school, Harry had a crush – and I mean a real big crush – on her. He was always on at her to let him take her out but she was having none of it. Even though he wasn't the best looking of chaps he had that bad-boy thing going on, full of charm, you know and the girls all went wild for it; slick as an oil spill he was and he used

131

to have a different one every week. But none of them
could hold a candle to Liz and it drove him mad that the
only one he really wanted wasn't interested in him. Of
course, Harry being Harry he couldn't resist a challenge
and the more she rejected him the more determined he
was to get her. It went on for years him trying new tactics
to get her interested. At first, he tried playing it cool and
ignored her then when that didn't work, he did the
opposite and turned the charm on. He used to sneak
round to her house early in the morning and leave
flowers and chocolates on the doorstep for her to find
and once he even left a poem in her desk he'd torn out of
a book from the library, but someone saw him and
everyone took the piss out of him. Liz told him she cared
about him, just not in that way, but Harry insisted she
was just playing hard to get. And then, one day someone
said they'd seen Frankie Bell and Elizabeth at the flicks
in Hadley Saturday night and Harry went on the
defensive saying he didn't care but everyone could see he
was gutted. I think he hoped it was just a flash in the pan
and that it would peter out but of course, it didn't; they
were smitten and the longer it went on the more upset he
got. Well, we all left school and got jobs and Liz and
Frankie announced they were engaged. At the same time
Harry started going to what used to be Mallory's
nightclub over in Hadley and getting drunk and starting
fights and waking up in the cop-shop. Once night he
threw a brick through a shop window and ended up in
court with a fine and that was the wake-up call he needed
because after that he got his act together and got a job
driving trucks. When Liz and Frankie got married – even
though he was invited – he never went, away on a job

132

apparently. By the time he got back it was all done and dusted and Liz was Mrs. Frank Bell. Whenever he and Frankie crossed paths, even though they were polite enough to each other, it was always awkward between them."

"He never married anyone else?" Carter asked, unable to imagine the surly Harry Bennett he'd met the day before having a soft side like that.

Jack shook his head. "Never. I asked him about it in the Lion once and he said he wasn't interested. He said if Liz was never going to be his wife, no one was! Not that he was ever lonely – he had women all over the place but I don't think any of them actually *meant* anything to him, not like Liz did, anyway."

\* \* \* \* \*

*In his small, untidy bedsit, pacing nervously, Norman stopped and pulled another cigarette from a packet, his third in the last half hour. Stooping, he poked it through the metal grid of the small gas fire on full blast. Not that that was helping any – ever since his swift exit from the lab, he'd been chilled him to the bone with a deep, numbing cold he couldn't shake.*

*Only too late had he realised that by letting his curiosity get the better of him he'd screwed up big style because as soon as he'd seen that thing, he'd known it was something no-one had ever been meant to see. At the memory of that tiny, horrific face, the hair on the back of his neck stood on end.*

*But that hadn't been the worst of it.*

*One minute he'd been standing there staring at it and the next thing he knew he'd been paralysed.*

*Still not the worst bit.*

*Unable to move and terrified beyond belief, all of a sudden, he'd felt something alien – like a slimy wet tentacle – enter his mind, probing ever deeper, reading it and examining every memory he'd ever had. Never before in his life had he been so powerless or felt so violated. And then, just when he thought he could take no more, it had suddenly squirmed back out again leaving him breathless with shock and revulsion, the paralysis disappearing as it did so. In that moment, heedless to any noise he might've made, he'd bolted, wanting nothing more than to get as far away from that thing as he possibly could. At the thought of it his stomach turned once more and, dashing into the bathroom he fell to his knees in front of the toilet, just managing to lift the lid in the nick of time.*

# XIX

After tucking into Seth's chicken curry that melted in your mouth then kicked you back in it, they moved to the cosy living room flooded with mellow afternoon sunshine, sipping bottles of beer.

"Someone told me Harry saw a UFO." Carter began, inwardly cursing himself, wondering why he couldn't just leave it alone.

"That's right – a flying saucer." Jack nodded. "At first we thought it was a joke."

"Either that or he'd snapped and gone round the bend." Seth added.

"You didn't believe him?"

"To be honest, we didn't know what to think but despite his faults, Harry's one of the most reliable people I've ever known; if he says he'll be somewhere at a certain time, you can bet your bottom dollar that's exactly where he'll be and if you ask him to do something it's as good as done. In all the years I've known him, so far as I know he's never lied about anything and I've never once heard anyone else say different either. He told everyone in the Red Lion first, something he regretted no end later, believe me." Jack went on. "But at the time he was in shock and wasn't thinking straight."

Thinking about Reg Tarney, Carter nodded. It wouldn't have been long before the whole village knew about it. "So, what did he see, exactly?"

"Apparently." Jack went on. "They were in the truck not far from the village when the engine packed up."

"They?" Carter asked.

"Him and Bess, his dog."

"Lovely thing she is." Seth added.

"At the time we were in the middle of that big heatwave and Bess started growling at something in one of the fields. Well, he thought she'd must've seen a rabbit or something but she carried on so once he'd pulled to the side of the road, he let her out. Now, Harry's been tinkering about with cars and stuff all his life and what he doesn't know isn't worth knowing. At first, he thought the engine must've overheated, but when he looked under the bonnet everything looked alright and he couldn't understand why it wouldn't start. He climbed back in the cab and fell asleep. The next thing he knew, he woke up a couple of hours later with Bess spark-out on the seat next to him. He tried starting the engine and it worked – the radio too – so he assumed it must have overheated after all. He said he was starving by then, so, instead of going to the Red Lion for a pint like he'd been planning to, he went home and had dinner."

"What?" Carter asked, frowning now. "But what about the UFO?"

"This is the thing." Jack said. "A few months later he saw a glider flying low over some fields and it must've jolted his memory or something because all of a sudden, he remembered the engine packing up and letting Bess out and trying to fix it and then hearing her barking like mad somewhere in the field. Sounding like she was in some kind of trouble he went into the field to find her and that's when he saw it, the flying saucer. He said he was driving at the time when he remembered what had really happened and he almost crashed, it was such a shock."

136

"So, what happened then?" Carter breathed, his heart racing.

"Well, like I say, he went into the field to try and find Bess and that's when he saw something in the sky. At first, he said he thought it was one of those light planes, you know, crop spraying or something but then as it started coming down, he realised what it was."

"What did it look like?" Carter asked, his voice barely above a whisper.

"Big – about sixty feet across he reckoned, silver, with a dome on top. He said it didn't look real, like a typical flying saucer in a film or something, only he knew it was because the corn underneath it was being blown about. All of a sudden it began swaying side to side and then it landed. He stood there staring at it for a while and then all of a sudden it took off again. When he flew into the Red Lion saying he'd seen a flying saucer, everyone presumed it had just happened, but it hadn't, it was months before and the reason he was in such a state was because he'd just *remembered* it happening."

"Yeah." Seth nodded. "And as if remembering what he'd seen that day wasn't enough, the fact he hadn't remembered any of it until then, shook him up even more – he couldn't get his head round it."

"I told him it was probably just shock." Jack went on. "And I suggested going back up there to see if we could find any trace of it, but he said he wasn't going anywhere near Bowers Hill ever again but I did, I went and had a look around."

"He asked me to go as well but I thought the place where it landed might be radioactive or something." Seth

137

added. "And I was scared it might come back while we were there."

Rolling his eyes, Jack shook his head at him.

"Did you find anything?" Carter asked, holding his breath.

"Not a sausage." Jack replied, giving his head a quick shake. "But by then it was autumn and the field had been ploughed. I didn't tell Harry I went up there though – he'd have thought we didn't believe him."

"Did he report it to the police or anyone?"

"What, Harry, go to the cops?" Jack snorted looking at him askance. "You're kidding aren't you – he *hates* them! It was bad enough with everyone talking about him saying he was mental and asking him when the little green men were coming back, that sort of thing never mind getting the cops involved."

"We couldn't help but feel sorry for him."

"And then because everyone knew we were friends, *we* started getting funny looks as well!" Jack said. "And that Parry woman made a snide remark to Liz as well in Pretty's the bakers, remember?"

"Yeah. But from what I heard Liz gave her as good as she got and she never said anything else to her again did she?"

"I don't think she dared!" Jack grinned, shaking his head.

"A reporter from the local paper wanted to do a piece on him." Seth said. "And Sally Chambers from the radio station in Hadley kept ringing him up about doing a live interview on air but he didn't want to know. But that wasn't all, was it, Jack?"

"No." Jack said quietly, his face solemn now.

With baited breach, Carter waited.

"After he remembered what had happened, he changed." Jack said quietly. "Harry's never been afraid of anything or anyone but all of a sudden it like he was scared of *everything*, not like the Harry we knew at all. He stopped going out and wouldn't see anyone except Liz."

"That's right." Seth nodded. "She was worried he might be ill or something. She kept asking him what was wrong but he wouldn't tell her. In the end they had a blazing row and she stormed out. A few days later we were at Liz's and he turned up in the middle of dinner and we were shocked at how bed he looked. Apparently, he was too afraid to sleep because of terrible nightmares he kept having. Said he couldn't stop thinking about it and he felt like he was going mad."

\* \* \* \* \*

*Stubbing his cigarette out in the ashtray, Norman cursed. Ever since he'd gone into that damned lab a few weeks he'd been a nervous wreck, unable to forget what he'd seen, the terrifying moment it had entered his mind, haunting him. Barely functioning, he was hardly sleeping at all now, sometimes managing to drop off through sheer exhaustion and even then, never for very long because of the horrific nightmares. Filled with terror, he felt like he was going crazy.*

*Scared someone might've found out what he'd done – that and knowing was in there – he'd called in sick for three days but in the end, he'd had no choice but to go in. To his amazement no-one had said anything and, filled with relief, he presumed he'd got away with it. However, terrified at the thought of having to go anywhere near the basement, so far, he'd managed to avoid having to do so.*

*Frowning, he thought about what he'd seen down there in that lab again. Little wonder Walberg had been so worried about someone hearing it – what the sick bastards had done was unthinkable and unethical, maybe even illegal. Suddenly he stiffened. In which case they'd probably do just about anything to keep it under wraps. Narrowing his eyes, his heart raced, an idea beginning to form in his mind.*

\* \* \* \* \*

The next morning Carter was in the kitchen when Elizabeth's head appeared round the back door.

"Is that coffee I smell?"

Smiling, he invited her in, pleased to see her back to her usual chirpy self, so different from yesterday. "You couldn't have timed that better. I'm just making some toast – want some?"

"Just coffee for me." She said perching on a chair. "I heard you were at Seth's yesterday."

"Yeah. I had lunch with him and Jack."

"Did they behave themselves?"

"They were fine." He grinned. Deciding not to mention the fact he'd seen her having a row with Harry in the car park, he asked: "How you feeling today?"

"Oh, you know, as well as can be expected." she replied, shrugging a shoulder. "What about you? Are you alright?"

140

"I'm getting by,"

"I had a phone call from your uncle's solicitor, Frank something..."

"Wallace." Carter said. "Frank Wallace."

"That's right." She nodded. "The secretary, a right snooty thing she is, wanted to know if I could come to the office at two in Hadley. I presume you know all about it?"

"Yeah." Carter nodded. "He's going to read the will. She said there are three beneficiaries, me, you, obviously, and someone else, but she wouldn't tell me who."

"Why would he leave me anything?"

"Why wouldn't he? Uncle Rob thought the world of you, Elizabeth. You were a good friend to him."

"I wonder who the third beneficiary is?"

"I have no idea." Carter shrugged. "I'll drive but I don't know where it is or how long it'll take to get there."

"Only about half an hour." Elizabeth replied. "If we set off about one, we should be in good time. Can you pick me up from the library?"

"Of course."

Glancing at her watch, she finished her coffee and got to her feet. "I've got to get going."

Following her down the hall Carter held the front door open for her before. Turning, she looked at him.

"I'll see you at one then."

Watching her as she crunched over the drive into the lane, he saw her and Harry in the truck yesterday morning, again wondering what they'd been arguing about. Telling himself it was none of his business he turned and closed the door, oblivious to the fact he was being watched.

# XX

Entering the reception of Wallace, Meakin and Meakin, Carter and Elizabeth stared at Harry in surprise. Turning from the window, his eyes hardened at the sight of Carter.

"Harry?" Elizabeth said, going towards him. *"You're the third beneficiary?"*

"Apparently so." he replied, looking at her.

"Why didn't you say?" Elizabeth asked spreading her arms. "You could've got a lift with us."

"No need." Harry replied gruffly. "I was out this way, anyway."

Taking her coat off, Elizabeth took a seat next to Carter on one of the black leather chairs, patting her hair into place. Turning his back on them, Harry stared sullenly out through the window again, Carter and Elizabeth exchanging glances as he did so, the atmosphere in the room thick with tension, the only sounds the quiet ticking of a clock on the wall and the faint hum of traffic from the street.

At last, a woman appeared in the doorway. In her fifties, with salt and pepper hair severely pulled back in a neat bun, thin-faced and pensive in an expensive-looking charcoal grey suit, she looked what she was – efficiency personified. Giving them a sweeping glance, she smiled tightly and introduced herself as Miss Watson before shepherding them along a short hallway into a spacious room dominated by a large modern-looking pale wooden table and eight chairs. Going to the window, she adjusted the louver blind, instantly reducing the glare of afternoon sunlight streaming. "If you'd like to take a seat, Mr.

Wallace will be with you shortly. Would anyone like coffee?"

No one did so Miss Watson left them to it, closing the door quietly behind her, her duty completed.

"She looks exactly how I imagined her on the phone." Elizabeth whispered to Carter with a smirk.

"Me too."

A few minutes later a middle-aged man in a grey suit appeared, a buff-coloured folder in his hand, sharp looking eyes weighing them up behind a pair of silver rimmed pince-nez. Above a somewhat haughty-looking face, thick grey hair and white side-burns gave him a distinguished look. Introducing himself as Frank Wallace, he took his place at the head of the table. After thanking them all for coming he cleared his throat and opening the folder, withdrew a sheet of paper and began.

To Elizabeth, Robert had left the sum of five thousand pounds, causing her to promptly burst into tears. As if by magic Mr. Wallace promptly produced a box of tissues before handing them to Carter who placed them in front of her. Moving his chair closer, Harry put an arm round her shoulders.

To Harry, he left the Jag.

Equally amazed, Carter and Harry's eyes locked other over the table. At the moment, his uncles' pride and joy, a black, XJ12 Jaguar was in the garage, Carter suddenly struggling with the idea of it going to Harry.

"For services rendered." Mr. Wallace explained.

Frowning, Carter stared at Harry over the table. What services? What could Harry possibly have done for his uncle to have left him the Jag? Was it something to do with the strange liaison between his uncle, his dad and

Harry? Realising Mr. Wallace was speaking again, he forced his mind back to the matter in hand. The last part of the will, any monies, the house and all its contents went solely to Carter, to do with as he pleased.

After the reading, the solicitor peered at Carter over the rim of his glasses. "If you wouldn't mind remaining behind for a moment Mr. Stanbrook." he said. "There's another small matter I need to discuss with you."

"We'll wait outside." Elizabeth said quietly, following Harry out before closing the door behind her. Taking their seats again, Mr. Wallace withdrew a slim white envelope from the folder and pushed it over the table towards him.

"It was Mr. Sterling's wish that you have this Mr. Stanbrook." He began. "With the understanding that I myself hand it to you personally in private, along with the condition that you disclose its contents to *no one,* the importance of which he insisted I convey to you. His final instruction on this matter is that once you've fully read and understood its contents, you are to destroy it completely."

Intrigued, Carter stared frowned at the innocuous-looking envelope. "Destroy it?" he snorted. "What's in it – *government secrets?"*

With the faintest hint of amusement in his eyes, nevertheless Mr. Wallace managed to keep his face professionally straight. "I'm afraid I wasn't at liberty to ask." he replied coolly. "My instructions were to simply hand the envelope over to you in private and to impress upon you the gravity of the conditions, that was all."

"Yeah, I understand that." Carter said his eyebrows still raised. "But all the same – why all the drama?"

Leaning back in his chair Mr. Wallace cleared his throat, then, with the tone of having seen pretty much everything, spoke again.

"Ours is not to reason why Mr. Stanbrook. When it comes to our clientele, you'd be surprised at the little idiosyncrasies we have to deal with on a day-to-day basis on their behalf. Here at Wallace, Meakin and Meakin, we pride ourselves on ensuring those instructions are carried out to in full, no matter how odd or eccentric they may be, this being one of the *least* dramatic, I assure you. Now, do you have any questions?"

*Plenty*, Carter thought, none of which Wallace would be capable of answering however, of that he was pretty sure. "No, I don't think so."

"In which case, I'll process the necessary paperwork and we'll be in touch." He said, pushing his chair back, intimating that the meeting had reached its inevitable conclusion.

Getting to his feet, Carter picked the envelope up. Following him to the door Wallace stepped forward to open it for him and, offering his hand said: "Once again, my sincerest condolences. Your uncle was a good client of ours. He'll be sadly missed."

Nodding his thanks, with curiosity running rife, he went back to reception, tucking the envelope into the inside pocket of his jacket as he did so – what on Earth was all that about? Apart from Elizabeth sitting quietly with her handbag on her lap the reception was empty.

"Harry had to dash off." She said, apologetically.

\* \* \* \* \*

*Frowning, as the traffic lights turned red, Hely braked, staring in the rear-view mirror at the car that had been following him ever since he'd left the house; always two cars behind, he couldn't see who was driving.*

*Rattled, even before the lights had finished changing, he quickly pulled away and, with a screech of tyres, shot over the road, horns blaring behind him. Rounding a corner, he sped along a narrow street before turning sharply into a half-filled car-park at the side of an office block. Deep in shadows, he shut the engine off and quickly slid down in the seat, his eyes just above the dashboard, waiting.*

*Sure enough, as expected, the car sped past, a dark-haired man at the wheel. As it disappeared from sight he glanced down at the luminous face of his watch, giving it a few minutes to go around the block. Two minutes later it went past again, albeit a little slower this time, the driver obviously searching for him. Once it was out of sight he straightened, the muscles in his jaw bunched, waiting to see if it would reappear again. When ten minutes had passed with no sign of it, he started the engine and drove back the way he'd come, filled with deep, resonating fear.*

\* \* \* \* \*

Driving back from Hadley, like Elizabeth, Carter was quiet and subdued albeit it for an entirely different reason, the letter burning a hole in his pocket.

Considering the strict instructions his uncle had left with Wallace, ensuring he and he alone handed the letter

147

to him personally, knowing his uncle never did anything without good reason, it must be something pretty bloody important, he surmised; not to mention the instructions to destroy it after he'd read it. Wanting nothing more than to be alone to find out, nevertheless, Elizabeth insisted he join her for a cream tea at the café while she told Millie about the money. Two cups of tea and a chocolate éclair later however – unable to stand it any longer – he made his excuses and left.

Alone at last, in the kitchen, he stared down at the envelope in his hand with narrowed eyes, finding himself loathe to open it, suddenly filled with an almost prophetic notion that it was nothing short of a Pandora's box and that once opened, there'd be no going back. Shaking his head, he tutted, chastising himself for letting his imagination get the better of him, elevating it from what was most likely nothing more than a simple letter to something of monumental proportion. Turning it over he slit it open and with bated breath, withdrew a single sheet of paper.

*Dear Carter* (it said)

*Firstly, I imagine what you've learned must have come as a terrible shock, leaving you, no doubt, appalled at my actions. All I can say is, as a man of science, yourself, I hope you'll be able to understand why I had to do what I did. The more boundaries we push back, the more there are making them infinitely limitless, my only regret having put you in the precarious position you now find yourself in and for that, I am truly sorry.*

*I have done everything in my power to safeguard you from danger, however there are forces at work beyond*

*my control and I fear it's not enough. By now you'll be in contact with Adkins and he'll know people who will protect you and hopefully keep you safe. Do everything he says and trust him with your life – literally.*
  Uncle Rob.

*what the*
Bemused, he read it again.

Lowering it, he stared at the window unseeingly. What was he supposed to have learned that had come as a terrible shock to him he wondered and what on Earth could uncle Rob possibly have done to make him think he'd be appalled? What precarious position was he in, who was Adkins and what danger exactly would he be keeping him safe from, *the forces?* Unnerved, he glanced round the darkening kitchen, Wallace's words returning to him as he did so.

*destroy it completely*
For a moment he wondered if he shouldn't just keep it instead. However, knowing his uncle never said anything without a good reason, he got to his feet and, finding a box of matches in one of the drawers, took the letter over to the sink. Striking a match, he touched the flame to one of the corners and angled it as it lit, the blue-yellow flames engulfing his uncle's final words to him, the letters glowing brightly not only on the paper, but in his mind as well. At last, he dropped it into the sink, and, turning the tap on, rinsed black ash down the plughole with his hand until nothing remained.

\* \* \* \* \*

*Instinctively feeling something was different without knowing what, Robert swept the room with his eyes before staring at an oddly shaped rock Becca had given him which he used as a paperweight, remembering quite clearly putting on top of some papers next to the computer this morning. Only now it was next to them, the papers in an untidy slew as if someone had riffled through them.*

*Spinning, he suddenly noticed other things, a small rectangle in the dust on the bureau where a book had been moved, the drawer in the bureau not quite closed, another box seemingly having been taken out of the corner, the tomes on top of it on the floor next to it now; someone had been in here, searching for something.*

*Knowing it could mean only one thing he raced from the room and bolted up the stairs, his heart plummeting like a stone as he saw the key in the lock. Pushing the door open he peered round it seeing the room was empty. Taking the keys from his pocket he went to the desk and unlocking the bottom drawer, sighed with relief at the sight of the tablet, still there. Taking it out he dashed down the stairs and out the house again, the door slamming loudly behind him.*

# XXI

*Grinning, Carter watched his dad stow the fishing gear in the bottom of the boat, his spirits high. He loved fishing here at Blacknoll Lake, just him and his dad, long, hot summer days full of promise stretching endlessly out before them. Even though it had only just gone ten, the sun was incredibly hot and even with his baseball hat on he could still feel the heat on his head almost as if the rays were burning their way right through the fabric.*

*Hearing shouts, he glanced over his shoulder at a dark blue camper-van pulling into the car park, its side doors opening even before it had finished moving, watching in amusement as three kids spilled out onto the sun-baked earth clutching inflatable toys and rolled up towels with their swimsuits inside. Not too long ago a couple of motorbikes had parked up and now two oil-slathered girls lay on a large chequered blanket their limbs neatly arranged, the boys in the water diving and laughing. And they weren't the only ones, cars and vans stirring up clouds of dust as they approached, sharp glints of sunlight twinkling off their bumpers and reflecting off their windshields as they did so. By afternoon the car park would be full to overflowing, the shores of the lake dotted with people sunbathing or sitting on travel rugs eating picnics, kids and adults in the water, dogs of every size and shape running wild, retrieving sticks or lying panting in the shade of sun umbrellas, the whole debacle playing out against a cacophony of assorted music.*

*"Right!" his dad said straightening. "Ready to cast off sailor?"*

*"Aye, Aye Sir!" he replied, saluting. Bending he slipped the rope off the post on the small, wooden jetty and climbed into the boat. Taking the oars, his dad began sculling the small, wooden boat through the water, the sounds of the day-trippers fading behind them. Following the curve of the river, it began widening out, the bright expanse of open lake in front of them.*

*Rummaging in the canvas rucksack between his feet, he took out a pair of sunglasses out and slipped them on, the surface of the water instantly transformed into a million points of glittering light, a swell of stars cradling the boat. To the right reed beds loomed, a wall of yellow stalks rising majestically from the water while to their left were the Mayward Hills, nothing more than a misty ridge in the distance. Far out in the lake a speedboat towed a skier behind it, the engine no louder than the hum of an angry hornet...*

Smiling, Carter opened his eyes; not a dream so much as a treasured memory, the remnants of it fading even as he tried holding on to it.

Last night he'd found a photo album in one of the cupboards in the living room and, taking it out had begun paging through it; faded snaps of his mom and uncle as little kids, armed to the teeth with buckets and spades on a sunny beach, the pair of them still visibly recognisable as the adults they would become despite their youth. Another of them a little older this time, standing hand in hand in a garden, their faces wreathed with smiles, a brown friendly-looking dog with its tongue lolling out of the side of its mouth on a leash in his uncle's hand. Lots his parents' wedding, his mom young and beautiful, his dad looking like the happiest groom in the world. After that most of the photos were of himself in various stages of development, his cherubic face staring out from the cellophane-covered pages, his first Christmas in a romper suit on his dad's lap on the floor in front of the Christmas tree, his first Easter as a toddler in hideous, bright yellow dungarees. Another of him sitting astride a dog on wheels he couldn't remember and one of him a bit older, a face shot of him grinning widely into the camera, missing his two top teeth. Turning the pages, he'd wept until there'd been nothing left.

Feeling catharised he'd gone to bed and fallen asleep almost instantly, unable to remember the last time he'd done that, recent events being far from conductive to a good night's sleep by any stretch of the imagination.

Getting out of bed he padded into the bathroom, yawning. As he shaved, he thought about the bizarre letter with its ominous warning of danger his uncle had left him, once more wondering what on Earth it was all about. Suddenly, downstairs in the hallway the telephone rang shattering the silence and, starting, he dropped the razor with a clatter, the head breaking off from the stem and skittering across the bathroom floor. Cursing, he shot it a look before hurrying down the stairs two at a time and snatching the phone up, put it to his ear – Elizabeth, inviting him over for breakfast.

Saying he wouldn't be long, he hung up and went back upstairs to get dressed. As he did so, he thought about his uncle's instructions not to speak of the letter to anyone else, deciding it couldn't do any harm to ask

Elizabeth if she'd ever heard his uncle mention the name Adkins or if indeed, she knew anyone of that name herself, maybe someone who lived in the village even.

When he asked her however, she shook her head.

"No. Why?"

"Someone by that name left a message on the answerphone, that's all but they didn't leave a number." He lied, thinking on his feet.

"I expect you'll have to be leaving soon?" she asked a few moments later, looking at him over the rim of her coffee cup.

"Thursday." He nodded, trying not to sound too relieved, however, the truth being if he never saw Brentwood Down again it would be too soon.

"It won't be the same here without you." She said quietly. "I've enjoyed having you around. What will you do about the house?"

"Sell it I suppose." he said.

"I can't imagine not living next to Rob anymore. It'll seem strange having new neighbours." She replied, sadly. "You wouldn't consider living in it yourself, here in Brentwood?"

*not in a million years*

"God no!" he said quickly, instantly regretting it. "What I mean is I've got my own place in Point Pleasant right on the beach and then there's work..."

"Of course, you have." She nodded understandingly. "And let's face it, Brentwood's not for everyone."

*you don't say*

Suddenly, she looked at him, her eyes wide. "I've got an idea – why don't I cook us all dinner tomorrow night, roast beef with all the trimmings, you, me and the boys?"

154

"That sounds lovely." Carter nodded.

"Harry too?" she asked quietly, her eyebrows raised. "He could pick the car up while he's here – what do you say?"

Clearly, they'd made up.

Even though the prospect of spending the night being alternately glared at and frozen out by Harry over the dinner table wasn't exactly his idea of fun, nevertheless, knowing it would make her happy, he forced himself to smile. "Why not?" he said. "The more the merrier."

"That's sorted then!" she beamed. "I'll give them a ring and let them know."

* * * * *

*Deep in thought, Norman frowned. He'd managed to discover the identity of the second scientist he'd heard talking whilst in the basement that day, Robert Sterling, a molecular biologist who he'd seen about from time to time at the institute. A renowned scientist and a bit of a celebrity in scientific circles who no doubt would do just about anything to keep their dirty little secret, secret. But first, he'd need evidence.*

*Considering the controversial nature of their experiment, the institute would be the last place they'd keep records of it he thought; it would be too risky, so maybe they were somewhere else, stashed away somewhere safe under lock and key.*

*Finding out where they both lived had been surprisingly easy – all he'd had to do was follow them home in the car when they'd left work. Frustratingly however, Walberg lived in an exclusive block of flats* with ultra-high security with no chance of him being able to get inside and have a look around. Sterling on the other hand lived a few miles away in Brentwood Down, a sleepy little village he'd driven through a couple of times.

With a large garden backing onto a field, and high hedges shielding it from the neighbouring houses, even during the day he'd felt safe enough to slip over the back fence while Sterling was at work. The lock on the back door had been harder to pick than he'd first imagined but with a little patience and perseverance, at last, he'd managed to get it open.

Inside the house, he'd searched the ground floor and the bedrooms and found nothing. Seeing the attic door, he'd gone up the short staircase towards it but when he'd tried it, it had been locked. Reaching up he'd hardly been able to believe it when his fingers had located a key on the ledge above it. Taking it down he'd gone inside and had just been going through the drawers in the desk when to his horror, all of a sudden, he'd seen Sterling's jag coming up the lane.

Without a second to lose, at breakneck speed he'd bolted down the stairs three at a time before darting back out the back door, locking it quickly quietly behind him. Hearing the car door slam and the scrunch of footsteps crossing the drive, he'd dashed behind the shed with his back to it, his heart pounding and his chest heaving, praying Sterling wouldn't come out into the garden.

After a few minutes however, unbelievably, he'd heard a door slam and footsteps on the gravel, hurrying this time. Angling his heard he heard the car door slam, his shoulders sagging with relief as the engine purred to life, *hearing the crunch of gravel as it backed off the drive into the lane. Remaining where he was for a few moments, at last he peeled away from the shed and, sprinting up the garden as fast as he could, vaulted the fence at the end. Once in the field, he'd hurried back to the Cuc-de-sac where he'd left the car. Driving through the village, he'd kept an eye out for the Jag but there'd been no sign of it.*

*Shaken, he couldn't believe how close he'd come to being caught, the worst of it being the fact he still hadn't found anything, the whole thing having been a complete waste of time and unnecessary risk. Thwarted, he frowned. He could always go back into the lab with a camera he supposed, instantly dismissing it even as he thought it – there wasn't enough money in the world to make him go back into that lab again. On the other hand, there was nothing stopping him going back down to the basement and listening and it might be the only way of getting the proof he so desperately needed.*

\* \* \* \* \*

Bathed in sickly yellow light from the fluorescent strip light above them, in the garage, side by side, Harry and Carter stood looking at the Jaguar. Turning, Harry walked down the side of it, the tap of his stick on the cement floor the only sound. "I've always wanted one of these" He said quietly, as if to himself before lapsing back into stony silence.

Remaining where he was Carter stood stiffly, watching him with barely concealed contempt. All through dinner Harry had barely looked at him never

157

mind speak to him, the atmosphere throughout dinner awkward and forced. Indignant, unable to work out why and not wanting to make a scene, he'd kept quiet but, now, out here, he knew there was never going to be a better time than this. Taking the bull by the horns he took a deep breath. "Okay Harry, what's going on?"

With one hand resting on the roof of the Jag, Harry stiffened, the air suddenly thick. Bending at the waist, he peered through the driver's side window, ignoring him as if he hadn't spoken. Undeterred Carter spoke again.

"Have I done something to upset you?"

Glancing at him fleetingly, Harry shook his head.

"Don't worry about it."

"What do you mean, don't worry about it?" Carter frowned, narrowing his eyes. "Every time I see you, you act as if I've shot your granny or something and I'm sick of it. I want to know what I'm supposed to have done."

With a look of annoyance, Harry straightened. "Just leave it."

"All I want you to do is talk to me!" Carter grated, stepping forward.

*"I said leave it!"* Harry hissed, his whole demeanour that of a man trying to keep himself in control.

*"Who the hell do you think you're talking to?"* Carter gasped, indignant. Taking a deep breath Harry stared at him, his eyes mere glints in the dark shadows of his sockets. Feeling they were at a critical moment Carter spoke again. "Is this something to do with my dad?"

At his words, Harry froze.

"What happened?" Carter asked.

Remaining where he was, Harry stared at him silently, his flint-like eyes inscrutable.

158

"I know Uncle Rob introduced you." Carter went on. "What I don't understand is why? Why was it so important that you meet? What was it all about?"

Silence.

"Tell me!" Carter rasped, stepping forward. "What was going on?"

"It's none of your business."

"Like hell it isn't! When we met at the church you looked...*terrified.*"

Facing each other rigidly, Harry's eyes filled with something Carter couldn't analyse – *fear?*

"I don't know what you're talking about."

*"Bullshit!"* Carter ground out taking a step back as Harry went past him only inches away. Realising he was leaving Carter stepped forward and, grabbing Harry's arm, swung him back round. *"Tell me!"*

In reaction, as quick as lightening, with his stick clattering to the floor, Harry lunged at him, seizing the front of his shirt with both hands before slamming him hard against the side of the Jag, his eyes glittering with rage. *"Don't ever do that again!"*

Speechless, Carter gaped at him.

Glowering down at him, at last Harry let go of him and, bending, awkwardly retrieved his stick.

*"What the hell's wrong with you, Harry?"* Carter gasped, peeling himself off the side of the car, staring at him wide-eyed, his face ashen.

"I'm sorry." Harry whispered tightly. "I shouldn't have done that."

*"No kidding!"* Carter retorted hotly, straightening his shirt. "All I wanted to know was..."

"You're better off *not* knowing, believe me!"

All of a sudden, Elizabeth came through the door into the garage, her eyes narrowed. *"What's going on?"* she demanded coming towards them.

"Nothing." Harry muttered, hanging his head.

"It doesn't look like nothing to me!" Folding her arms over her chest, she raised her eyebrows questioningly, looking at them each in turn. *"Well?"*

"It's nothing, really." Carter said, running a hand through his hair. "We just had a few words that's all."

"About what?" she demanded, eyeing Carter's rumpled shirt. "That temper getting the better of you again is it, Harry?" she asked. Meeting her eyes, Harry pulled his mouth to one side in a sardonic sneer.

"I think you should go home."

Taking his hat off, Harry ran a hand through his hair before donning it again. "I think you're right."

"I'll get the keys." Carter said quietly.

As he left the garage, he heard Elizabeth hiss something at Harry. Pausing, he pushed his head nearer the door, hearing Harry mumble something back. Plucking the keys off the hook, he went back into the garage and, handing them over said: "The paperwork's in the glove compartment and I filled the tank up."

"Thanks." Harry replied gruffly with mild surprise, the look in his eyes, as usual, inscrutable.

Going to the back of the garage, Carter pushed a button set into a panel on the wall. With a click and a slight grinding sound, slowly, the garage door began moving upwards, cool night air dispelling the stuffy, oily smell. Wordlessly Harry opened the Jag's door and, lowering himself in, closed it behind him with a resounding thud. Starting the engine, he steered it

160

carefully out of the garage, the pair of them following as he did so, Carter feeling a deep wrench at the sight of Harry behind the wheel. In the lane Harry honked the horn and Elizabeth raised her hand in farewell, her face still angry. As soon as he'd gone however, she turned to look at Carter, an eyebrow raised. "Now, do you want to tell me what was really going on?"

Shaking his head, he looked at her. "Honestly? I have no idea Elizabeth – I only wish I had." High above them, one by one, stars began disappearing, blotted out by a dark shape drifting slowly across the sky.

# XXII

*Blinking, Hely stared at a round vent in a wall seeing lightening stuttering beyond it, swiftly followed by a deep-throated growl of thunder. Spinning, he saw he was in a passageway, the smooth metal walls and floors seamless, the end out of sight, shrouded in darkness, realising he had no idea where he was.*

*Or how he'd got here.*

*Behind him, lightening flashed again, revealing a doorway halfway down the passageway, and, disorientated, he slowly went towards it, feeling a slight vibration travelling up through the floor into his legs as he did so. Stopping in front of a metal door, with the illogical reasoning that made complete sense in dreams, knew he had to go in there. Pushing it open, he stepped through it, inky darkness enfolding him like a cloak, the only illumination coming from a vent glowing with opaque light halfway up a wall.*

*All of a sudden, not far from the vent he saw a flicker of movement and, remaining where he was, he stared at it, trying to make out what it was before realising there was someone there. Suddenly the vent brightened and he realised he was in an empty room, nothing in it but a table on which sat a small child of all things – a toddler – holding a large yellow and white toy rabbit, it's manic smile and floppy ears blocking the child's face.*

*As his heart leapt, feeling a tendril of fear unfurl in his belly, he slowly went towards it, unable to take his eyes off the grinning bunny, the child completely still. Reaching the table, he raised a trembling hand and, taking hold of one of the rabbit's ears, slowly pulled it*

*down. As if becoming aware of his presence, all of a
sudden, the child turned towards him before staring
straight at him over the head of the bunny, it's face
visible now. Filled with the usual sense of horror and
revulsion at the sight of it, he recoiled, at the same time,
realising it wasn't alone.*

*With a cry he staggered backwards, unable to do
anything other than gape slack-jawed at the three spindly
figures that stood not far away, silently watching him.
Filled with panic he spun and bolted towards the
doorway. Bursting through it, he tore down the
passageway into darkness wanting nothing more than to
get as far away from that room as he could. All of a
sudden, seconds too late, he realised there was an
opening in the floor before him and, with a scream,
began falling...*

\* \* \* \* \*

The next day dawned bright and sunny, perfect
driving weather Carter thought, glancing out of the
window as he packed. In a few hours he'd be home and it
felting like an eternity since he'd been there last. After
stowing his bag in the boot, he glanced back at the house
thinking about the letter and his and Harry's altercation
in the garage last night. Unbelievably, it was only when
he'd left the village that he remembered the road would
take him back through the woods. As images poured into
his mind in panic he stepped on the brake, before pulling
to the side of the road, a horn blasting angrily behind him
as he did so. Raising his hand in apology, the driver
roared past, glowering at him angrily.

163

Gripping the steering wheel, his heart pounded in his chest, his mouth dry, with fear. Taking a deep breath, he stared at a cow in the field next to the road, deep in thought. Yeah, that night in the woods was, by far, the most terrifying thing that had ever happened to him and yeah, he supposed he *could* take another route out of Brentwood Down but what then? If he didn't face his fear and put a stop to it right now, it would end up taking over his whole life and, bad as his life might be right now it was still *his* life. Fed up with being scared, the time had come to face it head on, after all, what was the alternative?

Taking a deep breath, he steeled himself and swung out onto the road again. A few minutes later, with the village behind him, the road he'd hurtled down that first night rose steadily before him, the beginning of the woods in their autumnal colours, as if on fire, looming up before him. With his hands clammy on the steering wheel and his heart racing, the car passed out of the sunlight into an eerie yellow twilight created by the canopy of leaves yawning high above him. After a few moments the ridge loomed up on the right and terrified though he was, he couldn't help but stare at it, the trees beyond it pierced with beams of sunlight slanting down through the branches. In his mind's eye he saw the creatures

*you know what they were*

again

*just standing there*

starkly illuminated in the headlights and he shuddered, feeling panic stir. Forcing himself to concentrate on nothing but the road ahead, a little while later he shot out

164

from beneath the canopy into bright sunshine releasing breath, he hadn't been aware of holding as he did so – *he'd done it!*

After that, the rest of the journey was a breeze and a couple of hours later he pulled up outside the grey stone building composed of two flats, his, the one at the top, the bottom one occupied by a web designer who spent most of his time in London and who he hardly ever saw.

Taking his bag from the boot he went up the steps to the front door and, opening it, picked up a handful of mail from the mat. Going into the kitchen he dropped the mail on the kitchen table before going to the sink. Taking a deep breath he stared through the window at the desolate mud flats, the tide nothing more than a twinkling line, miles out. In all it's different moods, whether baking in sunshine or cloaked in misty rain, it never failed to lift him and he felt his spirits lift, suddenly wanting to be out there with the wind in his hair. Going into the bedroom he swapped his shoes for a pair of old trainers before leaving the flat again.

Crossing the road, he stepped onto the beach and drinking in the beautiful isolation, sucked tangy sea air deep into his lungs. Turning his head, he stared about him, trying to decide which way to go. To his right, a long finger of rock called Cooper's Knot jutted out from the landmass, while to his left the beach stretched away in an arc all the way to North Point, the lighthouse nothing more than a slender white stick in the distance. Pushing his hands in the pockets of his jacket, he started towards it. Apart from the clouds of snowy-white gulls which rose into the air every now and then, the only other living things in sight were a woman with a dog in

165

the distance. Fringing the beach, holiday homes and apartments, abandoned for the winter now, rested in a state of hibernation, waiting for the spring and the seasonal tenants to bring them back to life, curtains and blinds covering their windows giving them a blank, forlorn look.

Bathed in mellow sunshine and a light breeze behind him he walked the entire length of the beach – all three miles of it – enjoying the exercise, waiting to feel himself slip back into his normal life, an odd sensation he'd often had as a kid when they'd returned home after being abroad. Only this time it wasn't happening.

Drawing level with the lighthouse, he stared up at it for a moment before scaling the rocks at its base. Climbing up, at last he lowered himself onto a flat rock before staring around him, the desolate shore-line constantly morphing with light, as clouds scudded across the sky. Over the next few hours, the sea it would relentlessly roar its way back in again, completely inundating the mud-flats and transforming landscape, the bay hardly recognisable from what it was now – *everything irrevocably changing.*

Feeling better than he had for a long time, he was just beginning to relax when the image of the creature emerging from the shrubbery suddenly flashed into his mind with startling clarity.

*what is it dad*

Feeling his spirits plummet, he realised he'd been naïve to think that once he got back home everything would be okay and that he'd be able to just carry on as if nothing had happened, because since that night in the woods, everything had changed.

166

He'd changed.

All of a sudden, filled with a deep longing for something intrinsically lost, he realised the pre-woods Carter Stanbrook who'd sat here so many times before no longer existed. That night a curtain had been lifted, revealing a terrifying new reality on the periphery of human consciousness, irrevocably shattering his world view and changing him forever.

And not just him.

What with his dad's unexplained jaunts to Brentwood Down and his uncle acting completely out of character, clearly something strange had been going on, but for the life of him he couldn't imagine what, the whole thing making no sense at all. What had been the reasoning behind his uncle wanting to introduce Harry to his dad and what had his dad been writing down when Jack and Seth had seen them in the pub that day? What role had Harry played in all this and why had he reacted the way he had when they'd met outside the church the other day? Had they met somewhere before and if so, where, and when? And why did Harry hate him so much? Was it something to do with his dad?

High above him a gull screeched and, looking up he realised everything was bathed in the pearly tones of dusk, the sea closer and louder now. Surprised, he looked around him, not having realised he'd been out here so long. Incredibly cold, his body chilled by the rock leeching the heat from his body almost without him being aware of it, he got stiffly got to his feet, before jerkily making his way off the rocks, his teeth chattering as he did so. Once at the bottom he turned his collar up and thrusting his hands deep into his pockets, began the long walk home. Behind him, in one of the sand dunes cresting the beach, a man lowered a pair of binoculars, his eyes bright.

* * * * *

*Chilled, in the laboratory, Hely stared at the incubation unit thinking about the nightmare he'd had the other night, unable to shake the feeling that it had somehow been a warning.*

*"Well?" Robert asked, startling him out of his reverie, his face eerily lit from below by the incubation unit between them.*

*"I'm sorry." Hely replied, giving his head a quick shake. "What?"*

*"I said my house was searched."*

*"What?" Hely gasped in horror his eyes wide.*

*"Yeah." Robert nodded. "I think someone's onto us."*

*"Christ!" Hely muttered, his face blanching. "You may be right – someone followed me in the car yesterday."*

*"Are you sure?"*

*"As sure as I can be."*

*Thinking, Robert shook his head. "I don't understand what's going on – it doesn't make sense. These people don't mess around – they wouldn't waste time searching my house and following you – they'd just arrest us."*

*Suddenly Hely's eyes widened. "Oh my god..."*

*"What?" Robert asked, his voice barely above a whisper now. "What is it?"*

*"It might be nothing." Hely began. "But a few weeks ago, I was in here asleep when something woke me up*

168

*and the sheet was on the floor along with some paperwork...*"

"*Sheet? What sheet?*" *Robert asked, spreading a hand.*

*Realising he'd just dropped himself in it, Hely shifted awkwardly.* "*Just a sheet I put over the tank sometimes.*"

"*What? Why the bloody hell would you do something like that?*"

*Feeling like a kid caught with his hand in the cookie-jar Hely shrugged.* "*I don't know. Sometimes when I come in here...it creeps me out.*"

"*You're not serious?*" *Robert gasped, staring at him incredulously.* "*We're scientists – it's what we do!*"

"*I'm aware of that! But...*"

"*Just tell me about the sheet!*" *Robert hissed impatiently, still unable to believe what he'd just heard.*

"*The sheet had come off and there were papers all over the floor. It might've been a draught or something but I got the feeling someone had been in here.*"

"*No one can access this lab except for us.*"

"*I know but If I'm right, someone did.*"

"*Christ.*" *Robert muttered, his heart racing.* "*What do we do?*"

"*We need to act fast.*" *Robert said, quietly.* "*We need to get everything together, notes, files, records everything and hide them because if we don't it won't just them that disappears, we will too.*"

*Swallowing on a suddenly too-dry throat, Hely wiped beads of sweat from his brow with his sleeve even though it was relatively cool in here.* "*And that?*" *he whispered hoarsely, nodding at the incubator.* "*What do we do about that?*"

169

*Placing a hand on the incubator that was almost a caress, Robert spoke quietly. "I've got that covered."*

*"You have?" Hely gasped in surprise. "Already? How?"*

*Turning his head, Robert looked at him steadily, the trace of a smile playing about his mouth. "You think I'd embark upon something as important as this without a back-up plan? I know someone who will take it."*

*"Take it?" Hely gasped, astounded. "What the hell are you talking about? This isn't just some run of the mill..."*

*"You think I don't know how risky it is?" Robert hissed quietly fixing him with a look.*

*"Risky?" Hely whispered, spreading his arms. "It's insane that's what it is!"*

*"What would you suggest instead then – termination?" Robert growled his voice laden with sarcasm.*

*"Of course not! It's just...". "*

*"At least this way we can monitor the results and keep an eye on its progress, even more so than under laboratory conditions because this way any abnormalities or traits will be allowed to develop naturally."*

*"Are you're going to tell them?"*

*"Of course not!" Robert gasped, looking at him incredulously. "What the do you think I am? There's no need for them to know anything."*

*"But we have no idea what could happen..."*

*"In that case we'll deal with it just like we're doing now."*

170

*"Christ." Hely muttered, taking his glasses off and pinching the bridge of his nose in an effort to relieve the tension building behind his eyes. Putting them back on again he stared at him. "These people – they can be trusted?"*

*"Implicitly."*

*"What if they start asking questions?"*

*"They won't."*

*"I hope to god you're right."*

*"Trust me, I know what I'm doing." Robert said quietly. "Everything's under control."*

*Below them, in the passageway, Norman left.*

# XXIII

*There were three fish in the ice-cooler on the bottom of the boat now and Carter was feeling proud because he'd managed to catch one himself and, even though it wasn't as big as he'd hoped, it certainly wasn't the smallest. At the moment, his dad was leaning against the back of the boat asleep, his hat tipped over his face, his arms folded loosely over his stomach snoring gently and Carter couldn't wait for him to wake up so he could show him. He was going to be so proud of him, he knew.*

*Looking over the side of the boat he saw the lines bob up and down as if something had disturbed them from beneath, something swimming unseen through the depths. Idly he wondered what his dad would say if he landed a whopper – a fifteen-pound Carp – better still, a Brown Trout – all by himself. Smiling, he imagined the expression on his dad's face when he woke up and saw it lying on the bottom of the boat taking up a humungous amount of room...*

*Brought out of his daydream by a quiet splash, turning, he saw two old men in hats sculling through the water in a row boat heading towards the bend. Raising their hands in greeting he waved back before watching them make their way round the curve, the ripples from their oars hardly disturbing the surface. Bored again, he stared out over the lake, the speedboat nowhere in sight, replaced now by two jet-skis, their engines no louder than a bumble-bees.*

*All of a sudden, his eyes widened at the sight of a crouching figure in the reed-beds wearing what looked like a grey wetsuit with large goggles on its face, looking*

172

*directly over the water at him, its head and shoulders
protruding from the long stems. Wondering what it was
doing over there he shaded his eyes with his hands, the
way it was staring back at him so still and all, decidedly
creepy. Dropping his eyes, he turned his head and waited
a few moments before looking back at it, chilled as he
saw it was still there in exactly the same position, still
staring across the water at him. Despite the heat, he
shivered, the hairs on the back of his neck and his arms
standing on end. Frightened, without knowing why, he
wished it would go away.*

*To his surprise, all of a sudden, the figure twitched
and disappeared backwards into the reeds, a couple of
Canadian geese taking to the air as it did so. With his
heart pounding he leaned on the side of the boat,
scouring the reeds with his eyes, seeing no sign of it now,
nothing but the sluggish water and dancing insects...*

On the pillow, Carter's head moved head side to side,
his lips moving soundlessly.

*"Carter? Are you alright?"*
*Starting, he saw his dad had woken up and was
staring at him from beneath the peak of his cap. "What's
wrong?"*
*"Nothing." he replied firmly, shaking his head.*
*Concerned, his dad had narrowed his eyes at him.
"Come on, what is it? What's the matter?"*
*Suddenly upset for no reason he could explain, not
trusting himself to speak, he dropped his eyes lest his dad
see the tears forming in them. At the ripe old age of ten
he didn't want him to think he was a cry baby.*

"Jesus Carter!" his dad gasped, leaning forward before putting his hands on his shoulders. "You're shaking like a leaf!" Suddenly, pushing himself forward into his dad's arms, he clung to him for dear life, the image of the figure crouching on the bank, vividly imprinted upon his mind. "What the..."

"There was someone over there." Carter muttered thickly. "In the reeds, watching."

Frowning, his dad stared across the stretch of water. "What? Where?"

"Over there, in the reeds." He repeated, pointing.

"I can't see anyone..."

"They've gone now."

"You sure you didn't just fall asleep and have a dream?" his dad asked quietly.

"No." he said adamantly. "I wanted to but I someone had to watch the lines..."

"What do you mean?"

"You were asleep."

"I was asleep?" his dad gasped, hardly louder than a whisper now. Glancing at his watch, he did a double-take, visibly paling. Then, taking him firmly by the shoulders, he stared at him intently. "Carter, listen to me, this is important. This figure you saw – what did it look like?"

Twisting his mouth to one side, he shivered. "It had these huge goggles, big black ones and it just kept staring at me, big black ones and its face looked weird too."

"Weird how?"

*"I don't know." Carter replied shrugging a shoulder, giving the reeds a quick glance. "Sort of all wrinkled. Like it was really old or something."*

*For a moment his dad fell silent, his face ashen.*

*"Carter, we've got to go – right now!"*

*"Why?" he asked, confused.*

*Instead of replying however his dad grabbed the fishing lines and threw them into the bottom of the boat willy-nilly before taking his place on the seat.*

*"Dad?" he said, frightened for a completely different reason now. "What's going on?"*

*"Nothing." His dad replied quickly. "We've got to go, that's all."*

Sheathed in a fine film of sweat, Carter opened his eyes, his heart pounding, the memory of that long-forgotten day vivid in his mind. Just him and his dad out there under the blazing hot sun on a summer's day. And the strange figure crouching down there among the reeds with those ridiculous goggles that had frightened him so much. Or what he'd believed at the time to be goggles anyway, because now, twenty-four years later, he knew exactly what they'd been – *eyes* – belonging to the same kind of creature that had chased him through the wood that night. Just as terrifying had been the way his dad had reacted. Rowing them back to the jetty, he'd tied the boat up and stuffed him and the gear in the car before driving off as if the hounds of hell were chasing them. Looking back now, Carter realised his dad had been terrified.

\* \* \* \* \*

In a parking space a short distance from the main building, Norman checked his watch again, rolling his eyes as he did so, time seeming to crawl by past at a snail's pace. Crossing his arms, he stared through the rain-spattered windscreen at a service door at the rear of the building everyone used as a short-cut to the car park. Suddenly, it opened, Sterling's distinctive figure briefly silhouetted in it before stepping out into the darkness.

Sliding down in the seat, Norman watched his progress through the car park as he splashed through the shallow puddles dotting it, a large hold-all in his right hand. Unlocking the Jag, he put the bag on the back seat, his face briefly illuminated by the interior light before getting in the front. As the engine purred into life, the headlights splashed over the wet tarmac.

With his heart racing Norman straightened and started his own engine, watching as Sterling pulled up in front of the security barrier, his brake lights coming on. A few moments later the barriers were raised and the Jag slid beneath them. Giving the guard a quick wave of his hand, quickly, Norman followed.

Heading north. On the outskirts of Ashton, the next town, the Jag turned off the main road, weaving through darkened country lanes, heading east. Wondering where he was going, Norman maintained his distance. However, forced to slow in order to manoeuvre three tight bends in a row, at last the road opened up before him, the Jag nowhere to be seen! Slowing, he turned his head first one way then the other, searching for a turnoff or opening it might've gone down. Finding none, with a curse, he angrily slammed his hand on the steering wheel.

*Behind a hedgerow, cloaked in darkness with the engine off, Robert watched the car that had been following him – the same make of car that had followed Hely – drive past, slower now, the driver clearly searching for him. A car that had come out of the Institute car park behind him which could only mean one of two things; someone at Biochem was curious about what they'd been doing or they knew something.*

*Either way he and Walberg were in trouble.*

*Behind him, on the back seat, the bag moved.*

\* \* \* \* \*

*It was midday now, the sun having turned the day into a broiling cauldron of heat pressing in on them from every direction and sucking the faintest breezes from the air, everything quiet and still, stifling under its relentless bombardment. All about them the lake undulated sluggishly, smoothly lifting the boat every now and then as if on an oil slick. Above the surface bright dragonflies hovered and darted, bright flashes of vivid greens and blues, seemingly unaffected by the heat. The speedboat had disappeared now, replaced by three jet-skis weaving back and forth across the water, the sound of their engines like distant hornets.*

*Sinking his teeth into a cheese and ham sandwich, he looked at his dad, his eyes hidden behind dark sunglasses. "When will we get a bite dad?"*

*Taking his hat off, his dad ran a hand through his hair, damp with sweat before putting it back on. Glancing over the side of the boat he shook his head and clicked his* tongue. *"I don't know, son. They just don't seem to want to be caught today, do they?"*

*"You know, why don't you?" Harry suddenly demanded from beside him, making him jump. Shocked, he gaped at Harry wide-eyed, wondering how long he'd been here without him realising. Poking his head forward, with his eyes boring into his, Harry spoke again. "You forgot to bring the book!"*

With a gasp, Carter shot upright, Harry's words echoing through his mind as he did so – *the book! Adkins was the name of the author of the UFO book he'd found in his uncle's study that day!*

Leaping out of bed he snatched his dressing gown off the chair and hurried into the living room. Snapping the light on he went to the desk, and sat down before the computer, amazed he hadn't thought of it before. With a trickle of excitement, he waited impatiently for it to boot up, his mind racing. Was Adkins the author the Adkins his uncle had been referring to in the letter – *was it possible?* A minute later, with the computer up and running, drawing the keyboard towards him he deftly typed in *Adkins, author.* A few moments later a page filled the screen.

*'Never seen anything like it in my life' woman from Wisconsin says. Bob Adkins investigates...'*
*'Bob Adkins, guest speaker to give lecture at MUFON seminar in Pasadena.'*
*'B. Adkins says UFO phenomena spiralling...'*

He scrolled down.

*'Adkins refutes allegations of scare-mongering. 'Ten per-cent of all UFO sightings remain unexplained.' he claims.'*
*Bob Adkins official web-site.*

Clicking on the last one, Carter watched, intrigued as the page was replaced by another, this time headed by an image of a man in his fifties with a thick thatch of salt and pepper hair, beneath which a pair of friendly, intelligent-looking eyes stared out from behind wire-rimmed glasses, a half-smile on his round face. With raised eyebrows, he began reading.

*Bob Adkins, sixty-two, had become interested in ufology when working as a plumber in the nineteen-seventies after he'd seen something unusual in the sky above Lake Sakakawea not far from his home in North Dakota. He and a number of friends had watched a small silver disc flying slowly across the sky before it had suddenly changed direction, zooming off at incredible speed, the incident still without explanation to this day, and the onset of his obsession. Twenty years ago, he'd moved to Manhattan as one of the world's leading UFO investigators, founding NYCAAG (the New York City Alien Abduction Group) where alleged abductees were interviewed and counselled before being invited to attend group meetings along with other abductees, but most of all – listened to and believed. Over the years he'd given countless abductees a much-needed lifeline, helping them to understand and come to terms with what they were experiencing. Ten years ago, he'd toured all over the States, his lectures on UFO phenomena/alien abduction*

179

*being sell-outs and had been a guest speaker at innumerable UFO seminars and conventions. An author of four books to date, he'd co-authored another two and had been brought in as a consultant on Christian Slovenski's epic sci-fi movie 'Transcendental.'*

Leaning back, Carter stared at the screen, bemused. Surely this couldn't be *the* Adkins? So far as he could see, the only thing that linked them was the fact his uncle had known Harry Bennett who'd claimed to have seen a UFO once, Adkins' specialist subject. Or had Harry bought the book and lent it to uncle Rob? But why would his uncle have borrowed it in the first place? As a hard-nosed scientist, he'd have dismissed the subject as utter clap-trap and Bob Adkins as nothing but self-deluded imbecile along with it. And yet, undeniably, the book had been right there on his bookshelf. With his mind going round in circles, he decided to approach it from a different angle – had his uncle *known* Adkins?

Frowning, he turned it over in his mind.

If so, then maybe after hearing the UFO story he'd referred Harry to him which would explain why he'd got Elizabeth to bring Harry round in the first place. Shaking his head, he dismissed it. Never a people person at the best of times his uncle rarely showed empathy with anyone and so, that being the case, why would he have bothered? What possible reason would he have had for doing so? But then why had he then introduced his dad to Harry? So far as he was aware, his dad had never shown the slightest interest in UFO's so that made no sense at all.

Frustrated, he stared at Bob Adkins' image on the screen before him. No nearer to understanding than he had before, all tonight had done was muddy the waters further, the mystery deepening.

# XXIV

*It had been easy finding out who the car belonged to –
suspiciously so in fact – that suspicion deepening further
when the security guard on the desk told him it belonged
to Norman Kepple, the caretaker.*

*Thanking him, Sterling wondered if Kepple was a
'plant' to keep an eye on what they'd been doing,
however, if his amateurish blunderings were anything to
go by, nothing could be further from the truth. But why
then had he followed them? Had he somehow found out
about the experiment and if so, how? Andy why, if he'd
been in the lab and seen it for himself, why hadn't he
said told anyone else?*

*Later that night, in a rented car, he followed Kepple
to a shabby, run-down block in a slummy area a few
miles away. Snorting, Robert shook his head – either
Kepple's cover was good or he really was a nobody. A
few days later, in the mouth of an alleyway, steeped in
shadows, with his hat pulled down low over his face,
Sterling waited, staring at the block with narrowed eyes.*

*Inside, Norman bolted upright in bed as the front door
crashed inwards. Grabbing the baseball bat by the
bedside cabinet he leapt out of bed, wielding it. As the
bedroom door burst open, two burly policemen rushed in
before quickly overpowering him and snatching the bat
away. Convinced someone had discovered he'd been in
the lab, Norman's heart sank. However, when six bags of
heroin were discovered in a cardboard box under the
sink – bags he'd never seen before – he knew it for sure.
Over the road, bathed in flashing blue lights, Robert
smiled.*

\* \* \* \* \*

After reading a few more articles on the UFO
investigator, deciding it couldn't do any harm and might
even help him with his own, terrifying encounters,
entering his credit card number, Carter ordered a copy of
Adkins book. And, even though doubtful the author and
the Adkins in the letter were one and the same,
nevertheless he couldn't dismiss it out of hand until, he
was sure. He supposed he could contact him directly and
ask him if he and his uncle had known each other,
however, the letter with its warning of imminent peril
had rattled him more than he cared to admit, so for now
at least, he decided to err on the side of caution.

A few days later it arrived in the post.

Once more, at the sight of the cover, his heart leapt,
but, reminding himself it was just a book, he opened it,
and began reading. It opened with Adkins explaining the
term 'flying saucer' had been coined by the press after an
aviator, Kenneth Arnold, on June the twenty-fourth, in
nineteen-forty-seven, had seen nine flying objects flying
in tandem near Mount Rainier, Washington, likening
their movement to 'saucers skipping on water'. Before
that, during World War two, planes had been inextricably
dogged by unexplainable balls of light, the pilots naming
them 'Foo Fighters.' Although not hostile, the lights had
messed with their equipment, drawing alongside them
and performing incredible manoeuvres at impossible
speeds. At first, these strange encounters had been put
down to some new-fangled weapon developed by one
country or another and it was only when the war ended

183

that it came to light, they hadn't belonged to anyone. However, mounting evidence pointed to the fact that strange encounters and visitations been going on long before that. *Much* further back in time – as depicted in an ancient wood-cutting of Satan mowing hay with a scythe essentially creating a corn circle and Old Masters paintings depicting beings in flying machines in the sky behind the subject matter.

Chilled, Carter shifted uncomfortably.

Before his own experience he'd have dismissed this stuff out of hand; however, he knew different now. After the introduction, the first chapter opened with a couple who lived on a farm in McMinnville, Oregon, who, in nineteen-fifty had seen a silver cigar-shaped craft streaking across the sky. Two days later they'd seen it again, a spate of separate, unrelated reports collaborating their sighting. Then an elderly man walking his dog early one morning on a beach in Somerset, England in nineteen sixty-three who'd been surprised by a dark grey, dull-looking saucer-shaped craft which had suddenly shot up from the sea before streaking across the sky in the direction of Bristol at breath-taking speed. Terrified, the man had been treated for shock while the dog, usually placid and calm had been nervous and skittish for a long while after. Another man walking in woods not far from his home in Queensland, Australia in nineteen seventy-seven had watched a strange round craft descend behind a hill not far away. Believing it was about to crash he'd raced towards it only to see a circle of dried grass down below, that and a sulphuric odour which had lingered for many days over the site. He hadn't seen the craft leave and it was only when he returned home, he realised four hours had passed with him recollection during that time, a phenomenon known as 'missing time.'

Freezing, the words leapt off the page at him, and, suddenly filled with fear he thought about the day beneath the tree when the shadows had suddenly lengthened, it apparently having passed in seconds. And then the sense of shock he'd felt when he'd realised he'd somehow lost an entire day without even being aware of it, on his way to Brentwood Down.

*what happened to Monday then*

With his heart racing, he read on.

It was only when the man contacted the author and was hypnotically regressed that he began remembered seeing the craft on the ground at all and being taken into it by small, humanoid figures after they'd emerged from it, him at the time being rendered completely immobile. Once inside the craft the beings had examined him before carrying out, strange, surgical procedures on him.

As panic stirred, closing it with a snap, Carter leapt to his feet, the book falling to the floor as he did so, before agitatedly pacing, the implications of what he'd just read and what it might mean for him, beyond terrifying. The rest of the day he refused to think about it. That night, after tossing and turning, unable to sleep, he got up and, padding back into the living room, picked it up again.

\* \* \* \* \*

*In bed, the small boy turned his head and looked at the window, the curtains drawn back, bright stars appearing every now and then between the ragged clouds scudding quickly over the night sky. Closing his eyes, he listened to his dad's rhythmic snores coming from his parent's room, that and the occasional odd creak of the house settling. Suddenly, out in the darkness, an owl hooted and his eyes snapped open.*

*Slipping out of bed he put a small stool beneath the window and climbed up on it. Peering over the windowsill he stared down at the back garden, an ocean of inky blackness, save for a yellow oblong of light on the lawn from the office window. Narrowing his eyes, with his nose only an inch or so from the glass, he stared at the misshapen humps of trees and shrubbery silhouetted against the lighter backdrop of the sky, bright stars appearing every now and then between the slow-moving clouds. Chilled, he wished he could just go back to bed, just get under the warmth of the covers and go to sleep. Dropping his eyes back to the yellow oblong he stared intently at it for a moment or two as if searching for something.*

*Suddenly he saw a flicker of movement below – something crossing it before disappearing again, his heart leaping. All of a sudden something reappeared within the light and he sagged with relief, realising it was just a fox. A second later it disappeared back into the darkness. Shivering with cold, he climbed back into bed, noticing his dad was no longer snoring.*

*Outside, the fox trotted to the end of the garden and slipped through a hole in the fence into the darkened meadow. Realising something was standing by the fence, it froze and barred its teeth at it menacingly, a deep growl coming from its throat. Instantly the figure vanished, and, with a startled bark the fox turned tail and streaked through the meadow, only darkness remaining now.*

\* \* \* \* \*

Two days later, Carter finished the book, it being the most terrifying one he'd ever read simply because it rang so many bells with him. Chilled, at least he knew he wasn't alone now, a global community of ordinary, sane, people trying to come to terms with what had happened to them, his encounter with extra-terrestrial beings in the woods, that night, more than a common occurrence, apparently. People he'd once jokingly called 'a fully paid-up member of 'the mindless imbeciles with nothing better to do club', something which, in the light of current events, had come back and bitten him firmly on the ass. Worse, if Adkins was right, then considering his encounter in the woods and the park, not to mention the periods of missing time, not once but *twice* now, chances were, he was an abductee, a thought which didn't bear thinking about. On the verge of panic, he quickly turned his mind to other matters. He was still none the wiser as to whether this Adkins was the same one as in the letter so now what?

During his visit to Brentwood Down, he'd learned things about his family he'd never believed possible and, clearly, something strange had been going on. In which case he surmised, his best chance of getting to the bottom of it would be to do a little digging into his uncle's life

187

and see what he came up with. Which meant a return visit to the village because there he was sure, all the answers to his questions lay.

* * * * *

*Feeling the soft caress of a warm breeze on his face George opened his eyes, filled with surprise to see he was no longer in bed but standing on a pebble beach, the moon, almost full now, turning the mirror-like surface of water molten silver, the scene spectacular. Frowning, he saw a darkened ridge on the other side, realising with a jolt they were the Mayward Hills, a small cluster of lights, the tiny village of Brunton to the right, realising it was Blacknoll lake!*

*Suddenly, a small wave washed over his bare feet, the coldness shocking, realising with a jolt he really was here and not just dreaming as he'd first thought. Taking a step back he gaped down at himself, still dressed in t-shirt and Y-fronts, the same things he'd gone to bed in!*

*"Don't be afraid." A soft voice said from the darkness next to him. Turning, he stared at a tall blonde man in a white robe, his face turned from him, looking at something further on down the beach.*

*"Who are you?" George gasped. "How did I get here?"*

*Instead of answering however, the man pointed to a small figure on the beach. Narrowing his eyes, George stared at it seeing a small boy pick up a pebble before examining it and discarding it, repeating the action again, the earnestly and intensity with which he was*

*doing it evident in the way he held his body. Suddenly, he
gasped.*

*"Is that my son? Is that…Carter?"*

*"Yes."*

*"Why is he here?" George demanded loudly,
suddenly filled with fear. "What's he doing?"*

*"Searching."*

*"Searching?" George breathed, his teeth beginning to
chatter with cold. "Searching for what?"*

*"Us." The man replied.*

\* \* \* \* \*

Standing before the window with a mug of coffee in
his hand, Carter stared at the monochromic scene before
him, the sky a low slab of grey marble, the horizon
indistinguishable from the incoming tide, a tumult of
white-horses racing for the shore before breaking on the
beach in a crescendo of white foam, the turbulence
reflecting his own, inner turmoil. Above it all, snow-
white gulls soared, their wings spread wide, buffeted like
kites in the wind, their faint squawks hardly audible.

Narrowing his eyes, he sucked in a deep breath not
wanting to Brentwood Down, the village being the last
place he wanted to be, his brief stay there nothing short
of a hellish, white-knuckled ride of insanity and
emotional upheaval. On the other hand, there were too
many things he needed answers to; things he'd never be
able to stop thinking about until he did. Knowing he
wasn't going to find them by putting off the inevitable,
he tipped the remainder of the coffee down the sink and
turned from the window. In the doorway he paused for a

189

moment and gave the kitchen one, last, sweeping look, suddenly filled with the strangest notion he'd never see it again. Unsettled, telling himself he was being ridiculous, nevertheless, the feeling remained.

\* \* \* \* \*

*"I'm worried about you." Rebecca said looking at George over the breakfast table. "This morning there was mud all over the sheets – you've been outside again."*

*Looking up from the newspaper, George shrugged. "I've always slept-walked, you know that. As for the sheets..."*

*Rolling her eyes, Rebecca shook her head dismissively. "I'm not worried about the bloody sheets, I'm worried about you being outside, wandering about in the middle of the night again – Christ Georgie, anything could've happened to you..."*

*"But it didn't, did it?" he sighed, laying the newspaper down. "I'm fine."*

*"This time maybe." She went on. "But what about next time, or the time after? What if you wander across the road or over the edge of a cliff or something?"*

*"What cliff?" George asked, lowering the paper again, amused. "There aren't any cliffs around here..."*

*"Don't be flippant with me, Georgie!" she hissed, angrily. "You know what I mean and it's not funny. How would you feel if it was me – wouldn't you be in the least bit concerned?"*

*"Of course, I would. I just don't see what I can do about it that's all."*

"You could go to the doctor's, see if he can give you anything..."

"What and get hooked on sleeping tablets – no thanks." He snorted. Rolling her eyes, she was just about to protest when he lowered the paper again and, looking at her, shook his head. "Okay, listen, if you're really that worried, I'll get Tom to come round and put an extra lock on the door so I can't get out, how's that?"

"You'll give him a ring after breakfast?"

"I promise. Just as soon as I've finished my coffee, He replied, before looking at her pointedly. "And the paper."

# XXV

The next day Carter began searching the house for clues as to what his uncle might've been up to before he died, determined to leave no stone unturned.

Starting at the top of the house, he stared at the desk beneath the window, its surface littered with a slew of paperwork. As good as anywhere to start, he took the sheaf of papers off the chair and dropped down into it before beginning to leaf through page after page of equations and calculations. Written in his uncle's familiar scrawling hand-writing, most of them were completely illegible. A couple of hours later he decided to take a break and, getting to his feet, went downstairs.

Ten minutes later, carrying a mug of coffee and half a pack of biscuits, he returned to the task. Turning his attention to the drawers he groaned inwardly as he saw they contained even more paperwork, interspersed with a sprinkling of pens, pencils, paperclips and rubber bands. The bottom one however contained a sturdy-looking shoebox and, taking it out, he put it on the desk in front of him. Inside were letters in his mom's neat handwriting. Taking one out, he withdrew the letter from the envelope.

*Dear Rob* (it read)
*Well, here we are out in the Coatzacoalcos in the middle of mapping what could potentially be the most significant site we've excavated for a long time, albeit only a little one, but just as important as any of the larger ones we've worked on so far. You'd hate it out here – it's so hot we can hardly breathe! Georgie's*

*having trouble with his tooth again and as soon as we
get home, he's going to the damned dentist even if I have
to drag him there!*

Holding it in his hands, with the faint hint of her
scent, for a moment as if she were right there in the room
with him. Taking a deep breath, he read on.

*As for the strangeness we talked about before, so far
as I know nothing more's happened although I seriously
doubt Georgie would tell me anyway now. He says
there's nothing we can do about it and he doesn't want
me worrying but how can he say that – I'm his wife for
god's sake, we're in this together and I need to know,
doesn't he realise that? Sometimes he wakes up and
looks haunted, but when I ask him about it, he just shrugs
it off and says he had a nightmare and even though I
know he's lying, what can I do?*

Frowning, he wondered what she'd been talking
about. What strangeness? The rest of the letter was about
the dig, nothing else mentioned about it. Intrigued, he
took another from the box, this one dated two months
earlier.

*Last night I woke up and Georgie was gone again. I
don't care how common it is or what anybody says, it's
horrific and if I live to be ninety, I'll never get used to it,
ever! I called Bob and he managed to calm me down and
told me to just go back to bed. He told me everything
would be alright by the morning and it was. When I woke
up Georgie was right there next to me and didn't seem to*

*remember anything so I mention it. Does that make me a*
*bad wife, or worse – a coward?*

*Bob!*

*The* Bob Adkins, he wondered? Suddenly a thought
struck him. Maybe, being an author too, his parents had
known him, that would at least explain the book. What it
didn't explain however was why his uncle had left his
name in the letter, nor why he believed he'd be able to
help him. Clearly his mom must have been referring to
his dad's frequent sleepwalking. For years, his dad had
slept-walked and he remembered waking up in the
middle of the night once and hearing them out in the
back garden, his dad obviously out there again. It had
been a constant source of worry for her and even though
they'd had extra locks put on both the front and back
doors, somehow, he'd still managed to get out. But why
on Earth would she have called Bob about it and why
would he have told her to just go back to bed rather than
go out looking for him – *what the hell?* Quickly scanning
the rest of it, there were no more clues as to what
might've been going on or another mention of Bob.
Refolding it he slipped it back into the envelope before
taking another one out, this one dated six months earlier.

*We've arrived safely in Manhattan and the hotel is*
*magnificent. Bob seems like a nice man but nothing like*
*we expected – just ordinary-looking.*

Bob Adkins lived in Manhattan – so it had to be the
same one, didn't it, Carter thought, his heart skipping a
beat.

194

*We spent most of the weekend just talking about it all and I'm glad we went now because at least Georgie feels he's not alone and that this is happening to other people as well, not just him. Maybe all this stuff is real after all...*

Feeling as if someone had just thrown a bucket of iced-water in his face, Carter jerked – *what?* Filled with a deep foreboding, he read on.

*In the end, we decided to stay for the whole week because Manhattan's so beautiful in the fall as they call it over here! We went for a walk in Central Park and had some hot dogs and coffee by the boating lake*

Quickly taking another out, this one was dated two weeks earlier.

*Apparently, it's happening to people all over the world every day and how terrifying is that if it's true? He got this chap's phone number from this book he's been reading and he thinks he might be able to help him but I don't like it one bit. I still not sure what to make of it but at least we know he's not ill or going crazy now he's had all those tests done.*

*"Christ!"* Carter gasped, his hands trembling. Like Harry, had his dad seen some kind of UFO and contacted Bob Adkins, thus explaining the connection? Filled with fear, he felt panic awaken, a line from Adkin's book returning to him.

*this kind of phenomena often runs in families*
Filled with dread, he reached for another, three
months earlier.

*Georgie said he woke up in the middle of the night
and it was just standing there by the side of the bed
staring down at him with huge black eyes – like an insect
– and he was absolutely hysterical, screaming at the top
of his voice and shaking me like a rag doll but couldn't
wake me up!*

As shock lanced through him, Carter leapt to his feet,
sending the chair flying backwards, the letter see-sawing
to the floor. In panic, he flung the window open and,
leaning out, sucked in huge gasps of air, his mom's
words clanging around inside his head over and over
again like some huge, insane cymbal, knowing only too
well exactly what his dad had seen that night.

\* \* \* \* \*

Hearing a soft ping beep from the laptop, Stevenson
looked up at it before getting to his feet and going to the
window. On the bed, Rieker sat up, suddenly alert.
"What is it?"
Peering through a chink in the curtains, Stevenson
stared at the house over the road. Reaching for the
binoculars he raised them to his eyes. "I'm not sure..."
Joining him, Rieker stared at Carter leaning out the
window, gasping for air.
"Jesus, he looks like shit!"
"You think he's having a cardio or something?"

Taking the glasses from him, Rieker peered through them, adjusting the focus as he did so. "He's not clutching his chest or anything…he looks like he's had some kind of shock."

"What like?"

Lowering the glasses Rieker looked at him, his eyebrows raised. "How the hell would I know – it could be anything. Maybe, he stuck his finger in a socket or found his uncle's stash of gay porn – your guess is as good as mine."

"You think we should we call it in?"

"Give it a minute and see what happens." Rieker said staring through the binoculars again. "Hang on, he's gone back in." Lowering the glasses he narrowed his eyes, no sign of Carter now, the window cranked open behind him.

\* \* \* \* \*

*Staring round the ring of faces, the boy's eyes stopped at one in particular, feeling the floor lurch. Fumbling for his mom's hand he gripped it tightly, unable to tear his eyes from it, the room spinning around him, getting faster and faster like a carousel. Filled with panic, all he knew was he had to get out of there.*

*Letting go of his mom's hand he bolted from the room, almost knocking another child over as he did so before tearing down the hallway for the front door. Yanking it open for he shot down the garden path. Behind him, his mom shouted out to him, her voice full of shock. Vaulting the garden gate, he streaked out into the road. All of a sudden, the world was filled with the shockingly loud blare of a horn – that and the terrifying screech of brakes – and in that moment, it was as if everything slowed down, time itself slowly grinding to a halt. Only too late as the acrid stench of burning rubber on tarmac filled his nostrils did he realise what was happening and, propelling himself forward he hurled himself at the grassy verge on the other side of the road. As he hit the curb, he tripped and barrelled into a fence with a loud cry, hearing a loud crack as he did so, not sure if it was the fence breaking or him.*

*Frozen, he stayed where he was on the ground, filled with shock, unable to believe the car hadn't hit him and that he wasn't dead. And then, suddenly time sped up again with, everything happening at once, his mom on her knees by his side, screaming for someone to call an ambulance over her shoulder.*

*And then, suddenly, everything went black.*

*Back inside the house, some of the children were pressed against the window, including Billy Mason who, gaped at the car slewed across the road in horror, the driver jumping out, ashen-faced, his best friend Carter slumped against the wooden fence of the house on the other side of the road. Shocked and frightened at the sudden turn of events, he reached up and pulled the alien mask off his face, his tenth birthday party the last thing on his mind now.*

# XXVI

On legs that felt like rubber, trembling, Carter groped
for the chair, his mind pin-wheeling, the very idea of one
of those things
*you know what it was*
in their house in the middle of the night unthinkable,
knowing only too well the shock and terror his dad
must've felt when he'd seen it. Covering his face with his
hands he peered over his fingers, trying to remember a
time being woken up in the middle of the night by his
dads screams but couldn't. Nor any memories of his
parents behaving strangely at any time either.

Getting to his feet he hurried downstairs and snatched
the phone up before leaving a garbled message, his
words tumbling over each other as he spoke. Chilled to
the bone by his discovery, for the next few hours he
paced the hallway, willing the phone to ring. As daylight
faded into evening, his terror and anxiety grew, dreading
the oncoming night even more so now. Unable to face
going upstairs, he slept on the sofa, the lamp and telly on
all night.

The next morning, having hardly slept a wink, still
fully-dressed he padded into the hallway and, picking up
the phone, held it to his ear to make sure it was working.
Going into the kitchen he snapped the kettle on before
going back upstairs to the study. Standing stiffly in the
doorway, he stared at the letter, still on the floor where
he'd left it yesterday. Snatching it up, he quickly stuffed
them all back in the box before shoving it into the drawer
and slamming it shut with his foot.

Going to the window he stared out unseeingly, his mind racing, it taking a moment to register he'd seen a brief flash of light in a bedroom window in one of the houses opposite as if light had reflected off something. Wondering what it had been he waited to see if it would happen again but saw nothing.

Turning, he went back downstairs and had a strong cup of coffee, wanting to have a clear head if Adkins called back, especially after the hysterical message he'd left on his answer machine last night. Pottering about the house, it was almost seven that night before the phone rang. Skidding out into the hall he snatched it up, his heart pounding.

"Carter Stanbrook."

"Hi." A man's voice with an American accent said. "Bob Adkins – you left me a message?"

Opening his mouth, all of a sudden Carter froze, realising he didn't know how to even begin explaining why he'd called, a million-and-one questions popping into his head all at the same time. "I, yes…I did. I believe you knew my parents, George and Rebecca Stanbrook?"

"Yeah, I did. My condolences Carter. I couldn't believe it when I heard what had happened."

"Thanks." Carter said quietly. "You were at the funeral?"

"No." Bob said. "I was unable to attend at the time, even though I wanted to."

"Mr. Adkins…" Carter began, taking a deep breath.

"Bob please."

"Bob, I found one of my mom's letters saying they'd been to New York to see you. Was it about what my dad saw in their bedroom that night?"

200

After a shocked pause on the line, Bob spoke again.

"I'm sorry, that's confidential, the same with everyone I counsel."

"You *were* counselling him then?" Carter breathed, clutching the phone tightly.

Silence.

"Did you know my uncle, Robert Sterling as well?"

"No, not really." Bob sighed. "The only time I spoke to him was when he called me a few months ago, to let me know about your parents..."

"You never met him?"

"No, never. Why do you ask?"

"Okay." Carter said awkwardly, suddenly feeling like a complete idiot. "This is going to sound crazy but when he died, he left me a letter mentioning you..."

"Your uncle's dead as well?" Bob gasped, sounding shocked.

"Yeah." Carter said. "He passed away suddenly a few weeks ago."

*"Jeez!"* Bob breathed quietly. "Christ, that's hard on you Carter – I'm so sorry."

"He wanted me to get in touch with you."

"He did?" Bob said quickly. "Why?"

"I don't know." Carter said, still erring on the side of caution. "I was hoping you might be able to tell me."

"Sorry, I don't know anything about it. You said last night something was happening to you?"

After a slight pause, Carter nodded. "Yeah."

"Okay." Bob replied, not sounding in the least surprised. "Can you tell me about it?"

"I want to." Carter said, shifting nervously from foot to foot, once more filled with fear. "But I don't know if I can."

"Okay." Bob said evenly, automatically slipping into calm, counsellor mode. "At this stage I think it might be better if we talk face to face."

"What in New York?"

"No." Bob snorted, smiling now. "Online."

Five minutes later Carter sat before the computer in his uncle's study, Bob's friendly-looking face smiling out at him on the screen, looking much the same as he did on his website profile picture albeit with a little less hair. "Nice to meet you properly, Carter." He smiled, his eyes burning with curiosity. "Although I must admit, I feel as if I know you already – parents told me all about you."

"They did?" Carter, asked, surprised.

"Of course." Bob nodded. "They adored you."

"Thanks." Carter replied giving him a weak smile. "That means a lot."

"Now." Bob said quietly, leaning forward, his hands folded neatly in front of him, his voice gentle but firm, instantly putting Carter at ease. "What's been going on?"

Taking a deep breath, Carter hesitated.

"Is it okay if we just talk for a while first?"

"Of course." Bob said soothingly. "Take your time."

"I know you said my dad's case is confidential but that thing he saw by the side of the bed that night, I can't stop thinking about it, about what I read."

"Have you ever experienced something like that?"

"Was that the reason he contacted you?" Carter asked, deliberately dodging the question. "Please, I know what you said about confidentiality and all that but…there was something strange going on and I need to know."

Remaining silent for a moment, deep in thought, at last Bob made a decision. "No." he said quietly. Your dad got in contact with me because of something else."

* * * * *

Over the road, the two agents listened as they talked, Rieker at the window, staring over the lane at the house.

*"Twenty- four years ago, your parents had a UFO sighting and it changed their lives."*

All of a sudden, Rieker saw a flicker of movement in the front garden and, frowning, stared down into a sea of shadow. Seeing nothing more however, he'd just put it down to a trick of the light when a dark shape suddenly peeled itself from the shadows and disappeared round the side of the house. Spinning, he snatched up his SIG 9mm pistol from the table, Stevenson looking up from the monitor at him questioningly.

"We've got company."

"How many?" Stevenson asked already on his feet.

"One, that I saw."

Going into the bedroom opposite, Rieker went to the window before sweeping the back garden with his eyes, Stevenson watching him from the doorway. In the empty room behind them a voice spoke.

*"What? Where?"*

*"The Nubian Desert, five of them travelling east. He noticed them because of the setting sun glinting off them. The whole thing couldn't have lasted more than thirty*

*seconds and although everyone else was excited at what they were seeing, they frightened the hell out of your dad."*

Suddenly seeing something, squinting, Rieker stared at an indistinguishable shape slightly lighter than the darkness surrounding it halfway down the garden. Too small to be a man, it looked like a kid with no clothes on.

*what the hell*

"See anything?" Stevenson whispered, next to him, making him start.

"There's someone out there alright." Rieker whispered, his voice low. "A kid I think and naked by the look of it."

*"Naked?"*

Moving his head back into the shadows Rieker glanced at him giving him an almost imperceptible shake of the head. "Either that or it's wearing a light-coloured jumpsuit or something."

As he spoke, the shape separated, one of them streaking off down the garden before disappearing into a dark, shapeless mass of shrubbery at the end. Holding his breath so it wouldn't fog the glass he pushed his face nearer to the pane, staring intently at the remaining shape still there on the grass not far from the patio, doing something. "I was wrong – there's two of them. One went down the garden but the others still out there. We need to get closer."

Turning, they stealthily descended the stairs into the depths of the house, the hallway an inky pool of darkness, opening up into even darker rooms, the furniture inside them nothing more than humped shapes under the dust sheets draped over them.

Following Rieker down the hallway into the kitchen, Stevenson moved fluidly around the kitchen table before pressing his back against a tall unit meanwhile Rieker, on one knee now, peered over the windowsill. With a flick of his hand, he indicated Stevenson join him. Crouching low, Stevenson scooted over to him, careful not to bump into anything. Raising his head, he saw a shape squatting over something, blocked from sight by its slight, body, its hands working feverishly. Chilled, it dawned on him there was something wrong with its head, being way too large for its body – a helmet maybe? As if reading his mind, Rieker glanced at him, his eyes nothing more than dark sockets in his face.

*"What the hell is that?"*

"You think we should take a look?"

"The last thing we want is to draw unnecessary attention to ourselves." Rieker whispered back. "Let's wait and see what it does first."

Suddenly, without warning a bright flash of white-blue light briefly illuminated the kitchen, the agents ducking their heads as it did so, swiftly followed by a fizzing, electrical sound and a loud pop. As the kitchen plunged into darkness once more, somewhere outside, a dog began barking. Unable to see anything other than the after image of the flash, Stevenson peered blindly at him through the darkness. *"What the hell was that?"*

Without answering, Rieker cautiously raised his head above the window-sill again and peered out, the figure having disappeared now. "There's something out there only I can't make out what it is..."

Scooting behind Stevenson, he crab-walked towards the back door before straightening to the side of it, his gun in his hand. Joining him on the other side, motionless, Stevenson held his breath as Rieker quietly turned the key. Raising his eyes, Rieker gave him a barely perceptible nod and took hold of the handle. Pulling it open it squeaked loudly, the pair of them freezing as it did so. After waiting a moment or two, angling his head, Rieker peered through the gap, seeing nothing but the patio and the shapeless ridge of hedges bordering the garden. Pulling it open, he slipped out into darkness.

* * * * *

*Getting to his feet George stretched his legs, cramped after kneeling for so long on the hot, arid earth of the Nubian Desert. Pulling his neckerchief off, lifting his hat he wiped his face and head with it before glancing upwards at the sun, a blazing ball of molten fire in the dusty Egyptian sky.*

*From his elevated position on the ridge, he swept the site below with his eyes. A hive of activity, the workmen, their robes, stained orange by the setting sun, jabbered away to each other as they worked, the tinny sounds of their tools clanking and scraping in the dusty earth, floating up to him. Mingling with the scent of camels in the hot air was Koshari mint tea, his mouth watering at the thought of it.*

*Narrowing his eyes, he stared at Rebecca sitting on a rock with the ever-faithful Kamal who'd put this work-crew together and who oversaw everything from* transport, food and water to the safe delivery of rock samples to wherever they had to be sent – a godsend if ever there was one, he thought. Suddenly as if aware of his eyes upon her, Rebecca looked up and smiled. Returning it, he raised his arm and tapped his watch and, with a nod she got to her feet and blew on the whistle hanging from her neck on a piece of string, signalling the end of work for the day.

Shading his eyes with his hand, George stared over the desolate wasteland beyond, fringed by undulating red hills to the east, nothing but flat, sandy plains stretching all the way to the horizon to the west. Just about pick his tools up, he saw a flash of light in the sky. Wondering what it was, all of a sudden, he saw five discs skimming over the sky heading east at high speed, the sun reflecting off them. Filled with shock, the blood drained from his face.

"BECCA!" he shouted, his voice, high with panic, echoing around the site. Down below, heading towards a small group of tents, Rebecca spun and stared up at him, the men following suit.

"Over there!" he shouted, pointing towards the horizon. "In the sky!"

Turning, she shaded her face with her hands, seeing a flicker of light, then another and another. At the same time gasps and cries rippled through the site, the workers still as statues now staring wide-eyed at the discs as they skimmed across the sky, sunlight alternately glinting and sparking off them as they spun. Shocked, Rebecca gaped at them. As they vanished from sight, all about her voices rose, jabbering to each other excitedly, some of the men however remaining silent, stunned.

207

*Hardly able to believe what she'd just seen, turning, Rebecca looked up at George, standing motionless on the ridge high above her, still staring at the sky his face ashen. Wordlessly he turned and bolted out of sight before reappearing again a few moments later, careering down the scree of sand and loose rocks. Going towards him, all of a sudden, she stopped, shocked at the fear on his face as he charged past her before disappearing into their tent. Alarmed, she hurried after him. Inside, George was pacing and wringing his hands, his eyes bright with fear. "Georgie? What's wrong?"*

*Suddenly without warning, his face crumpled and, raising his hands to his face he did something she'd never seen him do before. Her husband of twenty-five years cried like a baby.*

# XXVII

"Your dad was deeply disturbed by the sighting, and kept saying he'd been *meant* to see them. When your mom asked him what he meant, he said he couldn't explain and that it was just a feeling he'd had when he'd seen them."

Stunned, Carter thought about that for a moment.

"How did my mom react to seeing them?"

"She took it all in her stride because back then didn't think they *were* UFO's. She thought they must have been some new-fangled experimental air-craft being tested or something. She was scared though, not so much because of what they'd seen, but at how upset George was and his insistence they'd been there for his benefit because none of it made sense. She couldn't understand what was going on. Weeks later, the sighting still haunted him and he had nightmares about it. Usually, after a sighting, most people do suffer from deep anxiety, a sense of unease and disquiet about nothing they can put their finger on. In the end he decided to do something about it."

"He contacted you."

"Not right then he didn't." Bob said quietly, giving his head a quick shake. "Before that he tried to get to the bottom of it himself." A very private person, Carter nodded knowing it would've been just like his dad to try to deal with it on his own first.

"How?"

"He started reading up on the UFO phenomena, anything he could get his hands on, almost to the point of obsession. At our initial meeting he said he'd also felt conflicted because even though the sighting terrified him, at the same time he couldn't help but be intrigued by the way they'd looked and moved and the level of technology it must've taken to create something like that."

Chilled, Carter was able to understood that only too well because even though the encounter in the woods had been the most terrifying thing that had ever happened to him, nevertheless, he couldn't deny a part of him had been fascinated by them; hence the need to constantly ask questions and force the issue, even though he wanted nothing more than to forget the whole damn thing.

"He told me reading up on it had helped him realise he wasn't alone and that there were a whole bunch of other people all going through the same thing and inevitably that led him to the subject of alien abduction. Of course, he'd heard stories about aliens coming down and taking people away and stuff – who hasn't – but until then he'd never actually *believed* any of it. Anyway, as soon as he began reading up on it, alarm bells rang and he realised he'd experienced some of the things they were describing himself. In the past he'd wake up convinced he'd been somewhere in the night, something he put down to sleepwalking."

"What are you saying Bob?" Carter whispered, holding his breath now, feeling a finger of ice travel down his spine.

For a moment, Bob dropped his eyes, his face serious. Looking up again, he held Carter's eyes levelly with his own. "There's no easy way to say this Carter – your dad believed he was being abducted by aliens."

\* \* \* \* \*

Out on the patio, Rieker swept the darkness with his
eyes, everything steeped in silence, the dog having
stopped barking by now. With his gun in his hand,
tucked into his shoulder he stared at a dark, angular
shape on the grass, halfway down the garden. Going
slowly towards it, behind him he heard the faint whisper
of Stevenson's shoes on the patio, covering him.

Suddenly he heard a loud screech and something
sailed towards him. Instinctively dropping into a crouch,
he brought the gun up in front of him before realising it
was only an owl. Cursing, as his heart pounded, he
straightened, annoyed that his momentary lapse in
backbone had been witnessed by Stevenson, a rookie.
Nevertheless, glancing over his shoulder, the sight of him
was strangely reassuring, the strange, crouched figure out
here, having spooked him more than he cared to admit.
Feeling foolish, nevertheless, the first thing he'd learned
was that listening to your instincts could mean the
difference between life and death, and right now his
instincts were telling him there was something very
wrong out here.

Sensing Stevenson's confusion over his hesitation, he
was just about to take another step towards the shape
when, to his astonishment, a circle of bright red light
appeared from the top of it before snapping into a cone of
light before disappearing again a few seconds later.

*what the*

Poking his head forward he trained his gun on it,
stiffening for a moment as the cone briefly appeared
briefly once more before flickering out again.

*What the hell was that thing?*

211

\* \* \* \* \*

To Carter, hearing those words, the room suddenly disappeared, instantly finding himself back in the woods, charging through the darkness on legs that felt like rubber, his heart pounding, whipped by branches as he streaked past, snagging his hair and clothes almost as if trying to prevent his escape from the things
*you know what they were*
pursuing him, things that
*knew his name*
gained on him with every stride. In full-blown panic
*what is it dad*
he leapt to his feet almost knocking the chair over behind him as he did so, gasping for breath as if he really *was* running, no longer able to stem the images flooding through his mind, remembering
*those eyes*
reliving every moment.

*"Carter?"* Bob gasped, alarmed. *"What's wrong? What's happening?"*

Planting his hands firmly on the desk in front of the monitor Carter dropped his head, gasping for breath, unable to speak had he wanted to.

*"Carter, you're having a panic attack!"* Bob's voice squawked from the monitor. "Just concentrate on my voice and breathe."

At last, trembling, he grabbed the chair and dropped heavily onto it, Bob staring intently out from the screen at him, his face a mask of concern. "You okay?"

"Yeah, I think so." Carter breathed. "That keeps happening."

"It does?"

"Yeah."

"When did it start?"

"Not long ago."

"Do you know why?"

"Yeah." Carter nodded. "I think so."

"Because of what happened? The thing you couldn't talk about earlier?"

"Yeah."

"Do you want to talk about it now?"

"No." Carter replied, giving his head a quick shake, his hands clenched together in front of him on the desk.

"I'm sorry, I just can't."

"That's fine." Bob nodded understandingly, leaning back in his chair. "If ever you want to, you know where I am, okay?"

"Thanks." Carter nodded, rubbing his hands over his face. Composing himself, a few minutes later her felt able to continue. "So, my dad – was it true? Was he being abducted?"

"In my professional opinion, yeah, he was." Bob nodded. "No doubt about it. At first, your mom refused to believe it, I mean, who wouldn't? On the other hand, she knew him inside out and naturally, she was scared, not only because of the things he was saying, but because she knew he really believed it was true. She wanted him to go see someone, a doctor or a shrink."

"She thought he was losing his mind?"

"At first, yeah. Later on, he had a battery of tests done, physical, mental, physiological – you name it, he had it – for his peace of mind as much as hers."

The tests she'd mentioned in the letter.

"When they proved there was nothing wrong with him, she realised he must have been telling the truth all along and that terrified her, even more than the thought of him losing his mind. At the time, your dad had just finished one of my books and he called me. We talked for a while and he made an appointment. Apparently, your mom was far from happy about it when he told her but in the light of the medical evidence and not knowing what else to do, there wasn't a lot she could say."

"Knowing my mom, I bet she found something!" Carter snorted, the ghost of a smile on his face.

"Did she ever!" Bob nodded. "At the time she was still struggling to accept the whole alien abduction thing and I think she came out here hoping he'd find out it was nothing of the sort, but, of course things didn't quite pan out that way and she ended up blaming me."

"What?" Carter asked in disbelief. "How could she possibly blame you for what was happening?"

"For writing what she called 'twaddle' and putting ideas in his head. I tried to tell her the only reason he'd read my book in the first place was because he'd already begun to suspect what was happening to him."

"She called your books twaddle?" Carter asked, his eyebrows raised.

"Your dad told me she thought I was a charlatan exploiting people when they were at their most vulnerable. It's not true of course. I don't charge for my services. I never have and never will."

"But you *did* help him though?"

Nodding sagely, Bob leaned back in his chair.

"During the first visit he told me everything – everything he could remember that is – and as soon as he started talking it was like the floodgates opened and he started he couldn't stop. He'd been bottling it up for so long it did him good to be able to get it all off his chest. I told him he wasn't the only one going through this, not by a long straw and he took a lot of comfort in knowing other people really were experiencing the same thing, it made him feel less isolated. They were out here two weeks and I saw him most days and I think your mom began to realise seeing me was helping. He started eating properly and sleeping better and even though he was still having nightmares, they weren't so often and even she couldn't argue with that; she was getting your dad back and to her, that was all that mattered."

"They loved each other so much."

Bob nodded. "They sure did; I could see that the minute I opened the door to them. And then, about three months later, out the blue, your mom called me in a right state. She said she was struggling to come to terms with it all. She said she the beings had no right to do what they were doing and she hated being unable to prevent it happening or do anything about it. I see that a lot with relatives and spouses of abductees; they feel like they're failing to protect the person they love and blame themselves. It's worse for parents when it comes to kids because it's natural for parents to protect them, but they're powerless to do be able to do anything and it drives them crazy."

"How can things like this happen?" Carter gasped. "How can people live with something like that going on?"

"I don't know." Bob replied quietly, shaking his head. "But they do."

"My mom was right – they can't treat people like that!"

Leaning forward, Bob adjusted his glasses before peering through the screen at him. "Well Carter, I hate to say it but the truth of the matter is it happens all the time and let's face it, the way they treat us is no worse than we treat animals."

"But we're not animals though, are we?" Carter demanded indignantly. *"We're humans!"*

"Maybe so." Bob replied, shaking his head. "But maybe in the eyes of the aliens – beings I prefer to call them – that's exactly what we are, animals. Or insects."

\* \* \* \* \*

Roughly the size as a family-size cereal carton, the shape was actually some kind of box, completely black and reflecting no light whatsoever, more like a shadow, Rieker thought, rather than a something solid. Only a foot or so away from it, behind him Stevenson crossed the patio, sweeping the darkness with his eyes. Joining him, he was just about to speak when the cone of light suddenly appeared once more, the pair of them taking a step back. *"What the hell is that?"*

Shaking his head, Rieker frowned. "I don't know, I've never seen anything like it before..."

216

"We need to call this in!" Stevenson gasped, his eyes wide. At that moment, the cone suddenly expanded, bigger and taller than the two men. Taking a few steps back, they gaped at what looked like dust motes swirling around inside it like a mini-tornado, their faces stained a deep blood-red. Suddenly, it shrank to a few inches high again. Moving forward, Stevenson cautiously touched the box with his foot, a slight vibration travelling through the sole of his shoe as he did so.

*"Stevenson!"* Rieker barked quickly. *"What the hell are you doing – get away from there!"*

"I just want to see if…"

Before he'd finished speaking however, with a loud buzz, all of a sudden, the cone expanded again, completely encompassing him.

*"Stevenson!"* Rieker gasped, cold with fear now. *"Get the hell out of there!"* As if he hadn't spoken however, Stevenson remained where he was, staring around him, transfixed. Just about to step forward, all of a sudden, the cone expanded again, at least ten foot tall now, engulfing Rieker now as well. About to step back, to his horror he realised he couldn't move his legs and feeling something akin to warm sunshine on his skin, raised his hands before staring at them in horror, every vein and capillary standing out in stark, relief against his skin.

All of a sudden, the light deepened, his skin beginning to tingle as if the light was seeping through his pores into the very depths of him, sure he could actually *feel* it in his gut. Knowing he had to get out of there and quick, filled with fear, he fought against the paralysis with everything he'd got, his eyes, bulging with the effort, all

217

to no avail, the light simply too powerful. Turning his head, he looked at Stevenson, his shoulders sagging and his head bowed as if he'd fallen asleep standing up.

Suddenly, with a crackling electrical sound, for a moment the light flickered, before winking out of existence, both the men and the box vanishing in an instant. With a loud pop, cold night air rushed in to fill the void, a faint mist hovering in the air over the spot where they'd been in the now empty garden.

## XXVIII

Turning, Carter frowned, sure he'd just heard something outside, a car back-firing perhaps.

"So old was my dad when it started?" he asked, looking back at the monitor. "When he was a child?"

"No." Bob said, shaking his head. "Strangely enough, his experiences only began as an adult. It's not unheard of but most people I deal with have been having them since childhood. At the time, they don't realise anything else has happened and it's only when they're regressed that everything comes out."

Staring at him, Carter opened his mouth before closing it again, too many questions popping into his head all at once for him to be able to ask a single one.

"It's almost as if the Beings don't *want* people to remember, not straightaway, at least." Bob went on. "Maybe they think it would be too traumatic. When I first suggested hypnotic regression to your dad he refused point blank, saying what he did remember was bad enough. After a few months later he changed his mind."

"Why?" Carter asked.

"Natural curiosity." Bob sighed, leaning forward. "Good or bad, people want to know what's been happening to them."

"So how long had it been going on for then?"

"You were a baby when he had the first one. Without going into too much detail, one night he woke up and realised he wasn't in bed anymore but somewhere else with a nightmare creature standing over him looking down at him and he completely freaked. He had no idea

219

where he was or how he'd got there. The last thing he remembered was going to bed as usual."

"And the last?"

"That must've been about a month before the accident. He was driving home when he suddenly saw a bright light in the sky in the direction of the house. You and your mom were there at the time and terrified, he put his foot down and drove like a mad man but before he could get there he blanked out and woke up in the car on the side of the road three hours later."

*"Oh my God."* Carter gasped, his mind spinning. *"The night my mom broke the vase!"*

"You remember it?" Bob asked, leaning forward, his eyes bright.

"Yeah." Carter nodded. "I'd gone over to their house for dinner because they'd only been back in the country a few days and we hadn't seen each other for God-knows-how-long..."

"You lived close to them?" Bob asked, employing a method of asking mundane questions to normalise the conversation, in effect allowing memories to form properly.

"Yeah, about half an hour's drive, no more than that." Carter replied, his mind spinning, remembering every little detail now. "When I got there, mom said he'd had to pop out but that he'd be back before dinner. We had a drink in the kitchen while it was cooking but by dinner time, he still wasn't home. Mom rang his mobile but it went straight to answer-phone; he was a stickler about not answering the phone while he was driving so, we thought he must be on his way. When he still hadn't arrived about an hour later, we tried a few more times..."

"You couldn't get hold of him?"

"No – it just kept going to answerphone."

"What happened then?"

"We waited another hour and by then mom was frantic in case he'd had an accident."

"She thought he might've crashed the car or something?"

"Yeah. She wanted to call the hospital but I told her to give him another half hour. Not long after we heard his car pull up on the drive and she jumped to her feet and dashed out into the hallway and as she did so she knocked her favourite vase off a little side-table."

"How was your dad when he arrived?"

"He was okay." Carter murmured quietly, his mind racing. "But he looked drained. He said he'd had a flat tyre and it had taken him ages to change it only for some reason I didn't believe him. Mom just stood there staring at him in horror something passed between them, something I wasn't a part of and then all of a sudden, she grabbed him and they hugged each other and I remember wondering why she was so upset…"

"She was upset?"

"Yeah, almost crying. At the time I couldn't understand why she was over-reacting the way she was but it must've been because she'd guessed what had happened to him!" Covering his face with his hands, he groaned. *"Christ!"*

"What happened then?"

"Nothing. We had dinner and I stayed over in the spare room. I can't believe we were in the house waiting for him while he was…with *them."*

221

Unbelievable, isn't it?" Bob said matter-of-factly again. "Like I said before – it happens all the time."

*  *  *  *  *

Opening his eyes, Gueshe started at the sight of a tall, figure standing in the shadowy corner next to the window, completely motionless, only the tip of its nose and its chin showing beneath the hood of the long cloak it wore. As he got to his feet, the figure came towards him. Bathed in silvery moonlight, they stared at each other.

Without speaking, all of a sudden, his mind was filled with thoughts and images that weren't his, understanding a decision had been made, one that would affect every living thing on Earth, a global event greater than anyone could ever imagine. An event which he would be part of. He had to prepare, get ready. Suddenly, in the blink of an eye, the figure vanished. Going to the window, filled with expectancy and great excitement, he stared out at Mount Kailash bathed, silver in the moonlight.

Something big was coming.

*  *  *  *  *

*Blinking, Hely stared into the darkness, sure he'd just heard something – a sound. Suddenly convinced that he wasn't alone he quickly snapped the bedside lamp on, relieved at the sight of the empty room. Nevertheless, the feeling that something wasn't right, remained.*

*Pulling the covers back, he picked his revolver up the nightstand and, slipping out of bed, went quietly to the door before standing before it, listening.*

*Hearing nothing, he took a deep breath he opened it and stepped out into the hallway, the apartment completely silent. All of a sudden, he heard movement behind him and, bringing the gun up, whirled, seeing movement behind the curtains. "Whoever's there – come out with your hands up!" he barked.*

*Silence.*

*"I know you're there!" he shouted. With the reassuring weight of the gun in his hand he quickly strode forward and grabbing a curtain, whipped it back. At the sight of the creature standing there, the gun dropped uselessly to the floor, an image of himself screaming, reflected in its huge, bug-like eyes.*

\* \* \* \* \*

A few hours later, propped up against pillows, Carter thought it would be a miracle if he ever slept again. After reading his mom's letter, he'd known only too well what his dad had seen.

*standing there by the side of the bed*

Nevertheless, having it confirmed that his dad had been an abductee had shaken him to the core, his experience in the woods, paling in comparison to what

223

his dad must've endured all those years, the thought of it, beyond terrifying. But why, he wondered? Why had it started out of the blue the way it had? His dad hadn't been abducted as a child so why had the beings suddenly taken an interest in him? Had he done something to catch their attention and if so – *what?* Filled with fear he shook his head in disbelief that he hadn't been aware of any of it.

Still, he thought, at least he knew who Adkins was now and, even though he was no nearer to understanding why his uncle might've believed he was in danger and might need his help, nevertheless, it was reassuring to know he was there should he need him.

Before they'd logged of Bob had asked him again if he was ready to talk and once more, he'd declined, something stopping him at the last minute. No doubt the same kind of thing that had prevented him and Uncle Rob opening up to each other after the accident. An act of sheer avoidance, knowing if they did there'd be no going back; no more denial and no more hiding. Right now, it was as much as he could do to hang on to his sanity, terror seeming to be his constant companion of late and panic never far away, like a coyote circling a campfire. No, he thought, he wasn't ready to talk about it yet, no matter how much he wanted to – *if ever.*

Somewhere outside a dog barked and fell silent again, followed by the faint whine of a motorbike at a distance, a lonely, haunting sound before it too faded, leaving him alone with nothing more than his tortured thoughts to keep him company in the deep, stillness of the night.

\* \* \* \* \*

High above the village a full moon hung sedately in the winter sky, it's light alternatively dimming and brightening as ragged clouds scudded fleetingly across its face.

Completely silent, a dark craft glided over the crest of hills to the West before moving silently over a field, causing a family of badgers to stiffen, their night-time foraging momentarily forgotten. Sensing danger all around them but unable to pinpoint it, the boar turned and bolted, the rest of the clan quickly following quickly behind. As the shadow the craft cast fell on the hedgerow, small nocturnal creatures scattered in all directions, scampering into burrows and undergrowth for cover, frozen into immobility, their tiny bodies trembling with fear, waiting for the danger to pass. Perched in the branches of an ancient oak tree, startled, an owl hooted loudly before taking flight in the opposite direction, its wings spread wide, swooping through the cold night air, fleeing for safety from the unknown menace behind it.

Drifting over fields, the craft headed for a cluster of farm buildings at the end of a dirt lane. Inside the house, two Jack Russell's lifted their heads, cocking them side to side before leaping to their feet barking like mad with their hackles raised, waking the whole household. By the time the farmer flung the front door open, shot-gun in hand, the craft was out of sight, heading for the dark ribbon of road which snaked through the silvered countryside, leading to the village. Passing over the park, it sailed over the cedars bordering it with only inches to spare, the tops of the tall trees dipping and swaying in its wake before falling still again. With the lights of the village to its right, the craft drifted towards a house on the edge of a darkened wood before hovering over an area that from this height resembled a crash site, the ground below littered with the carcasses of old cars. Far below, a dog began barking.

* * * * *

*Still shaking from head to toe after finding the Being in his room, just as terrifying was the realisation that two hours had inextricably passed in the blink of an eye, the implications almost as bad as finding that thing there in the first place. Filled with terror, all he knew was that he had to get to Rob's as quickly as he could, because surely, this had to be connected to what they'd done.*

*Driving into a bend, his hands slick with sweat on the steering wheel, the twin cones of his headlights sliced through the darkness like knives. Suddenly he saw something in the middle of the road and, realising what it was, gaped at it in shock before yanking the steering wheel to the left. Without moving, the Being turned its head, watching without emotion as the car smashed headlong into a tree with a sickening whump, the sound of shattering glass filling the air.*

* * * * *

Roused from sleep by a crescendo of barking with a curse, Harry hobbled down the stairs as quick as he could. Just about to turn the key in the lock however, all of a sudden, outside, Bess fell silent. Pausing, he lowered his head to the door.

*Nothing.*

With his stomach a cold slab of ice, filled with fear he took a deep breath, and, turning the key and pulled the door open, the cold night air stinging his skin. After pushing his feet into his boots, he went out onto the veranda and limped to the low railing, the motion-sensor light coming on, illuminating the kennel he did so.

Narrowing his eyes, he stared at it seeing Bess facing away from him on the far side of it, hackles up and head down, a low, growling menacingly at something in the darkness. Feeling his blood freeze, Harry's fingers tightened on the railing.

"Bess?" he called trying to keep his voice low, expecting her to whip round with her tail wagging, the tension broken; instead, she remained where she was, unmoving, as if unaware he was even there.

*"Bess – what is it?"* he hissed a little louder now, the sight of her standing so still like that giving him the creeps. Wanting nothing more than to just turn around and go back into the house, nevertheless he clumped down the wooden steps, pain flaring in his leg as he did so. Stepping onto the frozen ground, he looked at Bess realising she wasn't even growling now, the only sound being that of his heart flinging itself against his ribs; that and the screaming silence, deafening in its intensity.

*"Bess?"*

Limping forward, he went to the kennel and, just bout to stretch his hand out to her, all of a sudden, she whipped round and lunged at him with the whites of her eyes showing, emitting a deep growl from her tooth-filled, saliva-dripping maw, Harry just managing to step back out of reach in time. Losing his balance, he

227

staggered backwards and tripped before falling heavily onto the hard ground. Winded, pain shot through his ribs and he gaped wide-eyed at Bess straining against her collar to reach him, her jaws manically snapping the air inches from his face.

And then the light went out.

* * * * *

"What do you mean you can't get hold of them?" Bruce McCarthy asked, staring at the agent that had just hurried into his office, looking anxious.

"They didn't check in at twenty-two-hundred-hours. When we still hadn't heard anything by zero-two hours we tried contacting *them* but there was no response."

"What about their cell phones?"

"Straight to answerphone Sir."

"When was the last communication?"

Looking down, the agent consulted a piece of paper he held in his hand. "Just before eight pm Sir, right on schedule."

"They didn't report anything unusual?"

"No Sir."

"Okay, leave it with me – and Miller – not a word to anyone about this, not until we know what's going on, is that clear?"

"Yes Sir."

"Meanwhile, keep trying."

"Yes Sir."

# XXIX

*From beneath his black umbrella, Robert stared into the grave with conflicting emotions, the rain beating a steady tattoo on the lid of the coffin.*

*Raising his head, he looked at the other mourners gathered around the graveside – five of them in all – including Walberg's sister and aunt, wondering what they'd say if they knew what they'd done.*

*And now he was dead.*

*Dressed only in jogging bottoms and a t-shirt, at three in the morning his car had left the road and hit a tree head on, killing him instantly, the general consensus being he'd swerved to avoid something in the road, maybe a fox or a deer, a theory which the skid marks left behind on the road appeared to back up.*

*Only Hely had been an excellent driver.*

*Where had he been going at that time of night dressed like that, he wondered? What had happened? Looking round the faces of the mourners, his fear deepened.*

\* \* \* \* \*

Jerking awake, Harry's eyes flew open, the image of Bess's snapping jaws only inches from his face filling his mind. Spooked, in that moment, she'd hardly been recognisable as the dog he knew and loved, not his faithful companion so much as a hound from hell!

Filled with guilt he ran a hand over his face.

As soon as the light had gone off, as if in response to something, Bess had whipped round again, barking into the darkness, going berserk as if trying to physically snap the chain that bound her to the kennel, as if her very life depended upon it. Rigid with fear, he'd squinted into the void seeing nothing. And, then he'd heard something.

Footsteps.

Lots of them, running towards the house.

Filled with terror, he'd rolled onto all fours and hauled himself up the steps before diving through the front door, slamming it shut and bolting it behind him, leaving Bess to fend for herself. Closing his eyes, he'd leaned back against it sucking in deep breaths, his heart pounding, terror coursing through him like an electric current. After a moment or two he'd turned and, with his hands planted against the door, tilted his head first one way then the other, listening.

Hearing nothing.

No footsteps.

No barking.

*Nothing.*

Filled with shame at his cowardice, he got off the sofa and reached for his stick. Shivering not just with cold, but trepidation he pushed his feet into his boots before pausing before the door, suddenly afraid of what he might find. Taking a deep breath, he pulled it open and hobbled over the veranda, his breath pluming out before him in the pre-dawn air, filled with relief at the sight of Bess's head resting on her paws just inside the kennel. Raising her head she got to her feet, before standing and staring at him, her head low, the expression in her eyes unmistakable.

*You left me.*

\* \* \* \* \*

230

Stirring sugar into his coffee, Carter thought about the lengthy conversation he'd had with Bob last night, the horror of finding out his dad had been an abductee hitting his afresh. Filled with disbelief, he likened it to watching a play with events unfolding on the stage right before his very eyes, the people he knew saying and doing things he'd never have believed possible.

*standing there right by the side of the bed*

However, even though it might explain his dad's solo visits to Brentwood to see Harry, it still didn't explain why his uncle had would've arranged it. Nor did it explain the letter, what he'd done and why he'd thought Carter would hold it against him. Or what he hoped Bob would be able to protect him *from*.

Feeling the need to escape Brentwood Down for a few hours, to just get in the car and drive aimlessly like he did now and then when he was stressed, picking up the car keys, he left the house. Avoiding the woods, he turned towards Hadley. High above him, bruised and swollen with unshed rain, towering thunderheads loomed malevolently in the leaden sky, looking like huge, crouching monsters about to pounce on the tiny humans scuttling across the surface of the earth far below.

* * * * *

Back in the village, in the lane, a white transit van with *Tailor's house and grounds maintenance* printed along the side pulled onto to the drive of one of the houses. Partly obscured by the tall hedge shielding them from the road and the neighbouring houses, the front

231

doors opened and two men wearing dark blue overalls got out, one of them carrying a tool bag. Going down the side of the house they went round the back and, finding the back door open, disappeared inside.

* * * * *

Passing a sign for Blacknoll Lake, Carter did a double-take, not realising he'd come this far already, chilled as he remembered the figure in the reeds.

Filled with morbid curiosity, he turned off the main road onto a narrow, country lane heading north half a mile or so before driving between two boulders onto what was nothing more than a wide gravel track. At the end, the track opened up into a gravel car park overlooking the lake, empty apart from one other car. Turning the engine off he folded his arms on the steering wheel and stared through the windscreen at the body of the lake, looking a lot smaller than he remembered, dark, slate-grey water, uninviting and cold. *Had he really seen one of those things out there among the reeds?*

Opening the door, he got out and stared out over the lake at the misty ridge of the Mayward Hills in the distance, before heading towards the beach. As he did so his eyes widened at the sight of a small wooden pier – albeit a newer version now – picturing his dad standing there, the Bristol University baseball cap he always wore whenever they went fishing (the one with extra hooks threaded through the fabric just in case they were needed) on his head. Turning, he stared at the bend, the reed beds out of sight beyond it.

232

Pushing his hands into his pockets, he watched a flock of Canadian geese make their way over the lake. As he did so, a light rain began to fall, forming ever widening circles on the still surface of the water. As it got heavier, hunching his shoulders he hurried back to the car. Once inside he stared at the lake once more, blurred by fat raindrops trickling down the windshield, the sound of them drumming on the roof. Leaning his head back against the seat, he watched the geese reach the other side of the lake, all of a sudden feeling incredibly tired. Before too long, he was asleep.

* * * * *

On the patio, one of the men stared at what appeared to be the remains of a bonfire, although why anyone would have had a bonfire this close to the house was a mystery. Frowning, he went towards it, realising it wasn't the ashy remains of a fire at all, but a blackened stain on the grass as if something had exploded.

"Anything?" The other man asked, from behind him, coming out of the kitchen doorway.

"I'm not sure." The first one answered, prodding the blackened grass with the toe of his boot.

"What is that, someone let off a firecracker or something?" Realising that was probably exactly what it was he nodded. "I guess. Come on, let's get out of here."

Turning they crossed the patio and went back into the house, the strange black mark on the lawn, forgotten.

# *XXX*

Jerking awake, Carter stared about him in confusion for a moment, seeing he was no longer in the car at Blacknoll Lake but was in bed, at home in his own flat.

*what the*

Jumping out of bed he went to the window and, swooshing the curtains open was met with bright sunlight blazing from a cloudless blue sky. Wide-eyed he gaped with disbelief at the sight beyond the window, the mud flats replaced by a field of golden now, stretching all the way to the horizon, rippling and undulating, stirred by gentle.

All of a sudden, he saw movement, a flash of red, realising it was a scarf fluttering, belonging to a woman, two men standing either side of her, all of them facing away from him, one of them an Asian-looking man with short hair wearing a robe – a monk maybe, he thought.

*what the*

Narrowing his eyes, Carter stared at them, wondering who they were before suddenly realising the woman was his mom! Suddenly, almost as if sensing he was watching, the man in the red robe turned and looked up at the window, their eyes locking. As they did so however, all of a sudden, the woman grabbed his arm and, swinging him round, pointed at something off in the distance, speaking excitedly.

Pushing his face closer to the glass, Carter squinted into the bright sunlight, seeing a line of small figures pushing their way through the corn dark towards them, six of them in all, suddenly filled with horror as he or he realised what they were.

234

*wall monsters*

Tearing his eyes from them he looked back at his mom and the two men, all three of them unmoving now, as still as statues now. Knowing they were too far away to hear him, nevertheless he rapped his knuckles hard against the glass before trying to open it, it not giving an inch. Meanwhile, the figures came closer, parting the corn before them, black almond-shaped eyes in their over-sized head clearly visible now. Spinning, he ran for the door, his only thought to get down there and reach them before those things

*wall monsters*

did but no matter how hard he tugged on the handle it refused to open. er to it. Frustrated he tore back to the window, his eyes darting between the two lines of figures. Raising his arm, he crashed his elbow into it in an attempt to smash it but unbelievable it held. Knowing it was already too late, nevertheless he hammered on the glass with his fists again, the line of figures closing in on them, only a hundred yards away now...

With a cry, he jerked awake, staring in horror at the darkness pressing against the windows of the car, realising he must've dropped off and had another nightmare. Covering his face with his hands, he groaned, the image of the six Beings weaving their way through the field towards those people vivid in his mind. Raising his head he stared at the dark water of the lake, a crescent moon reflected in its mirror-like surface now. Turning his head, he saw the other car had left, nothing but dark shrubbery behind him now.

*Time to go.*

235

Just about to turn the key in the ignition, all of a sudden, he saw movement out of the corner of his eye, and turning his head, almost choked at the sight of the face staring in at him on the other side of the window a few inches away. Opening his mouth he screamed, the sound of it in the enclosed space deafeningly loud...

With a cry bolted upright and, spinning, gaped at the window in horror, for a moment completely disorientated as he saw everything bathed in the purple haze of twilight – *no moon, no face, nothing!*
*a nightmare within a nightmare*
*"Jesus Christ!"* he gasped weakly. With his heart slamming against his ribs, turning his head he saw the other car really had gone. Not wanting to be out here a second longer, reaching for the keys he started the engine and, shoving it into reverse, swung the car round before speeding for the track, haunted by the back-of-the-spoon effect image of himself reflected in the huge, almond-shaped black eyes framed in the window, his face so contorted with terror he'd hardly been able to recognise it as his own.

\* \* \* \* \*

In the wood panelled library, Bruce McCarthy sat awkwardly in a brown leather club chair, barely big enough for his large frame.
"So, what are we talking about here exactly, McCarthy? Kidnap, ransom – *defection?"* The old man growled, his voice surprisingly deep, scowling at him over the wide expanse of the mahogany desk. Looking at

him McCarthy was once more reminded of some prehistoric bird – a Pterodactyl – his scrawny, buzzard-like neck protruding from the shirt collar easily two sizes too big for him, the cords on his neck, stretched and sinewy and dark, piercing eyes beneath reptilian-looking lids. *A man of great power and a very dangerous one.*

"Absolutely not." McCarthy replied, giving his head a quick shake. "Rieker's one of the most patriotic men I've ever met."

"And yet his Biolink, along with Stevenson's indicated they were no longer in the country – Tibet in fact?"

"That's right." McCarthy conceded, dipping his head. "We received the signal a few hours after they failed to check in, not long enough for them to have got there."

"So, how do you explain it?"

"We can't." McCarthy sighed, spreading his hands. "It's impossible. One minute they were in the U.K, the next they were in Asia."

"It's not an equipment malfunction?"

"No, that's the first thing we checked."

*"Men don't just vanish!"*

"I think we both know that's a lie." McCarthy snorted loudly. "Especially in our line of work."

"What, so that's *it?*" the old man gasped, glowering at him, his hands bunched into fists on the desk now. Swallowing his impatience, McCarthy spread his hands.

"I don't know what else you expect me to do. We've done all we can – I don't know what else we *can* do."

Taking a deep breath, the old man's eyes glinted in their sockets. "In your opinion – what do *you* think happened to them?"

Meeting his eyes levelly, McCarthy paused, choosing his next words carefully. "I think they're dead, otherwise they'd have found a way to contact us by now."

\* \* \* \* \*

*Breathing heavily from the unaccustomed exercise, Sterling leaned back against the wall, his pounding heart drowning out the sound of traffic whizzing past the entrance to the alleyway he'd just torn up. Leaning forward, with his hands on his knees he sucked in a couple of deep breaths.*

*Having come to Hadley to see his solicitor, it hadn't taken him long to realise he was being followed. Pretending to stare at something of interest in a shop window, behind him in the reflection he'd seen a man in jeans and t-shirt stop in mid-stride. Casually he'd continued down the street, the man following slowly behind at a safe distance. Going into the market he'd swerved between the stalls, before hurrying through the back alleys, coming to a halt next to a blue dumpster, shielding him from sight.*

*Two days before, with the accident only a month behind him, unable to sleep, he'd got up to use the bathroom when he'd seen something through the open curtains – a quick flash of light in the bedroom window in the house opposite, a house which was supposed to empty, the owners being away on a cruise.*

*Wondering if it was being burgled, he'd padded over to the window. Almost sure he saw movement, he'd remembered the infra-red binoculars in the cupboard under the stairs, a birthday gift he'd bought Carter years ago for watching badgers at night. Fetching them he'd positioned himself to the side of the window and raised them to his eyes.*

*What he'd seen had filled him with terror.*

*Inside the bedroom in the house opposite – invisible to the naked eye but brought out in sharp relief by the binoculars, in lurid green, a man had been standing with his back to the window, his arms and hands moving, obviously talking to someone. Turning, the man had picked up a pair of binoculars very much like his own before training them on this house. Ducking back into the shadows, clutching the binoculars to his chest, he'd known there could only be one reason why anyone would be watching him – the Creation!*

*But how, he'd wondered, especially after all this time?*

*Surely if someone knew, they'd have disappeared by now? Why would they be watching him, what were they waiting for? Maybe, he'd thought, all they had were suspicions. Maybe he should get rid of the box, just in case. He should have done it years ago, but somehow, he hadn't been able to. And so, yesterday he had got rid of it – or made sure it was somewhere safe at least. And now, things being what they were, knowing there was no other option, there was one last thing he had to do.*

*Taking a deep breath, he peered round the dumpster and, seeing no one, hurried down the alleyway before stepping cautiously out onto the street. Without further ado he drove home, acutely aware of the house over the road when he arrived. Without looking at it he went inside.*

*In the hallway his eyes fell on a framed photo next to the telephone. Picking it up he smiled down at it sadly, the faces tugging at his heart, his eyes moist. At last, returning it to the table he hurried into the living room and, poured himself a large whisky before taking it with him to the armchair. Sitting down, frowning deeply, he sat stiffly, ticking off a mental checklist, not once but twice, making sure he hadn't forgotten anything.*

*Satisfied he'd done all he possibly could, at last he took a small glass phial containing two yellow pills from inside his jacket, something he'd kept on him for years now in case an occasion such as this ever arose.*

*One for Walberg. One for him.*

*Removing the rubber stopper, he shook them out onto the palm of his hand and stared down at them in morbid fascination, knowing this was the only way he could prevent himself revealing all under the influence of drugs or torture. Getting to his feet he went to the French windows and, opening them, stepped out onto the patio before pushing the empty phial into a tub containing a small fir tree. Straightening, he gave the garden a quick glance, the sky a blaze of red with the setting sun.*

*Returning to the chair he reached for the tumbler and, feeling he should dignify the moment with some final, parting words, with a defiant look on his face now, he raised his glass in a toast.*

*"Rot in hell, you bastards!"*

*Before he could change his mind, he tossed the pills into his mouth and swallowed deeply, savouring the rich, expensive taste of the fifteen-year-old malt whisky, not*

240

*stopping until the glass was empty. Setting it on the table, he rested his head against the back of the chair and waited.*

# *XXXI*

As the kettle boiled, the phone rang. Padding into the hallway Carter picked it up.

"Carter Stanbrook?" A crisp, business-like voice asked on the other end of the line. "Miss. Watson." Still drowsy with sleep, for a moment his mind remained blank. "Of Wallace, Meakin and Meakin?" she added with a hint of sarcasm. "We recently handled your uncle's will."

"Oh yes of course." He said. "You're the secretary…"

*"Personal assistant."* Miss Watson replied icily.

"Yes, of course." Carter gabbled. "I do apologise…"

"Don't give it another thought." Miss Watson replied crisply, her tone implying she was fully aware that as a simple mortal he was incapable of functioning at the levels of efficiency to which she so effortlessly aspired.

"Mr. Wallace has some documents regarding Mr. Sterling's property that need signing. Are you available next Thursday?"

"Yeah…I suppose…" Carter stammered, all of a sudden feeling not as if he were a grown man anymore but a ten-year-old schoolboy having been asked an impossible question by his teacher, the answer to which he was fully aware he should know the answer to, but nevertheless didn't.

"Shall we say eleven o'clock then?" Miss Watson went on, clearly feeling she had to take control.

"I should think that would be okay…."

"In that case we'll see you at eleven o'clock Thursday morning Mr. Stanbrook. Thank you for your time."

242

"Thank *you*." Carter replied, hearing a loud click at the other end, Miss Watson, clearly needled from his secretary comment. With a smirk, he put the phone down.

\* \* \* \* \*

"Well?" The Pterodactyl asked, sitting at his desk, the telephone to his ear, a beam of bright sunlight slanting in through the library window behind him, giving him a saintly appearance. On the other end of the line McCarthy spoke. "I have a replacement for Rieker."
"Who?"
"One of ours. Harrison Clarke. He's was with Homeland Security but I've been mentoring him for a while now."
"Whoever he is he'd better be good." The old man growled. "Because so far, this whole thing has been one giant fuck-up and believe me McCarthy if there's another, *the consequences will be dire, is that clear?"*
Silently, McCarthy nodded.

\* \* \* \* \*

Redialling, Carter called Elizabeth to ask her if she'd like to join him when he went to Hadley. They could make a day of it and have lunch.
"That sounds lovely!" Elizabeth replied. "There's a smashing little restaurant me and Millie always go to for lunch when we're there – I think you'll like it."

\* \* \* \* \*

243

Alone in his cell, Norman stared down at the newspaper in his hands, wide-eyed with disbelief, the words seeming to leap off the paper at him, mocking him. Robert Sterling was dead.

*Only days before he got out.*

And how ironic was *that*, he thought with a scowl, the rug having been pulled from beneath him, cheating him of the justice he so richly deserved. No, not justice – revenge. The fire that had burned so fiercely for so long inside him, giving him the strength to carry on. The only thing he'd lived for.

With a loud curse he threw the paper at the wall and, getting to his feet, began pacing back and forth in the small cell, going over the events leading to his incarceration as clear as if they'd happened only yesterday, filled with blistering rage.

When the cops had raided his flat and discovered the drugs in his cupboard, it hadn't taken much working out who'd been behind it, realising he'd drastically underestimated the lengths Walberg and Sterling would go to, to keep their dark research and the monster they'd created secret. And what better way than to get rid of him and discredit him *before* he started blabbing, because who'd believe some common little drug-pusher over the word of not just one, but *two* renowned scientists of imminent standing? Considering what was at stake, he supposed he'd been lucky they hadn't bumped him off, but, after spending thirty years in prison for a crime he didn't commit, looking back, he wished they had. At least then he wouldn't have had to wake up every morning in hell, to the smell of piss, to the sights and sounds, the beatings and the never-ending boredom.

*And the fear.*

Haunted by the memory of the thing in the lab, he shuddered, remembering the sickening, slithery feeling as it had entered his mind, probing it, instantly knowing everything about him, his memories, *everything*. And how many nights, had he lay in the darkness, his arms wrapped around his head, filled with terror so deep he could hardly breathe, wondering if it was still alive? During those nights, the only thing that had got him through had been the thought of getting out of here, finding them and exacting revenge.

And exposing that thing.

*Maybe even killing it.*

Stooping, he picked the newspaper up and, straightening it, continued reading, his eyes widening as he did so. *Sterling was succeeded by a nephew.*

\* \* \* \* \*

On his second cup of coffee, Carter made a start sorting through the stacks of papers in the office at the top of the house, going through them and deciding which, if any, he wanted to keep. As he worked, he thought about the figure in the reeds, that and the words which kept popping into his head.

*wall monsters*

Sounding familiar, he hadn't been able to come up with anything, nevertheless, like an out-of-reach itch, annoyingly, it continued to needle him. Around noon, he went downstairs and made a sandwich and was just leaning against the counter eating it when, suddenly, without warning, an image appeared in his mind, one of himself as a little boy

*standing before his bedroom wall, a black marker pen in his hand, hot with shame at being caught red-handed, his dad having just appeared in the doorway. Coming into the room, his dad froze, his eyes wide with shock, his face ashen. Dropping to his knees he pulled him roughly into his arms. "NO! You leave him alone you bastards!"*

*Shocked and confused by his reaction, crushed against his dad's shoulder, he burst into tears. A second later, his mom dashed into the room, hairbrush in hand.*

*"Georgie! What's with all language? What on Earth's going on?"*

*"The wall." His dad replied quietly, his voice a flat monotone now. Turning, his mom stiffened and, seeing what he'd drawn, dropped the hairbrush with a cry, her hands to her face, now. "Oh God...oh no!"*

*Grabbing him by the arm, she dragged him from the room, her cries echoing through the house all about them while behind them, his dad wept...*

Wide-eyed with shock, Carter jerked.

\* \* \* \* \*

With his hands steepled together on the desk before him, McCarthy stared at the agent detailed to preplace Rieker. At five-eight, weighing a hundred-and-fifty pound, Harrison Clarke was solidly built, his chestnut brown hair cut neatly into short back and sides. With

246

dark, brown eyes that were almost black and a chiselled jaw, he looked what he was – ruthless and efficient.

After finishing college he'd joined the police academy and had sailed through it with flying colours. After applying for the C.I.A he'd trained as a political bodyguard but had found the job dull and boring without challenge. He'd applied for a placement with Homeland Security and to his delight had been accepted. He'd worked hard and kept his nose clean, applying for ever higher and higher promotions until one day he'd been called into the head honcho's office and informed he'd been selected for mentoring within in a sector of intelligence known simply as the Bureau, a governmental department that on paper, didn't officially exist. That mentor had been McCarthy, Chief Director of the elite Bureau, a black ops sector of American security, a man of formidable reputation.

Under McCarthy's wing he'd seen and learned things which might've broken lesser men, mentally and physically pushed to his limit, reminding himself it was all part of the process of being moulded into the perfect spy. To say McCarthy had had taken him to hell and back might've been a bit of an over-exaggeration – but not by much, Clarke more than tempted on a few occasions to drop him where he stood.

"Rieker and Stevenson were on surveillance hoping the mark might give us a lead but then he died suddenly. Nothing suspicious, he just died. Heart failure, apparently. There's a nephew though – his details are all in here." he finished, handing Clarke a file.

"Rieker and Stevenson – no one knows what happened to them?" Clarke asked quietly.

"No." McCarthy replied shaking his head. "One minute they were there, the next they'd disappeared. Needless to say, their disappearance has caused major ripples and the powers that be are baying for blood, sticking their noses in, wanting to know this that and every other damned thing and I've got nothing to give them; I need answers quick and I don't care what you have to do to get them, *is that clear?"*

"Yes Sir."

* * * * *

Pulling to a stop, Carter stared through the gate-posts at it the house, the gravel drive dotted with weeds now, only too able to imagine his parents inside. Taking a deep breath, his hands tightened on the wheel. Ever since the accident he'd avoided coming here, his grief still to raw, and the last thing he wanted to do was go in there.

*you have to know*

Reluctantly he drove between the gate-posts, accompanied by the strange sensation that he was crossing a threshold between the real world and one of half-remembered nightmares, all of a sudden filled with dread. Outside the front door he killed the engine, and taking a deep breath, got out of the car.

Taking the key from his pocket, he unlocked the front door and, pushing it open, was met by the faint hint of violets – his mom's favourite perfume – the delicate scent like a knife in his chest. On the floor were a pair of brightly coloured, woven rugs his parents had bought back from their travels, the walls covered with framed photographs, everything from archaeological sites and

248

artefacts to them at their book launches or charity functions, suited and booted. On an oak sideboard a mixture of family photos sat among ornaments and figurines of stone and metal. Swallowing, he heard his mom's voice coming from the living room.

*in here Carter – come in*

The living room was a juxtaposition old and new furniture, nevertheless still aesthetically pleasing, and following the family tradition, books and papers everywhere. Draped over the corner of the sofa was his mom's favourite red silk scarf, the one she'd brought back from Tibet, looking for all the world like she'd just left it there. Picking it up he held it in his hands, thinking of the nightmare he'd had in the car, about seeing her down there in the cornfield wearing it. Putting it back where he found it, reminding himself why he was here, he turned and left the room.

At the top of the stairs, he paused for a moment, staring at a door at the end of the landing, suddenly filled with fear. With his heart pounding in his ears, he slowly towards it, before hesitating in front of it. Taking a deep breath, he swallowed on a dry throat.

*you've got to know*

Lifting his hand, he put it against the cool wood and slowly pushed it open before going in, and turning, stared at the wall, the swirling patterns of the wallpaper forming themselves into strange, distorted faces, hearing a faint chorus of voices in his head once more.

*Caarter*

Curling his hands into fists, he dug his nails into the palms of his hands until they hurt, the patterns just meaningless swirls once more.

249

*Do it.*

Taking a deep breath, bending, he worked a corner of wallpaper loose before pulling it away from the wall. Tugging gently, the paper was so thick, it came off with surprising ease. Pulling it upwards, the last couple of inches beneath the picture rail, it held tight. With another tug it let go and as it fell to the floor, he staggered backwards in shock, gaping wide-eyed at the drawing on the wall.

*he'd done when he'd woken up from a nightmare so bad, he'd wet himself. Angry and filled with shame, he'd grabbed a marker and had drawn the things from his nightmares for all to see...*

Before him, a gangly-looking Being rested on its haunches, an arm resting on its knees, looking at him with huge, tear-drop shaped eyes
*blacker than anything*
insect-like in the elfin shaped face, its extended cranium bulging. Behind it stood two others, their heads and bodies bisected by the strips of wallpaper bordering them, one of them with its head tilted to the side as if studying him curiously.
*Wall Monsters.*
*Just standing there, looking at him.*
No wonder his parents had reacted the way they had, seeing the creatures that had torn their lives apart right there on their sons' wall, knowing it could mean only one thing.
*Like father, like son.*

Like a dam bursting, all of a sudden, long-forgotten memories flooded into his mind inundating him and, weak-kneed, he slid down the wall onto the floor, his hands dangling limply on his knees, remembering how

*he'd changed from a bright, happy, contented child to one filled with a dark, brooding anger so fierce he'd even frightened himself, violently rebelling against everyone and everything, because of the nightmares. Ones which he woke up filled with panic and screaming from, shaking from head to toe, his heart pounding against his ribs. Sometimes he'd be too afraid to close his eyes, only falling asleep when dawn broke through sheer exhaustion. In the end he'd been afraid to go to bed at all, becoming hysterical, convinced there was something in his room, hiding under his bed.*
*Or in the wardrobe.*
*Waiting to get him.*

As the room swam back into focus again, he stared at the drawing, struggling with the idea that he could've forgotten such a dark, terrifying chapter of his life.

Suddenly, there was a flicker of movement in the doorway and, turning his head, saw a small figure framed within it. Before he could scream, it was on him.

# XXXII

*"Jesus, you look like shit – what happened?"* Bob gasped, pushing his face closer to the screen.

Narrowing his eyes, Carter stared at him accusingly.

"You *knew,* didn't you? You knew all about it and you said *nothing!"*

Taken aback, Bob stared at him. "What?"

*"You know what!"* Carter hissed. *"The things behind the wallpaper, the things I drew when I was a kid!"*

"You remember that?" Bob gasped, his eyes bright.

*"I do now!"* Carter ejaculated. *"No thanks to you!"*

"Carter, listen to me…"

*"No, you listen to me!"* Carter hissed angrily. "You knew all about them because my dad told you what I'd done, didn't he?"

Dropping his eyes, Bob nodded.

*"Why the hell didn't you say anything?"* Carter gasped, gaping at him, his face ashen.

"I couldn't."

*"Couldn't or wouldn't?"*

"Couldn't." Bob replied. Pausing, he took a deep breath. "It would've compromised your memory."

"Compromised my memory?" Carter gasped. "What does that even *mean?"*

"It means if I'd have told you, I'd have led you, influenced you. You had to find out for yourself."

"I can't believe this is happening, *any of it."*

"Tell me what happened."

Running his hands over his face, Carter shook his head, his anger spent, and, dropping heavily down onto the chair haltingly, told him about how he'd remembered drawing

252

something on the wall one morning after a particularly horrific nightmare, one of many he'd had around that time.

"I'd been having some problems at school and had been playing up a bit at home but until I saw the drawing, I'd forgotten just how bad things actually were, like I blanked it all out. Lately the words 'Wall monsters' kept popping into my mind only I couldn't work out what it meant. Then, this morning, out of the blue, I remembered."

"Is that what you called them at the time, Wall monsters?" Bob asked, jotting it down on a pad.

"Yeah."

Knowing they were at a crossroad, one that would have the potential to irrevocably change everything, for a moment Carter was on the verge of telling Bob about what had happened in the woods at the same time acutely aware that if he did there'd be no going back; Bob would want to know every little detail and right now it was as much as he could do to *not* think about it, never mind talk about it. Feeling panic stir, at the last moment he changed his mind.

After logging off, he decided to have a shower. Turning the hot water on, all of a sudden, he gasped, his shoulder blade feeling as if it were on fire. Getting out again he quickly wiped the mirror with his hand and, angling his back towards it, stared in amazement at a bright red, perfectly-shaped triangle on his right shoulder-blade.

*"What does it mean?"* Carter gasped, showing it to Bob a few minutes later, a towel wrapped round his waist.

"Hang on – I just want to get a screen-shot." Bob said excitedly, his eyes bright, quickly typing on the keypad before him. After he'd taken three, he looked at Carter, his face serious now.

253

*"Well?"* Carter asked fearfully, his face pale. "What is it?"

"It's a PAM mark."

"A PAM mark?" Carter asked with a frown. "What's that?"

"Carter." Bob said quietly, holding his eyes steadily, his face serious. "There's no easy way to say this – a PAM mark is a Post Abduction Mark."

*"What?"*

"A Post Abduction Mark, and pretty fresh by the look of it." Bob said. "Maybe only a few hours old."

*"Oh my god!"* Carter gasped weakly.

"Is there any time during the past few hours you can't account for?"

"No."

"Have you ever noticed any marks like this on your body before?"

Thinking of the injuries he'd inflicted during the chase through the woods he wondered if there had been and he'd missed them.

"Carter?"

Knowing he couldn't be anymore terrified than he was right now, swallowing his fear, Carter decided to take the bull by the horns. Dropping down onto the chair once more he took a deep breath and, raising his head, looked at him.

"Bob, that thing I couldn't tell you about before…I still don't know if I can but…I don't know what else to do."

Able to see only to clearly that he was desperate to unburden himself, instead of pushing him, Bob leaned back in his chair, waiting.

Clearing his throat, slowly Carter told him all about the incident in the woods, everything from seeing the figure

254

dash across the road in his headlights, to only just making it back to the car in time before driving off and almost crashing.

*"They chased you?"* Bob gasped, shocked, his eyes wide behind his glasses.

"Yeah." Carter nodded, his hands clenched together in front of him. "And they almost caught me too."

"How many?"

"A lot. I could hear them all around me in the darkness and then when I was in the car they began appearing over the ridge, more and more of them..."

*"Jesus!"* Bob gasped, scribbling furiously on the notepad, his hands shaking with excitement. "I've gotta tell you Carter, this is a new one on me; in all the years investigating this stuff, I've never heard of them chasing anyone before."

"What, never?" Carter gasped, his eyes wide.

"Never."

*"So, I'm the first?"*

"Calm down." Bob said quietly. "Just because it's never been reported doesn't mean it hasn't happened to anyone before. Now, was there any missing time?"

"No. I just ran for the car and drove off." Suddenly Carter froze. "Oh my God..."

Quickly, he told Bob about the conversation he and Elizabeth had had the night before the funeral when he realised he'd lost a whole day, which in turn had led to him remembering that strange day beneath the tree when the day had passed, seemingly in a moment.

"I think on all three occasions – like today – you were abducted Carter." Bob said quietly, looking at him sombrely. "If they chased you through the woods there's no way

255

you've have escaped, not unless they allowed you to; do you honestly think beings with that level of technology and mind control wouldn't be able to catch you if they wanted to?"

Numb with shock, Carter realised things had just got a hell of a lot worse.

Over the road, wide-eyed with shock, the new agents glanced at each other.

* * * * *

The next day, in Hadley, Carter dropped Elizabeth off before heading to the solicitors. As she made her way along the high street however, she almost collided with a scruffy-looking man hurrying in the opposite direction. Tutting loudly as if it was her fault, he disappeared round the corner. Annoyed by his rudeness, she shook her head at him and went on her way.

* * * * *

"Just one more." Wallace said, replacing the sheet of paper Carter had just signed with another. Watching while he signed that too, he grunted quietly with satisfaction.

"That's it, the house is now officially yours. Have you decided what you're going to do with it?"

"Sell it." Carter replied.

"You wouldn't consider living there yourself?"

"No." he replied, frankly unable to think of anything more unlikely. After Bob's shocking revelations the other night, once he left, he didn't want to come within a million miles of the damned place ever again.

"I can't imagine it being on the market for very long. It's a much sought-after area. Now, if that's everything." Wallace said getting to his feet, extending his hand. "I'll bid you good day Mr. Stanbrook..."

"Actually." Carter said, clearing his throat. "There was something I wanted to ask you."

"Of course."

"The envelope my uncle left for me – the one you gave me last time – when exactly did he leave it with you?" Carter asked.

Pursing his lips, Wallace frowned, thinking. "Let's see, about a month ago."

"Only recently then?"

"Yes." Wallace nodded. "I remember he came in one day and asked if he could see me as a matter of urgency."

"He said it was urgent?"

"Yes. That's when he gave it to me."

"And that was the last time you saw him?"

If Wallace was at all surprised by Carter's questions, he didn't show it. "Yes unfortunately."

"How did he seem?"

Frowning, with his head to one side, Wallace studied him. "I'm not sure I know what you mean..."

"Well, did he seem upset in any way, or anxious? You know, was he behaving any differently from when you'd seen him before?"

Removing his glasses, after a slight pause, Wallace nodded "Yes, I must admit, he did seem a little perturbed and insisted I follow his exact instructions when I handed it over to you."

"He wasn't acting oddly, thinking straight and knew what he was doing?"

257

"Absolutely." Wallace replied, all of a sudden looking concerned. "Why do you ask? Is there a problem?"

"No, not at all." Carter said, shaking his head. "It's just that the contents were a bit confusing, that's all."

"Really?" Wallace asked, misunderstanding. "I'd be more than happy to go over it with you if you'd like."

"No, that's not necessary." Carter replied. "It's nothing like that. It's just some of the things he'd written didn't add up, that's all."

"I don't know what to tell you Mr. Stanbrook." Wallace said. "My instructions only went so far as to make sure the envelope was handed over to you in person. I have no idea what it contained."

\* \* \* \* \*

Glancing at her watch, Elizabeth saw she had half an hour yet before she met Carter, time enough to pop into a little junk shop she liked. Heading toward it, she saw the scruffy-looking man again on the other side of the street, cigarette in hand. Just about to carry on, all of a sudden, he darted quickly behind a tree, his behaviour, at best, suspicious, arousing her curiosity. Turning to see what he was looking at, she saw Carter coming out of the solicitors, the glass door swinging closed behind him before turning in the opposite direction. Looking at the scruff, to her surprise she saw him step forward, all the while staring at Carter's retreating back, before crossing the road, realising he was following him! Concerned, she hurried after them, the follower having become the followed.

As carter paused before a cafe, the scruff also slowed and as he in, the scruff stopped. Not sure what was going on, she decided to watch and see what happened. Sitting on a bench partially obscured by a rubbish bin where she could see the café door and watch the scruff unobserved, intrigued, she waited. Leaning against the wall he lit another cigarette.

After a while it opened and a couple of teenage girls emerged, chattering and laughing. Dropping the remains of his cigarette, the scruff crushed it underfoot before pacing back and forth impatiently. Suddenly, he stiffened as Carter came out of the café. Glancing at his watch he turned and headed back the way he'd come, the scruff frozen like a rabbit in the headlights. Turning, he leaned forward, pretending to look at something in a shop window, Carter passing by him only inches away.

On her feet again, she hurried after them, turning the corner just in time to see Carter outside Luigi's where they were due to meet, the scruff not far behind. Pausing, no doubt making sure it was the right place, Carter straightened his tie and, pulling the door open, disappeared inside. Slowing, Elizabeth narrowed her eyes, wondering what the scruff was going to do now. Crossing the road, he came to a stop beneath a red and white awning over a shopfront, standing in its shadow, his eyes on the front of Luigi's.

As casually as she could Elizabeth headed for the restaurant, all the time keeping her eye on the scruff reflected in the shop windows; glancing at her, if he recognised her as the woman he'd bumped into earlier, he showed no sign of it. Pushing the door open she went inside, thankful for the tinted windows at the front making it harder to see in than out. With half a dozen tables already taken, the restaurant was obviously gearing up for the lunchtime rush. Seeing Carter at the bar she hurried over.

"Hello." He said brightly. "I was just about to get a drink. What are you having?"

"Never mind that!" Elizabeth muttered, her hand on his arm now.

"What's the matter?" Carter asked, surprised.

"See the man over the road under the awning in a denim shirt?"

"Yeah." Carter said looking at him. "What about him?"

"Do you know him?"

Craning his neck, Carter studied the man with narrowed eyes. "No, I don't think so."

"Are you sure?"

"Positive." He said, frowning now, wondering what this was all about. "Why? Who is he?"

"I have no idea."

Confused, he shook his head. "I'm sorry Elizabeth, I don't get it – what's going on?"

"You may well ask – he's following you!"

Chilled, for a moment Carter found himself unable to respond, his uncle's cautionary words

*forces at work beyond my control and I fear it's not enough*

resounding ominously through his mind like the deep tolling of a bell.

"I've been following you both, watching him."

*"What?"* Carter gasped, feeling a sliver of ice travel down his spine as the man gave the restaurant a lingering look.

"I bumped into him earlier on a corner and that's what made me notice him in the first place. I was just on my way to this little shop I like to have a mooch in and I saw you come out of the solicitors and I saw him acting funny, staring at somebody, and I realised it was you. When you went around the corner, he followed you so I followed him – well both of you – and while you were in the café, he hung around outside a shop a few doors away so I went and sat on a bench not far away and waited for you to come out. When you did you went *straight past him* and he followed you again just like I knew he would, and then I followed you both here! Who *is* he Carter and what does he want?" Elizabeth asked, staring up at him, her face full of concern. "Are you in some kind of trouble?"

"I don't know." Carter muttered, unable to look tear his eyes from the man. "But I think we should get out of here."

"Hang on." Elizabeth said. Catching the barman's attention, she went down to the bottom of the bar before leaning over it, speaking to him in hushed tones. Wondering what she was saying Carter glanced at the window again, the sight of the man still there, chilling him.

*"Carter!"* Elizabeth hissed, from the end of the bar, beckoning to him. "He's going to let us out the back!" she said quickly as he joined her, her eyes bright. Heading down a short hallway to the rear of the building the bar man opened the door at the end and, with a

knowing smile, let them out. Thanking him, they stepped out into the car park into bright daylight once more, the door closing quietly behind them.

"This way." Elizabeth said. Crossing the car park, they made for a short alleyway before emerging onto a busy street. Turning left, they hurried towards the car park. Once inside the car they sped through the streets in the opposite direction to the restaurant, heading north. Constantly glancing in the rear-view mirror to make sure the man hadn't somehow seen them and was following them. With no sign of anyone following them and the town behind them now, Carter shook his head. "That was brilliant, Elizabeth. What did you say to them?"

"I told them my husband was outside and that we needed to make a quick getaway."

*"You didn't!"* Carter gasped, staring at her amazed, his eyes wide.

"What else were we supposed to do?" she asked. "And it's not like I lied, is it, I mean I didn't *say* we were having an affair, I just let them think whatever they wanted to." Looking pleased with herself, she chuckled.

Smiling, Carter shook his head. "Genius."

As he drove, he wondered if the man was still there, unaware they'd given him the slip. Frowning he wondered who he was and what he'd wanted. As if reading his mind Elizabeth turned her head to look at him. "So, who do you think he was then?"

"I don't know." Carter replied giving his head a quick shake. "But it might have something to do with Uncle Rob – he warned me something like this might happen."

"What?" Elizabeth gasped turning in her seat to look at him fully now. "When?"

Quickly, Carter told her about the letter his uncle had left him. One of the conditions of the letter was that I wasn't supposed to tell *anyone* about it. At the time, it seemed so far-fetched…I wasn't sure he hadn't written it simply because of the state he'd been in after the accident."

"So, I take it we're going to the police now?"

"Not yet." He replied quietly, glancing at her.

"There's someone I need to speak to first."

# XXXIII

*"You're joking!"* Bob gasped, staring out from the screen at him, his eyes wide.

"I only wish I was." Carter said quickly. "If it hadn't been for Elizabeth, I wouldn't have known about him at all – I don't know who he was or what he wanted but it's shaken me up, that's for sure."

"I'll bet!" Bob breathed. "And she's sure he was following you?"

"Absolutely." Carter nodded. "She might be getting on a bit but she's as bright as a button. I went into a cafe to kill some time and she watched him hanging around waiting for me to come out. When I did, she followed us to the restaurant and when she came in, she pointed him out me and there he was, waiting about on the other side of the street."

Over the lane the agents exchanged glances, surprised.

"Was that us?" Morgan asked quietly.

Looking at him askance, Clarke spread his hands, his eyebrows raised. "Of course not – we were here."

"I didn't mean that, Sir." Morgan said. "I meant us as in the Bureau."

"I know what you meant." Clarke replied, rolling his eyes. *"Shut-up!"*

"I wonder if this is what uncle Rob warned me about in the letter." Carter went on, his voice filling the room.

"What letter?" Clarke asked, his eyebrows raised. Spreading his hands, Morgan shook his head silently, his face blank.

Leaning forward, Bob frowned, as Carter told him about his name being mentioned in connection with the

264

warning of imminent danger. "You don't have any idea what it might've been about?"

"No." Bob replied, leaning back in his chair, rubbing a hand over his face. "This is the first I've heard of it. Where is it now?"

"I burned it."

"You burned it?" Bob gasped. "Why?"

"He left instructions to destroy it as soon as I'd read it."

*"Christ!"*

"I know – but at the time I put it down to him well, maybe not being right after the accident, you know, grief-stricken." Carter explained, unwilling to reveal the real reason – that there was a chance his uncle might've done something he shouldn't have.

"And he mentioned me?"

"Yeah."

"I don't like this."

"Believe me, I'm not too happy about it myself!" Carter snorted.

\* \* \* \* \*

"So, if he's not one of ours – who *is* this guy then?" Morgan asked, looking at Clarke, after Carter and Bob had finished talking, his face thrown into sharp relief by the light from the laptop on the coffee table in front of them.

"Beats me." Clarke growled. "But I'm damned well going to find out!"

"How?"

Getting to his feet Clarke crossed the room and, parting the curtains with a finger, stared out, quickly outlining his plan.

"It's a bit risky, isn't it?"

"We need results fast." Clarke muttered. "And if that means interrogating the whole damned neighbourhood, so be it. We'll wait till dark." Clarke went on. "I can't imagine the night life round here's too hot so I guess most folks will be in bed early. As Sterling's nephew he might be able to tell us something."

Turning, he took a small case from beneath the coffee table. Opening it he took out a small, glass phial filled with clear liquid, one of seven.

"We get the info and he's none the wiser."

\* \* \* \* \*

With his fork halfway to his mouth, Harry froze.

*"What did you say?"*

"I said there was a man following Carter today." Elizabeth said, looking at him over the table before telling him about the day's events, ending in their back-door escape from the restaurant and the mysterious letter Robert had left Carter.

*"What, and you're only telling me this now woman?"* Harry gasped, thinking of the day Sterling had turned up at the house, afraid. Afraid of someone getting hold of the box.

*guard it with your life*

Now he was dead and someone was following Carter.

"I don't know why I told you at all, the way you are around him. It's not like you care one way or the other, is

266

it?" she said, surprised. "And I've told you before – *don't call me woman!"*

\* \* \* \* \*

Taking his eyes from the road, Norman glanced at the revolver lying on the passenger seat next to him, his jaw locked, his eyes burning with anger. He'd waited for hours for Stanbrook to come out of the restaurant, until eventually, it had dawned on him he wasn't. Just to make sure he'd rung it and asked for him by name, only to be told he'd already left. Fuming, he'd hurried back to the car. Tonight, he was going to get revenge for all the wasted years of his life. But before he did, he wanted answers to all his questions.

*Every single one of them.*

\* \* \* \* \*

By the time he and Bob had finished speaking, daylight was already fading, Carter's anxiety at the thought of the oncoming night, deepening.

Unable to stop thinking about the man beneath the awning, out here in the sticks, he was aware of just how easily someone could approach the house without being seen. Chilled, he quickly went through the house making sure the windows were all closed and the doors locked, wondering if the man was out there somewhere, watching the house. Feeling like a sitting duck, his uncle's words in the letter sounded more ominous by the minute. Earlier Bob had suggested he go to a hotel for a few nights but he couldn't stay there indefinitely and what happened when he went back to Point Pleasant – what if the man followed him back there? With hindsight, instead of running away, he should have gone over and confronted the man head-on, because at least then he'd have known who he was and what was going on. As things stood, he was none the wiser and in self-imposed limbo. After pacing for a while, alert to the slightest sound in the house, in the end he grabbed his jacket, picked up the car keys and went out to the garage.

*  *  *  *  *

"He's on the move!" Morgan said, looking up from the laptop now emitting a low pinging sound as a small blue dot – Carter's car – moved along a digitalized map on the screen. Coming into the room Clarke went straight to the window and, snatching the binoculars up, stared at the rear lights of the car as it wended its way down the lane before disappearing into the darkness.

Quietly, the laptop continued to ping.

*  *  *  *  *

In Manhattan the phone rang. Picking it up, Bob's eyes widened as the voice on the other end of the line spoke to him, quickly and urgently.

After hanging up he punched in Carter's number, the phone clamped tightly to his ear, waiting for him to pick up. Frustratingly, it rang and rang before going to answer phone. Rolling his eyes impatiently, he called his mobile but after half a dozen rings, that too went to answer

268

phone. Leaving a brief message, he hung up again, pacing anxiously.

* * * * *

Concentrating on the road illuminated by the twin cones of light, Harry forced himself to ease up on the accelerator, cursing himself for being so bloody-minded. No matter what the circumstances, he'd failed to carry out Robert's instructions and put Carter at risk; he only hoped it wasn't too late.

Next to him, having been deprived of yet another meal for the second time in one day, starving and irritable, Elizabeth sat stiffly, her arms crossed over her chest. Confused by the sudden turn of events, she glared at him through slitted eyes. "Well, I would say thanks for dinner but we seeing we didn't have any, I can't."

Shaking his head Harry glanced at her. "Sorry Liz, I'll make it up to you, I promise."

"So, what's all this about then, what's going on?"

"Nothing."

"Don't lie to me Harry– I've known you too long. Everything was alright till I told you about that man following Carter today. Do you know who he was?"

"What?" Harry gasped, looking at her askance. "Of course not, why would I?"

"He looked dodgy, like someone you might know."

"Thanks!" He muttered, rolling his eyes. "Says it all, doesn't it?"

Five minutes later they drew up outside the house, Elizabeth halfway out the door even before they'd

269

stopped. Cursing, Harry opened his door and, limping round the truck, called after her. "Liz, wait!"

Stopping, she swung round to face him.

"That man following Carter today was nothing to do with me, I swear."

Stepping forward she looked up at him, her eyes narrowed. "So, why the sudden urge to see him then? You can't stand him most of the time."

"Liz…"

"Well?"

Rubbing a hand over his mouth, Harry shook his head. "I'll explain later, I promise."

"So, you *do* know something about it then?"

"I'm sorry, Liz." He said turning. "I've got to go."

Shaking her head in frustration, she turned. Watching her go up the path he felt the same old tug on his heart strings; all they ever seemed to do lately was row. As the front door slammed behind her, rolling his eyes he swore again. Turning his head he stared at Sterling's house, lit up like Blackpool illuminations before hurrying towards it, his stick tapping on the pavement as he did so.

* * * * *

Putting his empty glass down, Carter raised a hand in farewell at the girl behind the bar and slipped off the stool. On the way to the chip-shop he'd decided to have a pint in the Red Lion half hoping Rick Morley would be working, a welcome distraction from the day's events; better than sitting in the house jumping at shadows. When he'd arrived however, the only people there had been an elderly couple having dinner, the girl behind the bar and a young man – either her boyfriend or hoping to be – perched on a stool at the end of the bar drinking a pint, alternately talking to her and watching the replays of the football from the night before on the screen on the wall. After being served he'd been all forgotten about, something he'd been more than happy about, just content to be in company. Pulling the door open he swept the car park with his eyes, once more wondering if the man was out there somewhere, watching him. Deciding there was nothing he could do about it even if he was, he took a deep breath and stepped out into the night.

\* \* \* \* \*

Taking a step back, Harry stared at the front room window ablaze with light, wondering why it was taking Carter so long to answer the door, the thought entering his mind that maybe he couldn't. Maybe the man that had been following him earlier was inside the house with him right now. On the other hand, there was no sign of the car so maybe he'd gone out. Determinedly he knocked and rang the bell again, the sound trilling through the lower portion of the house. After waiting a little while longer he crossed the drive and, went back to the truck. Resting his hands on the steering wheel he looked back at the house unwilling to simply leave. At last, slipping out of gear he headed down the lane, unaware that he too, was being watched.

\* \* \* \* \*

271

"Who's that?" Clarke asked from the armchair around a mouthful of sandwich. Picking the binoculars up Morgan trained them on the cab of the truck.

"No idea." He replied. "Looks like a tradesman of some sort."

"What, at this time of night?"

"Whoever he is, he's wasting his time."

As it pulled away, he watched its tail-lights heading down the darkened lane for a moment or two before lowering the binoculars. "The car's still there?"

"Yeah." Clarke nodded.

"I wonder where he is?"

"In a bar if he'd got any sense. This place is enough to drive anyone to drink."

\* \* \* \* \*

Standing in the exact, same place as he had all those years ago, Norman leaned back against the shed. Seeing the house ablaze with light he'd just hurried down the darkened garden when he'd heard someone at the front, crunching over the gravel drive. After a while they'd left and driven off in what sounded like a van.

Clearly, no-one was home.

Cursing, he decided to wait.

# XXXIV

As he came out the chippy, Carter saw Harry's truck go by, watching as it swung into the car park with a squeal of brakes before jerking to a halt three cars away from his own. Rolling his eyes, he swore under his breath, Harry Bennett being the *last* thing he needed. Crossing the road, Carter kept his head down, he wouldn't see him; or if he did, that he'd just ignore him. However, as if he'd been waiting for him, Harry's door opened. "Carter!"

"Harry." Carter muttered, hurrying past.

*"Wait!"* Harry said, climbing down from the cab. "I need to talk to you."

Stopping, Carter turned. "Not now Harry – it's been a long day..."

"I know – Liz just told me all about it."

Shaking his head, Carter cursed, having told her specifically not to mention it to anyone else.

"She's worried about you."

"There's no need." Carter said tightly, turning again.

"That man." Harry said quietly, glancing around. "I think it might have something to do with your uncle."

Mid-stride, Carter froze. Turning, he stared at Harry wide-eyed. *"What?"*

"Not out here." Harry said quickly, sweeping the darkness with his eyes. "Get in the truck."

Looking at it, Carter remained where he was.

"It's important." Harry insisted.

Knowing he had no choice, not if he wanted to find out what was going on, reluctantly, he went to the truck and, going round to the passenger side, climbed aboard.

273

As he did so, next to him, Harry leaned forward and turned the keys in the ignition, the engine spluttering to life.

"What are you doing?" Carter gasped.

"I've got something to show you."

"I thought this was about my uncle?"

"It is." Harry muttered, pulling out of the space. "He left something with me to look after. Something important."

"He did?" Carter asked, intrigued. "What?"

"You'll see."

"Where are we going?"

"My place."

"It's there?"

"Yeah."

As they drove through the deserted village, Carter couldn't help wondering what he'd gone and got himself into, unable to believe he was going to Harry's at this time of night. After a few minutes, they turned onto a breathtakingly narrow country lane, the truck hurtling through the darkness, Carter helpless to do anything other than clutch his chips, praying for his life, hoping against hope there wasn't another vehicle coming the other way. To his relief after a mile or so they turned onto a wider, two-lane road with low hedges bordering the fields beyond. High above them a dome of twinkling stars yawned, larger and brighter out here in the darkened countryside. Turning his head Carter looked at Harry, his face bathed in green light from the dashboard, wondering if he ever thought about his own strange experience, the day he'd seen the UFO. Suddenly, without warning, they went over a cattle-grid, making his teeth rattle in his head. As they did so, Harry glanced at him, a look of amusement on his face.

At last, they turned onto what was little more than a muddy track ending in what Carter thought at first was a scrap yard, seeing an assortment of dilapidated cars in the headlights. All of a sudden, an old house in desperate need of repair loomed up, a light burning in one of the downstairs windows, the whole place surrounded by trees. As they approached, a security light came on, revealing a wooden veranda with rickety-looking wooden steps leading up to it. Not far away, within the confines of the light was a kennel, a black and white Collie chained it, on its feet, barking it's head off.

"Home sweet home." Harry growled quietly, killing the engine. With the barking deafeningly loud, echoing round the yard, he got out of the truck, Carter following suit as he went over to the kennel and, kneeling down, petted the dog, silence instantly reigning. Unclipping the chain, he and the dog headed towards the steps.

"This is Bess." He said to Carter over his shoulder. "Don't worry, she doesn't bite."

Glad to hear it, Carter followed them up the rickety wooden steps, glancing round nervously as he did so, unable to believe anyone would choose to live out here, the whole place giving him the creeps. Opening the door Harry snapped a light on, flooding the dingy hall with light. In the kitchen at the back of the house, Carter stared at the half-assembled car parts, nuts, bolts, spanners and monkey wrenches lying around everywhere, his eyes widening at the sight of a car engine sitting on the draining-board next to the sink. After Harry let Bess off the leash she came to him, curiously nuzzling his hand with a cold, wet nose. After stroking her, Carter straightened.

"Take a seat." Harry muttered indicating a round, Formica-topped kitchen table and three grubby-looking chairs. Pulling one out, he sat, the chair creaking loudly as he did so, Bess disappearing beneath the table. Picking up a pair of chipped mugs, Harry rinsed them out at the sink, the tap spluttering for a moment as he did so. Giving them a shake, he brought them to the table and, picking up a bottle, sloshed a generous measure of amber liquid into them before dropping down onto a chair, his leg stretched out in front of him.

"So, Harry." Carter said. "What's this all about then?"

\* \* \* \* \*

In his apartment, Bob stared down at the street forty stories below, light rain turning the sidewalks into a riot of colour, the traffic a river of light snaking along the cavernous valley of buildings. Turning, he glared at the phone, willing it to ring. *Where the hell was he, and why wasn't he calling him back?*

\* \* \* \* \*

With his face thrown into sharp relief by the stark light from the bare light bulb above the table, Harry looked at Carter, the expression in his flint-like eyes impossible to read. "Drink."

"I didn't come here to drink." Carter replied. "I came here because…"

276

*"Get it down you!"* Harry growled, fixing him with a steely look. Realising it was a baptism of fire that was obviously expected of him before the conversation could proceed, reluctantly, Carter picked it up, Harry watching him as he did so. Taking a deep breath, he took a swig, the amber liquid scorching its way down his chest and setting his belly on fire. Spluttering, he choked and gasped for air. *"What the hell is that?"*

"Firewater." Harry replied. "I got it cheap when the firm went out of business."

*"You don't say!"*

"This bloke who followed you." Harry began, narrowing his eyes at him. "You ever see him before?"

"No." Carter replied, giving his head a quick shake. "In the car park you said it might have something to do with uncle Rob – what did you mean?"

Putting his mug down, Harry looked at him. "Just before he died, he came out here to see me. That was strange enough in itself, but it was the *way* he was while he was here that really got me."

"What do you mean?" Carter asked, stiffening. "How was he?"

"Like a cat on hot bricks."

"He was nervous?" Carter gasped, his heart skipping a beat, unable to imagine his uncle being nervous about anything. "What about?"

"He wanted me to look after something for him – a box – couldn't wait to get rid. He said it was important and that I had to guard it with my life."

"What? Was he joking?"

"No, he wasn't." Harry said quietly. "And that wasn't all he said only I didn't take it seriously at the time. He said if anything happened to him, I had to send it to an address he gave me."

*"He actually said that?"* Carter gasped, astounded.

"Yeah." Harry nodded. "A couple of times."

*"Christ!"* Carter breathed, chilled. "So where was this address?"

Turning, Harry opened a drawer in one of the units and, rooting about, took out a small sheet of paper before sliding it over the table. Picking it up Carter stared down at it in amazement, Bob's name and an address in Manhattan leaping off the paper at him.

*by now you'll be in contact with Adkins*

"You sent it to him?" Carter asked, wondering why Bob hadn't mentioned it.

Shifting uncomfortably on the chair, Harry shook his head. "I was going to but then Liz told me about you and said you'd be arriving in a few days so, I thought I might as well give it you instead, you being his nephew and all."

"Where is it, this box?"

"It's here." Harry said. "In a place no one would think of looking."

\* \* \* \* \*

In bed, propped up against pillows with the book she'd been intending to read face down on the coverlet, Elizabeth frowned. Unable to stop thinking about Harry's strange behaviour and their swift exit from the restaurant earlier, she couldn't help but be concerned. Why had he reacted the way he had? What was going on?

278

Deep in thought, it took her a moment to register she'd heard something downstairs. Wondering if it was the fridge making the clunking noise it did every now and then, she waited and, sure enough, heard it again. As she did so, her heart leapt, realising it wasn't the sound of the fridge at all, but the squeak of back door opening!

Flying out of bed, she whirled, wondering to do. Who the hell was it in her house this time of night? More to the point, how had they got in; she distinctly remembered locking it, just as she did every night. Suddenly a thought hit her – maybe it was the scruffy man from earlier! Maybe he'd found out where she lived! Glancing at the wardrobe, she knew if she hid in there she'd be trapped. On the other hand, if she screamed out the window for Carter, he might not hear her and it might make things worse. Picking up a can of hairspray, she tip-toed to the door and, taking a deep breath, opened it, her heart pounding in her ears. As she stepped out onto the landing, she looked over the banister into the hallway below. To her horror, wreathed in shadows at the bottom of the stairs, she saw a man looking up at her.

# XXXV

Outside in the yard, bathed in the security light, nervously, Carter swept the darkness with his eyes again, once more wondering how anyone in their right mind could live out here alone, miles away from anywhere. Next to the kennel, Harry spoke. "Under here." he said simply.

"What?" Carter asked, staring at him uncomprehendingly. *"You buried it under the kennel?"*

"Not buried exactly." Harry said. "More like stored it. All we've got to do is lift it off."

Although not large, the kennel however, was big enough. Bending, Harry put his hands under the lip of the roof, and following suit, Carter did the same. After a count of three, with a creak, they lifted it and moved it aside. Embedded in the ground in the centre of a wooden frame he saw a metal safe.

"Sometimes I get stuff fallen off the back of a lorry – stuff I'd rather not be found with. Like I say, no-one would think of looking down there." Taking the torch from him, Harry trained the beam on it. Reaching down he took hold of the handle and pulled the door open. Inside was a cardboard box, a few inches to spare either side. Leaning down he grasped the edges and lifted it clear. After returning the kennel to its rightful place, they went back inside the house, Carter relived to be inside once more. Putting the box on the table, with mounting excitement he pulled the flaps open, the tape already having been cut through. Turning his head, he looked at Harry, an eyebrow cocked.

"I wanted to check what it was." Harry shrugged, non-committedly.

Inside, the box was full of paper, page upon page of calculations and formulae's, some in his uncles scrawling hand, others in a different one altogether. Taking a couple out Carter began reading them, trying to make sense of them.

With an air of a man relieved of his duty, Harry sat down and, after rubbing his leg, clearly in pain after the exertion said: "You understand any of it?"

"A bit." Carter nodded, glancing up at him. "I think it's something to do with genetics."

"I thought you were a scientist as well?" Harry asked, reaching for the bottle.

"I am." Carter replied crisply. "But this isn't my field. I'm an astrophysicist."

"What, stars and stuff?"

"Yeah."

"You think that bloke was following you because of that?" Harry asked, indicating the box.

"I don't know. Maybe."

"I asked him if it was classified."

"You did?" Carter asked, surprised. "What did he say?"

"He said the less I knew, the better."

"Christ."

"I should've sent it off like he wanted me to, shouldn't I?"

"Too late now Harry."

Silently they regarded each other over the table.

Feeling he had Harry at a disadvantage, clearing his throat, Carter decided to take the bull by the horns.

"Harry, someone told me something. About you. They said you saw a UFO."

"What the hell's that got to do with anything?" Harry demanded, staring at him intently, the expression on his face unreadable. Reaching for the chair, Carter lowered himself down onto it, his eyes never leaving Harry's for a moment. "Is it true?"

"That's none of your bloody business."

"The reason I ask." Carter went on. "Is because something happened to me, something terrifying. Something I can't believe actually happened, even now."

"What?" Harry asked, his voice barely above a whisper, his eyes wide.

Snorting, Carter shook his head. "You wouldn't believe me if I told you." Under Harry's intense scrutiny, he shifted uncomfortably on the chair.

"Aliens." He said quietly. *I saw aliens, Harry.*

Ashen-faced, for a moment Harry studied Carter intently before speaking again. "You *do* remember it then?"

"Remember it?" Carter gasped, staring at him aghast. "I'll never be able to forget it. But how do you know…"

Leaning forward, rubbed a calloused hand over his face. "Seeing that thing…it was the worst day of my life and then, seeing you at the church – you of all people – I couldn't believe it. It was such a shock."

"I'm sorry?" Carter asked with a frown. "What do you mean, you of all people?"

"What do you think I mean?" he asked. "I thought you said you remembered?"

"I do but…"

"I saw you carter – you looked right at me!"

282

*"You were in the woods?"* Carter gasped.

"What you talking about?" Harry snorted, frowning at him uncomprehendingly now. "What woods? I don't know anything about any woods! On the UFO I meant when they took me inside. We were both there, Carter – *I saw you.*"

\* \* \* \* \*

"Did Robert ever talk to you about anything strange?" Clarke asked. "Something he was working on, maybe."

Shaking her head, Elizabeth yawned. She had no idea who the men in her kitchen were and didn't care; all she wanted to do was sleep. "No, he never talked about his work." she murmured drowsily. "Ever."

On his chair before her, Clarke glanced at Morgan standing silently behind her. "Do you know who the man was who was following Carter earlier today?"

"No."

"Did Carter?"

"No."

"You ever see him before?"

"Carter?"

"No, the man."

"No."

"You know what he wanted?"

"No."

"Did Carter?"

"No."

"Do you know Bob Adkins?"

"No."

"You ever hear the name before?"

"No."

"Never?"

"No."

Sighing, Clarke, narrowed his eyes. "Do you know where Carter went, where he is now?"

"No."

"He didn't say anything about going out, about meeting anyone?"

"No."

At last, after jotting down the man's description, that and a somewhat burbled version of events, Clarke slid his notebook back into his pocket and, getting to his feet, nodded at Morgan. Stooping, Morgan picked Elizabeth up, her arms dangling like a rag doll as he carried her from the kitchen.

* * * * *

*"What?"* Carter gasped, recoiling as if slapped.

"The day I saw the UFO – there was a lot more to it than I told everyone. They took me up there with them and you were there too."

*"What?"* Carter gasped hoarsely, once more feeling reality recede. *"It wasn't me – it couldn't have been!"*

"I'm sorry Carter, but it was. You were wearing a white t-shirt with a gold dragon on the front and there was blood all down it..."

Feeling the room tilt, Carter stared at Harry numbly. About to say something, all of a sudden, he stopped, remembering...

*looking down at himself, wondering how he could've been bleeding so much before he'd noticed. A crimson river pouring from his noise onto his t-shirt, the one Anita, his girlfriend had bought him the day before in Camden Market. He'd only worn it to the restaurant in Soho for Max's birthday lunch to please her because, despite her appalling taste in clothes, he liked her a lot.*

feeling something inside him fell apart because

*Dimly aware of the other diners turning their heads curiously towards them to see what was going on. Everyone frozen in their seats almost as if time had stopped. Then Charlotte suddenly turning away from him with cry, her hand flying to her mouth looking as if she were about to be sick and Max jumping to his feet knocking his wine glass over as he did so, a dark, red tide spreading over the starched white tablecloth. Anita snatching up a serviette and pressing it to his nose, once hand resting firmly on his shoulder...*

there was no way Harry could know about that.

"*Oh my God!*" In panic, he leapt to his feet, Harry staring up at him in shock.

"Carter I'm sorry...you said you remembered..."

"*Mine!*" Carter cried hysterically. "*I remember my experience...in the woods!*"

"*Christ!*" Harry gasped, his face almost as pale Carter's now.

"*I can't believe it!*" Carter gasped hoarsely, his hands on his head now. Turning, he snatched up the mug of Firewater, and took a deep gulp from it before putting it

285

down. Leaning on the table for a moment he hung his head, trembling from head to toe.

"What happened?"

"Carter." Harry said looking up at him. "I don't think now is…"

*"Tell me what happened, Harry!"* Carter exploded.

Sitting back in the chair, dropping his eyes, haltingly, Harry told him how he'd gone into one of the fields after hearing Bess barking at something and seeing a group of men standing about. Only they hadn't been men at all. How Bess had tried to attack them and how they'd knocked her out before standing there with them watching a UFO descend and being taken aboard it. He'd been experimented on and had ended up suspended in some kind of tank filled with gel up to his neck.

Frozen with terror Carter waited.

"There were five or six of them looking at me and then, all of a sudden, I saw you. There was blood all down your face and your T-shirt and you looked sort of dazed as if you didn't know where you were or what was happening. You just stood there looking up at me among them."

*"Among them?"* Carter breathed weakly.

"Yeah."

*"Christ!"*

"Ever since then…your face…I couldn't forget it. Then when we met…I couldn't believe you were George's son, I mean – what are the odds? How messed up is that?"

Dropping down heavily onto the chair, Carter covered his face with his hands.

"All I knew was I had to get away." Harry went on. "That's why I left after the funeral the way I did. Me and Liz had a row about it the next day."

The argument in the truck.

"She had no idea what happened that day and she never will."

"Is that why Uncle Rob introduced you to my dad?" Carter asked. "So you could talk about your experiences?"

"Yeah." Harry nodded. "He thought it might help us somehow."

"But why?" Carter asked, spreading his hands. "Why did uncle Rob care about it enough to do that – he and my dad couldn't stand each other."

"It bothered him I think." Harry replied, simply. "Or maybe he was worried about how it was affecting your mom. It couldn't have been easy for her having to deal with all that."

"Maybe." Carter breathed. "So, did you tell my dad about seeing me...up there?"

"Yeah." Harry nodded. "But at the time neither of us knew it was you, *his own son.*"

\* \* \* \* \*

Back in the house over the road, Clarke stared at the monitor. "He can't have gone far – his car's still there."

"Maybe he's picked a chick up." Morgan suggested. "Apart from getting wasted – what else is there to do in a place like this?"

\* \* \* \* \*

As the room spun around her, leaning over the side of the bed, Elizabeth threw up on the bedside rug. Flopping back onto the pillows, she gasped for air, freezing with shock as she suddenly remembered seeing the man at the bottom of the stairs, everything a complete blank after that.

*what the*

Throwing the covers back she got out of bed, her legs weak, her heart pounding in her ears. Bathed in the peachy glow of the bedside lamp she stood rigidly, listening.

*Silence.*

Going to the door she cranked it open an inch or two, seeing the landing light was on. Hearing nothing, with her heart pounding in her chest after a slight hesitation, taking a deep breath she quickly slipped through it before cautiously peering over the bannisters, filled with relief at the sight of the empty stairs and hallway below.

Tilting her head, she listened, hearing nothing but screaming silence. All she knew was she had to get out of the house and over to Carter's as quickly as possible.

Taking a deep breath, she hurried down the stairs, wincing as the bottom stair creaked loudly. Freezing, she waited for the man to appear.

*Silence.*

Just about to make a bolt for the front door, all of a sudden, an idea occurred to her and she stopped.

*What if it had never happened?*

What if it had been nothing but a nightmare, brought on by what had happened earlier? Maybe the incident with the man following Carter had frightened her more

288

than she'd cared to admit, after all, what was the alternative? Suddenly, full of self-doubt, she stared at the darkened kitchen before slowly going towards it and clicking the light switch on, releasing her breath as she saw there was no one in there. Going to the back door, she checked it was locked before taking a large knife from one of the drawers and, armed, went through the whole house, finding no-one. Wondering if she was losing her mind, she was just about to put the knife back in the drawer when, she stopped, instead deciding to take it upstairs with her – *just in case.*

\* \* \* \* \*

Back in the house, glancing at his watch, Clarke frowned. After the conversation between Stanbrook and Adkins about being followed, his sudden absence was alarming; clearly someone else was keeping tabs on him as well as them, but who? Who had the man been and who did he work for, the military, the government or someone else? Either way all it was a complication they didn't need, only serving to muddy the waters further and after Rieker and Stevenson's disappearance, another screw-up was the *last* thing the Bureau needed.

*Where the hell was he?*

# XXXVI

Inside the fringe of trees bordering the cluttered yard, cloaked in shadows, a man moved from foot to foot to keep warm, his gloved hands thrust into the pockets of his long overcoat, his breath freezing in a plume in the air in front of his face. Behind him the darkened woods were steeped in silence while high above, bright stars glittered, startlingly bright in the clear winter sky.

From the pocket of his coat, he took out a pack of cigarettes and, lifting it to his face, pulled one out with his teeth, unwilling to remove his gloves to complete the action. Cupping his hands, he lit it, sucking warm, fragrant air into his lungs. Leaning against a tree, he stared at the one light-filled window in the house.

Suddenly, behind him he heard the rustle of undergrowth and he spun pulling a small torch from his pocket as he did so, seeing a small figure standing only a few yards away in the narrow beam of light. For a moment, man and Being stared at each other before it turned and disappeared back into the darkness. Flicking the torch off again the man turned and continued to watch the house.

\* \* \* \* \*

Glancing at the kitchen window Harry saw it was beginning to lighten outside, he and Carter having talked through the night. As they had he'd realised he'd been wrong treating Carter the way he had, after all what had happened that day hadn't been his fault, and, from what he'd told him about his own experience in the woods,

290

clearly, he was as much a victim of the aliens as he and his dad had been.

"Harry, do you have a phone?" Carter asked.

"In the hallway." Harry nodded. "Just so long as you're not calling Australia."

"New York actually." Carter replied, already on his feet. Raising his head Harry looked at him, his eyebrows high. "But I'll pay for the call."

With a grunt, Harry nodded.

In the hallway Carter punched in Bob's number. A few moments later in Manhattan, the phone was picked up. *"Where the hell have you been?"* Bob ejaculated, obviously just having been woken up. *"I've been trying to get hold of you for hours!"*

"I'm at a friend's house."

"Carter, listen, I've been doing some research on your uncle and I discovered he was only working with Hely Walberg – a geneticist renowned for his cutting-edge research and practically a genius – conducting secret military research for both the British and the U.S!"

*"What?"* Carter, gasped loudly, clutching the phone tightly in both hands now. "Are you sure?"

"Absolutely." Bob said quickly. "And guess what they were working on?"

"I don't know."

"Samples of biological material found aboard a crashed UfO!"

*"What you mean like…"*

"Yeah." Bob finished for him. *"Alien DNA!* And that's not all. Just before he died, *someone* was watching his every move and keeping a very close eye on him, maybe even watching the house. I haven't been able to

291

find out who just yet but it explains the letter he left you."

Shocked, he stared through the doorway at the box sitting on Harry's kitchen floor before telling Bob about how his uncle had turned up at Harry's house out of the blue before leaving a box with him for safe-keeping; a box full of calculations on genetics.

*"My god."* Bob breathed. "They could be the research records. If they are, these people will stop at nothing to get them – you could be in real danger Carter, you and Harry!"

*"Christ!"* Carter gasped weakly. "What can we do?"

"There's no time to lose." Bob replied quickly. "I'm going to call someone and call you straight back!" After what seemed an eternity but which in fact was only a few minutes, the phone rang again, Harry appearing in the kitchen doorway as it did so. Snatching it up Carter held it firmly to his ear.

"Right." Bob said. "Do you have a pen and paper?"

"Hang on a minute." Carter said looking down at a battered old telephone book, the cover almost obliterated with darkly smudged, oily-looking fingerprints, a stub of a pencil next to it. Flipping it open, as Bob spoke, he quickly jotted it down.

"You need to go there right now." Bob said urgently. "Someone will meet you there and take it off your hands."

"Hang on." Carter said quickly. "What's going to happen to it?"

"Carter, believe me when I say I'm more concerned about what's going to happen to *you* if it stays in your possession. You and Harry could both end up disappearing!"

A few minutes later, hearing the door open, the man watching the house stiffened. As the security light came on, he saw Carter cross the porch carrying with a cardboard box, Harry close behind him. Getting into the truck, the engine spluttered into life before roaring out of the yard, heading for the track. Turning, the man disappeared into the depths of the woods, darkness closing in behind him as he did so.

Inside the cab, shivering with cold, Carter stared through the windscreen at the narrow ribbon of road unwinding before them as they sped along, everything bathed in the pearly tones of dawn.

Turning his head, he looked at Harry next to him, resplendent in a donkey jacket topped by a red and black chequered deputy-dawg-style hat, the earflaps flapping up and down with every bounce of the truck, the suspension clearly on its last legs like the rest of it. Surprisingly sober even after the copious amount of Firewater he'd been drinking up till only less than an hour ago, bright and alert, clearly Harry didn't mind this impromptu dash into the middle of nowhere, his attitude one of eager willingness, seeming more than happy to be a part of it all. "How long now?" Carter asked over the roar of the engine.

"Five minutes at the most."

"And you're sure you know where it is?"

Turning his head, Harry narrowed his eyes at him. "Of course, I do! I've lived round these parts all my life – I know where Gallows Hill is!"

* * * * *

With the sound of Morgan's snores filling the room, sitting before the monitor, Clarke stared at the small blue dot, the digital representation of Carter's car.

*"Where the hell are you, you bastard?"* he muttered.

* * * * *

Suddenly, through the windscreen, Carter saw a car in the headlights.

*"There!"* he said quickly.

"I can see it." Harry said slowing down before pulling onto to the side of the road behind a black Land Rover. As he did so the driver's door opened and a large, well-built, blonde-haired man in his mid-thirties emerged before striding towards them. Opening the door of the truck, Carter got out, the two men staring at each other in the merged headlights.

"Bob said you have something for me?" The man asked with a trace of an accent that was either Scandinavian or Dutch. Taking the box from the truck Carter gave it him. With a nod the man turned, Carrying it to the Land Rover. After stowing it on the front seat, he climbed in next to it and shut the door. Raising his hand in farewell he swung it round and disappeared off down the hill into the gloom, the covert exchange complete.

* * * * *

In silence, Harry drove the truck back towards the village. Despite having spent the night hauling a kennel about, drinking the equivalent of hydraulic acid and learning he'd been aboard a space-ship surrounded by aliens, not to mention a cloak and dagger drop-off to a stranger in the middle of nowhere with a box that might or might not eventually get him killed, Carter realised he was actually feeling better than he had for a long time. At last, they pulled into the car park.

"Thanks for everything, Harry." Carter said, turning to look at him. "You took a hell of a risk looking after that box for Uncle Rob and helping me just now. I really appreciate it."

In the gloom, Harry nodded. "You're welcome. And I'm sorry about the way I told you about…well you know, seeing you up there. It must've come as a hell of a shock. Your dad would've been proud of the way you handled it."

"Thanks Harry, that means a lot." Carter said, moved.

Silently, Harry nodded and, putting his hand on the gear stick, turned his head and stared through the windscreen at the car park. Taking that as his cue, Carter turned and opened the door. As he climbed out, he realised everything seemed tame compared to the bizarre events of the night.

"Carter?"

Turning his head, Carter looked back at Harry.

"Your dad was a good man – your uncle too in his own way – and I'm sorry about what's happened."

"Thanks Harry." Carter nodded quietly. "That means a lot."

295

\* \* \* \* \*

Inside the darkened room, the laptop pinged alerting Clarke who'd been on the verge of nodding off in the chair. Leaning forward, he stared at the screen before rolling his eyes with relief. On the bed, Morgan stirred and, lifting his head stared at him, his voice thick with sleep. "Is that what I think it is?"

Without taking his eyes from the screen, Clarke nodded. "Yeah – he's back."

Slowly, the blue dot moved up the lane.

\* \* \* \* \*

Just having pushed his key in the lock, Carter heard movement behind him before being suddenly pushed from behind, gasping with pain as his face slammed against the door. Then something hit him on the back of the head and everything went black.

\* \* \* \* \*

Just about to go round to the back door like she always did, Elizabeth stopped and stared at the key in the front door. Thinking Carter must've left it in accidentally, she was just about to take it out when she noticed what looked like a drop of blood on the doorstep. All of a sudden, an image of the man beneath the awning flashed into her mind and she glanced quickly over her shoulder, seeing nothing but the empty lane, her nerves jangling. Turning, she stared at the drop, wondering if it was Carter's blood.

296

*Harry…*

Telling herself she was being ridiculous, nevertheless she took a deep breath and, taking hold of the key, opened the door.

*"Carter?"*

Getting to his feet, Morgan shook his head. "He's not gonna be happy considering what time he got in. I'm going to make coffee – want some?"

With a nod, on the monitor, Clarke watched Elizabeth make her way down the hallway towards the kitchen. Downstairs water ran as Morgan filled the kettle. A moment later she reappeared, stopping at the bottom of the stairs, looking up.

*"Hello?"*

"Jesus, just leave him be, why don't you?" Clarke muttered, irritated. Never a morning person at the best of times, after being up all night he was as grumpy as hell this morning.

*"Carter? Are you there? Are you alright?"*

Downstairs the kettle began boiling accompanied by the sound of Morgan opening cupboard doors. Slowly, Elizabeth went up the stairs, the camera on the landing showing her approaching. Going along the landing she stopped before a door. Downstairs the kettle reached a crescendo and clicked off. *"Carter, are you okay?"*

Downstairs the fridge door opened.

On the landing Elizabeth opened the door and went in.

The clink of a spoon against a cup.

Silence.

The whisper of Morgan's stockinged feet on the stairs, coming back up.

Elizabeth back on the landing.

297

Coming into the room Morgan put the mugs on the table and took a seat.

On the screen Elizabeth went to the main bedroom and, opening the door, peered round it.

*"Carter, where are you?"*

Frowning, Morgan glanced at the screen, Clarke looking equally confused.

Over the road, Elizabeth stood at the bottom of the short flight of stairs staring up at the attic.

*"Carter?"*

# XXXVII

With a jolt, Carter's eyes flew open. Bolting upright pain stabbed through his head, everything spinning giddily about him for a moment. Blinking, he stared at the mouldy wall a few feet away in surprise. Wondering where he was, for a moment his mind remained alarmingly blank before suddenly remembering being back at the house and putting the key in the lock. Then…a sound. Being shoved forward and something hitting him in the back of the head.

*what the*

Raising his hand, he winced as he felt a lump on the back of his head, relieved to see there was no blood on it. Under a tattered blanket on a filthy mattress in what looked like an old cellar, his disorientation deepened. To his right creepers partially covered a small, grime-covered window halfway up the wall through which weak light filtered, the whole place infused with a cloying, damp, odour. On the other side of the room a pair of old dining chairs were stacked one on top of the other next to a door, a cardboard box containing half a dozen empty jam jars on the other side. In the far corner rested an old wooden crate, it's lid half off, containing what looked like rusty metal tools. As he moved, he felt something round his ankle, and, throwing the blanket off, with horror, realised there was a manacle round his ankle, a chain leading from it, wrapped round a wooden beam and secured by a sturdy-looking padlock.

*what the*

Grabbing it he yanked on it a couple of times before getting to his feet and planting his hands against the post, putting all his weight against it but there was no give, it being way too solid for him to be able to do any serious damage to it. Thinking of the man beneath the awning he wondered if it was him that had brought him here, his uncle's ominous warning returning to him with startling clarity.

\* \* \* \* \*

At the window, Morgan watched Elizabeth leave the house. "How can he not be there?"

*"He never went in!"* Clarke gasped, typing on the keypad, replaying the footage. Beside him now, Morgan stared at the hallway on the screen, the minutes ticking by on fast forward in the corner, the front door however, remaining firmly closed.

"But we saw him."

"No, we didn't." Clarke muttered, tapping the keypad again. "We saw him come back but we didn't actually *see* him go in the house, did we?" Getting to his feet he said: "I'm going over there to take a look."

"What, now?" Morgan asked, getting to his feet. "In broad daylight? It's too risky – you'll be seen…"

"I won't." Clarke said, strapping on his holster. "I'll go round the back over the fields."

\* \* \* \* \*

In the kitchen, Elizabeth called Carter's mobile.
*Off.*

Just about to dial Harry's number, she jumped as it rang. *"Harry!* I think something's happened to Carter. I went over just now, and his key was in the front door and…I think there's blood on the doorstep and he's not there."

"I'll be right over!"

\* \* \* \* \*

On the mattress, wrapped in the blanket, Carter watched the window brighten, his mind fuggy, probably due to concussion, he thought. And the cold. And the fact he hadn't eaten for God-knows-how-long. Thinking of the man from yesterday he wondered if it had been him who'd knocked him out and brought him here, maybe because of the box

*you could be in serious danger*

If so, he wouldn't know he'd already got rid of it, in which case he might be able to use it as a bargaining chip. The man wouldn't kill because he'd never know where it was then and there was no way he was going to tell him – not unless he resorted to torture of course. Refusing to think about that, instead he forced himself to concentrate on getting out of here before he came back.

Suddenly, hearing movement from above he froze.

Getting to his feet, staggering, he turned, searching for something to use as a weapon.

*Nothing.*

In fear he stared at the door wide-eyed, listening to the clump of footsteps descending down a wooden staircase, growing louder with each passing second. Suddenly the footsteps stopped, followed by the sound of a bolt being drawn back. On the other side of the door, with bated breath, Carter waited.

301

* * * * *

"Something must have happened after I dropped him off, earlier. We went to mine last night."

*"What, you and Carter?"* Elizabeth gasped, astounded. "Why?"

"I'll explain everything later." Harry said coming towards her. "But right now, we really need to find him."

"Is this something to do with that man yesterday?"

"I don't know…maybe."

"What are you not telling me, Harry?" She demanded, folding her arms across her chest defiantly. Rubbing a hand over his face, he sighed. "A few months before he died, Robert came to see me. He wanted me to look after something for him – a box of papers – scientific papers. I think he was in trouble and he didn't want it getting into the wrong hands."

"What kind of trouble?" she whispered.

"He didn't say."

"Why didn't he ask me to look after it?"

"Mine would be the last place anyone would think of looking for it and he probably thought asking you was too risky."

*"Risky?"*

"And then he died."

"So, you've had it all this time?"

"Yeah."

"Is that why that man was following Carter, because of the box?"

"Maybe." Harry nodded his eyes dark.

"Harry, you've got to get rid of it!" she gasped.

"I have,"

*"Oh no…"* she said quietly, shaking her head. "You gave it to Carter last night, didn't you?"

"I did, yeah." Harry nodded. "But then we gave it someone else."

"Who?"

"I don't know, some bloke Bob knows."

"Bob who?" she asked, frowning in confusion.

"Someone Carter's dad knew…he was counselling him or something."

"Counselling him? For what?"

Holding his hands up, Harry shook his head. "I don't know – Liz we haven't got time for this – you said you've got the key to next door?"

"Yeah." She nodded. "I've got both of them now."

"Good." Harry muttered, turning. "Let's go."

\* \* \* \* \*

Concealed in shrubbery at the bottom of the garden, all of a sudden Clarke noticed a couple of cigarette butts. With a frown he picked one of them up and sniffed it – recent. Someone had been right here where he was now, watching the house.

Peering through the branches, he saw high hedges bordering the garden, shielding it from prying eyes. Parting the branches, he left the cover of the shrubbery and hurried down the garden toward the house.

Meanwhile, over the lane, Morgan cursed as Bell and the man from last night appeared in the front door, the pair of them looking over at Stanbrook's house before making their way toward it.

303

*"Goddammit!"* he muttered quietly, pushing the earphone into his ear. "Cobra, you've got company at the front – *get out of there!"*

Instead of a reply however, there was a loud burst of static. Unable to see the front door of the house from here, he'd only know if they'd gone into the house once the camera's picked them up.

*"Cobra, do you read me – I repeat, you've got company at the front!"*

Suddenly the static disappeared and, just about to speak again, all of a sudden, his earpiece burst into life.

*"Let's just get the hell out of here!"*
*"And go where?"*
*"Anywhere but here! It might be us they're looking for. Let's try and make it down there to that valley where there's cover…"*

Confused, Morgan blinked.
*"Cobra!"* he hissed urgently. *"Respond!"*
This time however, everything remained silent.

\* \* \* \* \*

"Bob's numbers got to be here somewhere."

"I've found his mobile!" Elizabeth cried, holding Carter's phone aloft. "I bet it's in here."

Turning, Harry narrowed his eyes at her. "Do you need a password to get into it?"

Pressing the buttons, she rolled her eyes. "Damn!"

Going into the hallway, she held up a notepad.

304

"This was next to the phone with a number on it, an overseas one I think – I'm ringing it."

*"No!"* Harry barked quickly, coming towards her.

"When Carter rang him from my house Bob told him the phone-line here might be tapped."

*"What?"* she gasped, dropping the phone as if it were a snake. "Are you serious?"

"I don't know." Harry replied, his eyes dark. "But it might be best to ring him from yours just to be on the safe side."

Nodding, Elizabeth was just about to answer when all of a sudden, a face appeared fleetingly at the window. With a cry, her hand flew to her mouth, her eyes wide with shock. Spinning, Harry stared at the window. Seeing nothing he turned back to her, his eyes wide.

*"What? What is it?"*

"The man from last night!" she gasped, clinging to his arm. "He was in my house!"

Doing a double take, Harry flinched. *"I'm sorry – what?"*

"He was at the bottom of the stairs looking up at me, that's all I remember. Later on, I woke up and checked the house but there was no one there so just put it down to having had a nightmare – *oh Harry, I'm so scared!"*

\* \* \* \* \*

Holding his breath, Carter stared at the door as it swung inward, his heart leaping at the sight of the man from beneath the awning on the other side, holding a gun. Coming into the cellar the man stared at him, his eyes glittering malevolently in his square face. "Thought

305

you were clever giving me the slip yesterday, didn't you?" he growled quietly, his voice deep.

Swallowing Carter stared at him. "Who are you what do you want?"

Smiling lopsidedly the man came a little closer. "Who do you think I am?"

"I have no idea."

"Are you sure?" the man asked, the gun wavering slightly in his hand. "Your uncle didn't tell you about me?" At the mention of his uncle, Carter's blood ran cold. "No."

"I'm Norman Kepple." The man replied, once more giving him a lopsided grin. "I was the caretaker."

"The…the caretaker?" Carter stammered.

"At the Biochem Institute Where your uncle worked." Norman said, walking slowly towards the window before stopping and staring up at it for a moment. "Him and Hely Walberg."

Once more Carter's heart leapt.

Spinning, Norman turned from the window to stare at him, his eyes glittering with barely concealed rage.

"They fitted me up."

Aware he was waiting for some kind of reaction Carter shook his head. "I'm sorry." He said quietly. "I don't know what you mean."

Coming back into the centre of the room, Norman stood before him, his eyes narrowed. "Three days ago, I got out of prison after doing thirty years. *Thirty long years, thanks to them.*"

"How?" Carter croaked.

"They stashed drugs in my flat and called the filth. I got six years and could've been out after three but every time my parole came up, something would happen. I'd get beaten up and end up getting slapped with a fighting charge, not just once, but time after time – *anything to stop me getting out again.*"

Frowning, Carter stared at him. "What makes you think they were behind it?"

"That, Carter is a very good question." Norman replied, spreading his hands, grinning manically now.

"What possible reason could he have for doing something like that – *any ideas?*"

Silently, Carter waited.

"No?" Norman asked, dripping sarcasm. "To get rid of me before I told anyone what they'd done."

"What they'd done?"

*"Like you don't know!"* Norman hissed, raising the gun.

*"Please!"* Carter cried, stepping back his hands up in front of him now. *"I don't know anything!"*

*"Liar!"*

*"I'm not!"* Carter cried, unable to see anything but the muzzle of the gun. *"I swear I don't know anything!"*

Remaining where he was, Norman stared at Carter intently, scouring his face with his eyes as if searching for any sign of duplicity. At last, he slowly lowered the gun, his voice quiet now. "One day I overheard them talking about an experiment they'd done, worrying about someone finding out about this thing they'd created in the lab, some kind of monster."

"A monster?" Carter gasped, hardly able to believe what he was hearing.

"That's right." Norman nodded. "A monster – *I saw it.*"

"When was this?" Carter croaked, thinking about what he'd found in the box.

"Years ago." Norman replied, his voice barely above a whisper now. "One night I managed to get inside the lab and even now, I still can't forget what I saw or what happened...like something forcing its way into my mind."

Freezing, Carter remembered the chorus of voices he'd heard in his mind during the chase through the woods that night. "What did it...look like?" he asked, filled with dread.

"Human." Norman croaked. "Except for its eyes...massive eyes...the blackest eyes I've ever seen."

"What happened to it?"

"You don't know?"

"No, of course not." Carter replied, spreading his hands. "How would I?"

"He was your uncle."

"That doesn't mean anything." Carter replied, shaking his head. "No-one knew what they were doing – their work was classified."

"Really?" Norman asked, his eyes arched. "And how would you know that?"

Realising he'd just tripped himself up, Carter literally thought on his feet. "He told me once."

*"Liar!"*

"I don't know what you want me to say." Carter said.

"If it's money you want – some kind of recompense – I have money. I'll give you whatever you want."

"This isn't about the money." Norman replied, taking himself by surprise as he realised it was the truth. "I want to know where that thing is now and if it's still alive."

"I've told you I don't know anything about it."
"I think you know more than you're letting on."
Norman rasped, narrowing his eyes at him suspiciously.
"Maybe you need time to think about it."

# XXXVIII

"Isn't it like closing the stable door after the horse has bolted?" Morgan asked with a frown.

"Maybe." Clarke muttered, giving him a disparaging look. Once he'd seen Bell and the man with the battered truck coming up the path he'd darted round the back and hidden in the garden. Once they were in the house he'd hurried over to Bells and quickly concealed a couple of bugs, one in the kitchen, the other in the living room. They should've done it the other night. "I think she saw me."

"Did she recognise you?" Morgan asked.

"If the look on her face was anything to go by, yeah."

"I thought you said she wouldn't remember anything about it."

"Most of the time they don't – dammit Morgan, what happened back there? Why didn't you warn me?"

"I tried." Morgan replied spreading his hands. "But then something happened and I could hear these two guys talking to each other…"

"What, on our frequency?" Clarke gasped, a look of disbelief on his face. "You couldn't have – it's secure!"

"You didn't hear them?"

"Of course not. Tell me what you heard."

"I was trying to get hold of you only you weren't replying and then there was all this interference – and then these two guys were talking."

"What, with radios?"

"No, that's the strange thing. They were having a conversation *together,* like we are now. And, that's not

310

all – the voice recognition software identified them as Rieker and Stevenson."

* * * * *

*"What?"* Bob gasped, on the other end of the line.

"I'm sure it's blood. And that's not all. While we were over there, something else happened." Quickly she told him about seeing the man's face at the window. Still reeling, with his face as black as thunder, Harry paced.

"At the time I thought I must've had a nightmare but when I saw him, I realised it had actually happened. "He broke into my house and I remember seeing him and then everything's a blank. When I woke up, I was sick. I searched the house but it was empty."

*"My God."* Bob breathed, horrified. "It sounds like he might've given you some kind of truth drug and questioned you."

"Harry's coming with me to the police."

"I doubt they'll do anything." Bob replied. "There's no evidence."

*"What, so he gets away with it?"* she gaped, angrily.

"Elizabeth, these people…they're a law unto themselves. Is there someplace you can stay for a while?"

"There's my sister here in the village." Elizabeth replied, clutching the phone. "But I don't want her getting mixed up in any of this. I'd rather stay here and stick it out if I can."

"Okay. But it's not safe for you to be alone. Is there someone that can stay with you?"

Turning her head, Elizabeth looked at Harry.

"Yeah." She said quietly. "There is."

\* \* \* \* \*

*"Let's get the hell out of here!"*
*"And go where?"*
*"Anyplace but here – it might be us they're looking for. Let's try and make it down there to that valley where there's cover…"*

"See?" Morgan replied. Tapping a small inset window which appeared at the top of the screen as each man spoke identifying them. "Rieker and Stevenson."

"It didn't locate the source?" Clarke asked, narrowing his eyes, staring at it intently.

"It *couldn't* locate the source." Morgan replied.

"Then how in god's name…"

"Beats me!" Morgan shrugged.

"Wherever they are it doesn't sound like they want to be found." Clarke muttered.

"You think they've defected?"

"I have no idea." Clarke read peaching for his phone. "But I'm damned well going to find out!"

\* \* \* \* \*

"What's going on?" Jack asked, coming into the hall, a mug of tea in his hand.

"It's Liz – she thinks Carter's gone missing."

"Is that Jack?" Elizabeth asked.

"Yeah."

"I don't suppose he's seen him, has he?"

"When was the last time you saw Carter?" Seth asked, turning to address Jack.

"Last time you did." He replied.

"I don't understand why you're so worried." Seth said. "He's probably popped out to the village"

Quickly, Elizabeth told him about the strange man that had been following Carter in Hadley and finding not only the key in the lock but the smear of blood next to it, finishing with the man that had broken into her house and drugged her.

*"What?"* Seth squawked, his eyes nearly falling out of his head. "My god Liz, did he hurt you?"

"No." Elizabeth said, shaking her head. "Although I was sick."

*"What's happened? Is she alright?"* Jack demanded.

"Hang on a minute Liz." Seth said quickly into the phone before looking at Jack. "She's fine!"

*"Let me speak to her!"* Jack hissed, trying to take the phone from him.

"Jack wants to speak to you." Seth said, passing it to him.

"Liz?" Jack gasped, clutching the phone tightly with both hands. "What's happened?"

\* \* \* \* \*

Flat out, half on and half off the mattress wearing only his jacket, having removed his T-shirt and jumper before knotting them together with one of his shoes for an anchor, Carter stretched as far as the chain would let him. Holding one of the jumper's arms, he tossed the bundle towards the wooden crate again, his shoe wedging itself firmly behind it this time. Afraid it might tip over and spill its contents out of reach he tugged gently. Annoyingly, it refused to budge an inch, clearly heavier than it looked. Moving at an angle to it, with the sleeve stretched around the corner, he pulled, the crate shifting this time. Encouraged, he tugged again and the crate slewed round with a dull scrape. After an excruciating eternity, at last it was within reach. Pulling it to him, with arms that ached and fingers that felt like blocks of ice, he unknotted his clothes and, with his teeth chattering with cold, put them on again.

Glancing at the window, he saw the light was beginning to fade, and, knowing there was no time to lose, fumbled the lid open seeing an assortment of rusty tools inside. Hardly able to believe his luck he found a screwdriver out and a heavy wrench. Angling himself so as to make as best use of the light that he could, he wrapped a corner of the blanket round the wrench to muffle the sound, and, jamming the screwdriver into lock of the manacle, began hammering.

\* \* \* \* \*

Hearing a loud metallic clank above him, Harry's eyes flew open, before widening with shock, as he realised he was in a chair, tilted back, a scream building in his throat as he realised where he was and what was happening

*OH-GOD-NO*

Incapable of movement he sat there, helpless, tasting the saltiness of his own blood pouring from his nose into his mouth.

Suddenly to his horror, one of them appeared above him before staring down at him with its huge black bug-eyes, tilting its head first one way them the other as if studying him.

In his mind Harry's scream rose.

Moving its head back slightly the Being raised an elongated hand before gently placing two fingers on the bridge of his nose, pain and terror vanishing in an instant.

Taking a step back the Being raised a spindly arm, indicating he stand up. Realising he could move now, looking down, Harry saw he was naked. Feeling shaky and weak he got out of the chair and, straightening, watched as the Being turned. Knowing he was meant to follow it, as they crossed the small space, Harry saw two more chairs, both empty. Going through a doorway he saw they were in a dimly lit tunnel, the ceiling so low he had to duck, passing beneath it with mere inches to spare.

Back in the spare bedroom at Elizabeth's house, the bed lay empty.

\* \* \* \* \*

In Manhattan the phone rang and, hurrying into the room Bob snatched it up, his heart pounding.

"Bob?"

Realising it wasn't Carter he sagged.

"Bob – you there?"

"Sorry – I just woke up."

"That's okay. Listen, I gotta tell you, that box of stuff you sent me is something else!"

"What did you find?"

"I hope you're sitting down."

315

Half an hour later he hung up, trembling with excitement. With no time to lose, he quickly punched in a number.

"It's me." He said breathlessly. *"I need your help!"*

\* \* \* \* \*

Narrowing his eyes Norman stiffened, hearing a dull clinking sound coming from somewhere below. Quickly unzipping the sleeping bag, he grabbed the torch and went down the hallway, light splashing over the walls as he did so. Hurrying down the steps he opened the door only to see Carter, standing on the mattress, brandishing a wrench.

"Give that to me!" Norman growled, storming into the cellar, his eyes glittering with rage. As he did so all of a sudden, somewhere outside a light snapped on, streaming through the window and filling the cellar with bright light, accompanied by a deep, rumbling, Carter suddenly filled with terror without knowing why.

*"What the…"* Norman gasped.

Shielding their eyes from the glare, they stared at the window for a moment as something in the room above them began rattling, watching in amazement as sifts of plaster from the ceiling drifted down towards them, caught in the beam of the torch. Suddenly there was a loud thud as something fell over, accompanied by the sound of clanking pipes. Turning in a circle, Carter gulped, his throat suddenly bone-dry.

*What is it dad*

As the rumble intensified, the jars in the box began clinking against each other, gently at first then louder,

316

while inside the crate the tools rattled. All of a sudden, the rumble changed frequency, and, gasping, they quickly clamped their hands over their ears. Filled with a pulsing vibration, all of a sudden, an image appeared in Carter's mind, him and his dad standing together with their arms wrapped round each other, looking up at something in terror before fading again. As it did so, in the blink of an eye, the light changed, the cellar filled with bright cobalt-blue light now, knifing down through cracks in the ceiling and gaps in the walls.

*"What's happening?"* Norman screamed, his eyes wide, stumbling backwards to join Carter on the mattress. Suddenly, overcome with a sense of weightlessness, with shock Carter realised he was no longer standing on the mattress but was hovering a few inches above it now, the man too, his eyes bulging from his sockets, wide-eyed with terror in his ashen face.

Drawn upwards, Carter jerked, his weight tugging against the manacle round his leg, the chain wrapped around the post preventing him from rising any further, anchoring him. Meanwhile, above him Norman cried out as he hit the ceiling, his hands pressed against it before flipping over on his back, his arms and legs flailing, as if swimming against an invisible tide.

*"Help me!"* he screamed down at Carter, his mouth a gash of terror.

Stretching his arms upwards Carter tried to grab hold of the man's legs but he was too high. With his head pressed hard against the ceiling and his chin jammed against his chest, all of a sudden, Normans began passing *through* it. Unable to do anything but hang in the air like a free-floating human balloon, Carter gaped in horrified

317

fascination as Normans head disappeared completely, his fingers clawing the air as his screams got fainter. Still kicking, the toes of his trainers were the last things to disappear, passing through the ceiling without a trace. *And how could that be,* Carter's mind screamed – *how was that even possible?*

And then, suddenly, without warning, the light snapped off, plunging the cellar into darkness once more and, with a clink of the chain, he landed heavily on the mattress. Unable to see a thing, for a moment, frozen with shock he simply lay there. After a while however, with the freezing air leeching the heat from his body, Carter knew if he didn't get out of here soon, he would die of hypothermia and with the man gone it was up to him to free himself. And they might come back, he thought, not sure which he feared the most, Norman or the Beings.

On all fours, he blindly groped around in the darkness before finding the screwdriver and wrench.

And something else.

At last, after what seemed an eternity, with a final bang of the wrench, Carter felt the two halves of the manacle separate. Hardly able to believe it, he pulled it from his leg and, getting to his feet, stumbled off the mattress. Going through the door, in pitch blackness he carefully mounted the wooden steps. At the top he felt his way along a wall before pausing at a doorway on his right, seeing a window, able to make out taps and a sink below it.

A kitchen.

All of a sudden, feeling a breeze, he turned his head and saw an oblong of light at the end of the hallway where the front door should've been. Going towards it he stepped through it into an overgrown front garden, the cold night air marginally warmer than the cellar had been. Seeing a car on the other side of what remained of a picket fence he hurried towards it and pulled the driver's door open, filled with dismay as he saw there were no keys in it. Straightening, he looked back at the house knowing he'd never be able to find them now, if they were here at all; for all he knew they might've been in the man's pocket when he'd been abducted.

Suddenly, like music to his ears he heard the sound of a car at a distance and, turning, hurried towards it.

# XXXIX

"Anything?" Bob asked, his voice high with tension.

"Not yet." The pretty brunette in the passenger seat said, speaking into the mobile phone. "We've driven through the village a couple of times but there's no sign of him, or anyone else for that matter. We're going to turn around at the train station and head back down in a minute though, maybe park up somewhere and just keep an eye out."

"Okay." He sighed resignedly. "And again, thanks."

"No problem." She replied. "Only too happy to help."

"Speak for yourself." The man beside her snorted.

\* \* \* \* \*

Cutting across a field, suddenly Carter saw a brief flash of headlights through some trees and, turning, hurried towards them. At last, stepping out from them, in front of him was a wooden fence beyond which was a dual carriageway, deserted. Wondering where he was, he ducked under it, at first seeing nothing but trees and stars as the road sloped upwards to the right. Turning his head however, his heart leapt as he saw a scattering of streetlights beyond the curve of the road sloping downwards. Ducking under the fence he hurried along the side of the road towards them.

Suddenly, rounding the corner he stopped dead, staring in confusion, at St. Laurence's the church not two hundred yards away, the lights of the Brentwood Down, spread out below it. Hardly able to believe it, following a narrow path down the side of the church he climbed over a small wooden style before emerging from it onto School Lane. Crossing the road, he hurried towards a plethora of houses nestled at the bottom of the hill, opposite the school. About to turn left however, all of a sudden, he froze, wondering if the house was being watched. Instead, he crossed the lane and followed the path leading to the fields behind the house.

Climbing the fence into Elizabeth's garden, he saw his uncle's house next door was in darkness, remembering the lights had been on when he'd left. Hurrying down the garden, he went to the back door but it was locked. Knocking as quietly as he could he waited in the darkness with bated breath. All of a sudden, a window opened above him, and, stepping back he saw Harry, staring down at him in amazement.

\* \* \* \* \*

*"Carter, where have you been – we've been worried sick about you!"*

*"It's a long story. I'll explain later I promise, but right now I've got to go next door without being seen – I've got to call someone urgently!"*

Shooting upright on the bed Clarke stared at Morgan in the chair, incredulously.

"I need to call someone only my phone's next door and…"

"It's not." Harry said. "It's right here."

A few minutes later, under a throw on the sofa, Bob bolted upright, snatching the phone up as he did so.

"Bob? It's Carter."

*"Jesus Christ! Where the hell have you been – we've been worried sick about you!"* Bob cried.

"You're not going to believe it when I…"

"Carter, listen to me." Bob cut in quickly. "You're in grave danger – *there are people looking for you!"*

"If you mean the man who was following me, I know." Carter sighed. "After we dropped the box off at the rendezvous, I came home and he hit me over the head from behind."

*"Box? What box?"* Clarke spluttered, looking as if he were about to explode. *"What damn rendezvous?"*

"When I came to, I was manacled to a post in a cellar in an old house not far from the village. Bob, they took him, beamed him up through the ceiling right in front of me…"

Over the road, the agents exchanged glances, Morgan's eyes like saucers in his pale face.

*"What are you talking about?"* Elizabeth gasped. Coming to her, Harry shook his head, his finger to his lips. "Calm down."

"What do you mean calm down?" she gasped, staring up at him, her face a mask of horror. "Didn't you hear what he just said? I don't understand what's going on!"

"You and me both, sweetheart!" Clarke snorted loudly.

*"You've gotta be kidding me!"* Bob gasped, gripping the phone tightly in both hands, his eyes wide. "Carter, it's not just him – there are others looking for you. You have to get out of there right now – *it's not safe!* Can anyone give you a ride?"

"My car's next door…"

"No!" Bob gasped. "They'll know it by now."

"Who?" Carter gasped, chilled. "Who will know it..."

*"Carter, for the last time..."*

"Okay, okay!" Carter gasped. "Harry's here – I'm sure he wouldn't mind giving me a lift..."

Giving him the thumbs up, Harry nodded.

"You need to get out of the village right now!" Bob said, speaking quickly. "Go back to the place you dropped the box off. Go with them."

"Go with who, where?" Carter asked, frowning.

"I'll explain everything when I see you – *go now!*"

*"Quick!"* Clarke gasped, on his feet now, pushing his gun into the holster. *"Stanbrook's about to disappear!"*

\* \* \* \* \*

"He's found him!" The woman breathed glancing at the man beside her. "He's on his way to Gallows Hill and he wants us to meet him there!"

\* \* \* \* \*

"Was that true what you said on the phone, about that man being beamed through the ceiling?" Harry asked, glancing at Carter in the passenger seat.

"Yeah."

"You saw them?"

"No, just bright light. And the sound of the craft above the house."

*"Christ."*

Looking at him, Carter shook his head. "I'm sorry you got dragged into all this Harry."

323

"It's not me I'm worried about." Harry muttered. "It's Liz." Quickly he told Carter about the man who'd broken into her house and drugged her, Elizabeth having simply having put the whole thing down to it being a terrible nightmare, that was until she'd seen his face peering in the window at them.

Horrified, Carter gaped at him. *"What?"*

"I don't know what the hell Rob did but we're all in serious bloody shit now, believe me!"

Mortified, Carter thought about the box of papers, the fact they some of the pages he'd seen had been something to with genetics, the conversation he'd had with Bob on the phone at Harry's and what the man had told him in the cellar.

*I saw it with my own eyes – the monster*

Was it true he wondered? Had his uncle and this Hely Walberg been experimenting with something not of this world and created something? A few months ago, if someone had suggested it, he'd have thought they were crazy but, knowing what he did now – after everything he'd seen and heard – unbelievable though it might be, he knew *anything* was possible.

At last, driving up Gallows Hill, heading for some trees, Carter couldn't believe it was less than twenty-four hours since they'd been here last; after what had happened, it seemed much longer. Pulling his phone out of his pocket he rang Bob. "We're here."

"They're on their way. Stay there."

"What's all this is about?" Carter asked.

"I'll explain everything when I see you."

Next to him, Harry spoke. "Are we waiting for the same bloke we met before?"

324

"Are we waiting for the man we met before?" Carter asked into the phone.

"Yeah." Bob replied. "Why?"

"Why?" Carter asked, turning his head to look at Harry.

"That's a different car."

Turning his head Carter saw a car speeding up the hill towards them.

"Did you hear that, Bob?" Carter asked.

"Yeah – what kind of car is it?" Bob asked.

"I'm not sure." Carter replied.

"A black Cadillac CTS-V Sport Wagon."

*"You have to get out of there!" Bob gasped. "Right now!"*

"It's too late." Carter whispered tightly into the phone. "They just pulled up."

\* \* \* \* \*

*"They've got them!"*

"Who?"

"I don't know but I think they're intelligence. Carter was on the phone to me when they saw the car pulling up, a black caddy!"

"Yeah, we can see it." The woman said, glancing at the man beside her. We've just pulled to the side of the road not far away. What do you want us to do?"

"Stay on the phone. Sit tight and see what happens. I don't want them seeing you or the car – *I don't want you putting yourself in danger."*

\* \* \* \* \*

325

"Carter Stanbrook?" Clarke asked walking slowly towards him, standing by the side of the truck now.

"Can I help you?" Carter croaked, his heart pounding.

"We'd like to ask you some questions regarding your uncle." Clarke said, coming to a halt a few feet away. Behind him, Morgan stood stiffly, his face a mask of angular planes of light and shadow in the bright glare of the headlights.

"My uncle?" Carter asked, taken by surprise by his American accent. "What about him?"

"About the legitimacy of his work."

"I don't know anything about that."

Narrowing his eyes, Clarke tilted his chin at him.

"You dropped a box off earlier. Care to tell me what was in it?"

"I don't know anything about any box." Carter replied a little too quickly.

"In that case, maybe you should come with us and we can discuss it further."

"I'm not going anywhere with you."

"We can do this the easy way." Clarke replied quietly, reaching behind him and withdrawing his gun. "Or we can do this the hard way."

Swallowing, Carter gaped at it, the second one pointed at him in the past twenty-four hours. "Who are you? Am I under arrest?"

"Not yet."

"Then I'm not going anywhere." Carter replied firmly, taking a step back towards the door of the truck. With a click, Clarke released the safety catch, Morgan bringing his own gun up, pointing it at Harry, through the windscreen.

* * * * *

*"Shit!"* The woman gasped, a pair of binoculars to her eyes. *"They've got guns on them!"*

* * * * *

*"Step away from the vehicle and put your hands on your head!"* Clarke demanded. *"Both of you!"*
Slowly Harry descended from the cab. A moment later, as if from nowhere, a man stepped out from the fringe of trees, into the open.
*"Let them go."*

* * * * *

"Who's that?" The woman asked, glancing at the man beside her in surprise.
"How the hell do I know?" He said squinting past her through the passenger window. "I didn't even realise he was there…"
*"What is it? What's happening?"* Bob squawked down the line.
"A man just came out from the trees." The woman replied, raising the binoculars again.

* * * * *

*"Rick?"* Harry gasped, dumbfounded.

"Let them go." Rick demanded, addressing the men with guns, ignoring him as if he hadn't spoken.

*"Who the hell are you?"* Clarke demanded.

"One of you."

"Show me your I.D!"

Instead, Rick remained as he was, his hands hanging loosely at his sides.

"I said show me your I.D!" Clarke shouted, training the gun on him.

"Let them go."

*"Put your hands on your head where I can see them and move over to the vehicle – now!"* Clarke shouted, confused by the man's lack of fear. Rooted to the spot, Carter and Harry stared from one to the other hardly daring to breathe, the atmosphere electric. Instead of moving however, Rick remained where he was, staring at Clarke disarmingly.

*"I said..."* Clarke began, stopping as he saw a flicker of movement among the trees behind him. Wondering if it had just been a trick of the light, all of a sudden, rustling came from amongst the trees seemingly from all everywhere at once, coming closer. At the sound of it, Carter's blood froze in his veins.

*what is it dad*

*"Whoever's there, come out into the open where I can see you!"* Clarke demanded, his voice echoing through the trees. Filled with fear, Carter and Harry exchanged glances, Carter desperately trying to decide which would be worse, being shot or having to face what he thought might be about to emerge from the darkness. Meanwhile, Rick, his hands at his sides, waited, an expression of amusement on his face now.

Suddenly, Morgan's eyes widened, and, taking a step back, he almost stumbled, his gun wavering as he did so. Freezing, Clarke's face was a rictus of shock. Rooted to the spot, he found himself unable to do anything other than simply stand there transfixed, all his training having gone out the window in an instant. Dropping their hands, Carter and Harry spun, staring at five small beings, standing silently not far from the truck.

* * * * *

Inside the car, the man craned his head forward, squinting at the little group on the hill intently with narrowed eyes. *"What the hell are those – kids?"*

Hardly breathing now, the woman shook her head. Even at this distance without binoculars, she had no doubt what they were.

"No Karl." she replied, her voice barely above a whisper now. "They're aliens."

* * * * *

Crying out, Harry staggered backwards his eyes wide with shock in his ashen face. Frozen to the spot, Carter gaped. Starkly illuminated in the headlights, the beings didn't look real, not like living, breathing creatures at all, more like plastic models off a sci-fi film set. Or kids in Halloween suits. At varying heights, the nearest to him was about five-foot, its skin white and pasty, its thin neck looking too fragile to be able to support its large, bulbous head, it's huge, tear-drop shaped eyes

*oh god, those eyes*

329

blacker than anything. With well-defined, almost muscular shoulders and thighs, its limbs however were stick-like with long, thin, bony hands which hung to its knees while its legs ended in small, four-toed feet. Suddenly, with a jerky movement, it turned its head to look at him and as it did so he gasped, feeling something almost physical enter his mind. Experiencing his shock and fear first-hand, their minds fused, Carter realising with utter disbelief that he was, in turn, reading *its* mind

*you know us*

knowing what it was.

*so old, so ancient*

As he did so, all of a sudden, he felt rather than saw soft white light, filling him like a vessel, his fear melting away, overwhelmed with a sense of

*coming home*

love and intense joy.

"Go."

As Rick spoke again, all of a sudden, the Beings mind withdrew from his and, reeling, he looked about him, dazed.

"Go." Rick urged again. "They can't hurt you."

"Don't move Stanbrook!" Clarke shouted. Unable to move, Carter stared at him, Harry on the other side of the truck, frozen to the spot unable to tear his eyes from the beings.

"Trust me, Carter." Rick urged. "They *can't* hurt you – their guns no longer work – *just go.*"

# *XL*

*"They can't be…they're not real…"* The man croaked weakly, pole-axed.

"They look pretty real to me!" The woman whispered, her eyes wide in her pale face.

*"Are you shitting me or what?"* Bobs voice squawked from the phone she still held in her hand sounding almost hysterical. *"What's happening?"*

Realising she'd momentarily forgotten all about him, she spoke. "Someone's shouting…I think the man that came out the trees is telling them to go."

"He's telling them to go?" Bob gasped. "What about the men with the guns?"

"Hang on a minute."

Next to her the man gripped the steering wheel tightly, his face as white as a sheet, unable to tear his eyes from the creatures on the hill.

\* \* \* \* \*

*"Move and I'll shoot!"* Clarke rasped, taking a step forward.

*"Harry!"* Carter barked, "Get in the truck!"

Looking up as if not sure where he was for a moment, Harry turned. At the door Carter paused and looked at Rick again, still unable to believe any of this was actually happening, before climbing in the passenger seat and slamming the door behind him. Dropping the muzzle of the gun, Clarke aimed it at one of the front tyres and pulled the trigger.

*Nothing.*

*"What the…"* he gasped, looking at it, checking the safety catch was off. Next to him Morgan levelled his own gun at the truck and fired.

*Nothing.*

Turning his head, Clarke stared at Rick.

*"How?"* he gasped.

As the truck lurched forward, Clarke suddenly leapt in front of it and rebounded off the side of it with a bang before falling backwards, spread-eagled on the grass. Turning, Morgan raced towards the caddy, but, just like the guns, it too refused to work.

\* \* \* \* \*

*"They're coming down the track!"* The woman cried.

"They've let him go?" Bob gasped, incredulous.

"Something's happened. I don't think the men's car will start…"

"They're not following him?"

"No."

"Either follow him or get him to follow you but either way make sure those men don't see you!" Bob hissed urgently now. "Pick him up further on down the road out of sight!"

"Will do." She replied, dropping the phone into her lap without hanging up. Turning to look at the man, she was shocked to see how pale he was.

*"Karl!"* she gasped quickly, grabbing his arm. *"Snap out of it – come on!"*

\* \* \* \* \*

"There's a car behind us flashing its lights – *I think it's them!*" Carter gasped, turning, one hand on the dashboard as the truck slewed from one side of the narrow lane to the other.

"They'll have to follow us for a bit." Harry said glancing in the wing mirror. "Cos I'm not stopping for anything!"

After a mile or so he pulled to the side of the road. A few moments later the Land Rover appeared and stopped in front of the truck, a woman emerging from the passenger side even before it had stopped moving. Opening the door, Carter got out, staring at her as she came towards the truck.

"You live an exciting life, Carter." She said breathlessly, looking up at him.

"Not through choice, believe me!" he snorted, shaking his head.

"Therese Vaughn." She said quickly, extending her hand. "I believe you've already met my husband, Karl." Nodding, Carter looked at the man in the driver's seat of the Land Rover, staring through the windscreen, un-movingly. "He's in shock, seeing those things…we both are."

"I'm not surprised. Do you have any idea what all this is about?"

"Not in the slightest." She replied shaking her head. "All I know is we've got to pick you up and get you as far away from here as possible and I mean, *right now.* We can't risk those men coming after us."

"Okay." Carter said, turning back towards the truck. Remaining where she was, Therese watched him.

333

Opening the door, Carter looked at Harry. "I've got to go – will you be okay?"

"Yeah."

"I mean after what happened back there…"

"I know what you meant." Harry replied gruffly, nodding. "You sure you can trust them?" he said indicating Therese.

"I don't have much choice, do I?"

Nodding silently, Harry stared at him.

"Thanks for everything Harry – I don't know what I'd have done without you." Carter said, suddenly, reluctant to leave him. Over the past twenty-four hours he and Harry had bonded like he'd never have imagined possible, their horrific experiences at the hands of extra-terrestrials, inextricably having drawn them together.

"I'm sorry about what happened to Elizabeth."

"She'll be okay." Harry said. "I'll make sure of it."

"I know you will Harry." Carter replied.

Closing the door, he hurried after Therese towards the Land Rover and climbed in the back, Karl barely acknowledging him as he did so. As it lurched forward, Carter turned and looked back at the truck, all of a sudden filled with the conviction he'd never see Harry again, his heart unexpectedly heavy.

\* \* \* \* \*

*"They can't have got far!"* Morgan growled pressing his foot down on the accelerator, trying to concentrate on his driving instead of what had just happened.

After the truck had disappeared from sight, the man called Rick had had turned and disappeared back into the trees again, the five Beings following suit. At the same time, the car engine had spluttered to life, and, holding his ribs, Clarke had hurried over and lowered himself onto the passenger seat with a grunt. With his nerves jangling he'd stalled the engine twice before turning in a wide arc and speeding down the hill towards the road. Beside him, unable to rid himself of the images of the Beings, Clarke knew his life had just been irrevocably changed forever.

* * * * *

As the Land Rover disappeared from sight round the corner, with hands that shook, Harry gripped the steering wheel tightly, his breath coming in short, little spurts, an icy hand gripping his stomach. Ever since the day he'd been taken aboard the UFO, he'd lived in terror of it happening again, of coming face to face with those things and, up there on Gallows Hill just now, his worst fears had come true.

*they came back*

Frozen to the spot with terror, he'd felt like he was about to collapse, part of him even hoping he would, just so long as he didn't have to stand there looking at them, in that moment, tempted to grab the gun and kill them all, imagining the ground littered with alien bodies, bleeding out onto the grass. And what the hell had Rick – *Rick who pulled his pints in the Red Lion* – been doing with them? Between them they'd helped him and Carter escape and, under the circumstances he supposed he should be grateful, but no matter how hard he tried, he couldn't forget what those things had done to him that day in the UFO.

*To his dying day, he'd hate them.*

Starting the engine, he reversed the truck over the road and killed the engine. Popping the glove box open he took the handgun out that Carter had given him earlier – the caretaker's gun he'd found on the mattress after the abduction. Getting out, he leaned on the bonnet, and, gun in hand, waited.

\* \* \* \* \*

"We've got him." Therese said.

*"Thank God!"* Bob gasped, his relief evident. To say he'd been on edge the past few hours would be an understatement and even though Carter was safe for now, he wouldn't be happy until everything was in place.

"Where shall we take him – ours?"

"Please." Bob replied. "I'll get the ball rolling this end. Can I speak to him?"

"He wants to talk to you." Therese said turning in her seat, handing Carter the phone.

"Thanks." Carter said putting it to his ear.

"Carter – are you okay?"

"Yeah, but you're not going to believe what just happened…"

"I've got a pretty good idea."

"You have?"

"Therese and Karl were parked up at the foot of the hill and I was on the phone the whole while. Carter, you'll be safe with them but I want you to do something. You need to throw your cell phone out the window."

"What?" Carter gasped. "Why?"

"Because your location can be traced through it, triangulated. Do it *right now."*

"But it's got all my numbers in it…"

"Never mind your numbers, just do it!" Bob insisted urgently.

"Okay, hang on a sec." Carter said wedging the phone between his ear and his shoulder while pulling his mobile out of his pocket. Winding the window down, after a slight hesitation he threw it out, Karl watching him in the mirror before glancing at Therese in amazement.

"I've done it – it's gone." Carter said holding the phone to his ear once more.

"Good. Now, don't contact *anyone* and stay inside when you arrive otherwise all this will have been for nothing, not to mention putting Karl and Therese's lives at risk, do you understand?"

"Yeah." Carter said, straightening in his seat. "But how long for? I mean, I've got work and…"

"Forget all that, Carter."

"What do you mean forget all that?" Carter gasped.

"Carter, I've got to go." Bob said quickly. "We'll talk later, I promise, but for now, put Therese back on, will you?"

\* \* \* \* \*

Hearing the sound of a car approaching Harry stiffened and, taking a deep breath, released the safety catch. As the caddy rounded the bend, Harry fired the gun at one of tyres, Morgan instantly losing control. As it hurtled towards the truck, he slammed the steering wheel

337

to the left. Missing the truck by inches, it ploughed headlong into the hedge at the side of the road with a loud crunch and a tinkle of glass, the wing mirrors snapping off as it did so. Propelled forward Clarke head-butted the windscreen while the steering wheel slammed into Morgan's mid-riff, knocking the air from his lungs.

Gasping with pain, Clarke pushed himself off the dashboard, everything around him spinning, his vision a swarm of black dots. As it cleared, he saw Morgan, slumped over the steering wheel. Grabbing his shoulder, he pressed his fingers to his neck, feeling a pulse.

*Alive.*

On the road behind them, the trucks' engine spluttered to life. Spinning, Clarke tried to open the door but it was wedged firmly shut against the hedge. With a crunch of tyres, the truck passed them, the sound of the engine dwindling as it roared off.

*"You God-damned red-neck piece of shit I'm gonna fucking kill you, you hear me?"* Clarke bawled hoarsely at the empty road. Five minutes later, Morgan leaned against the car holding his stomach looking pasty and sick. Glancing at him, Clarke spoke quickly into his cell phone. "Yes Sir...Yes Sir I understand that but..." As the other end hung up, he stared down at it in his hands, his eyes burning with rage, for a moment tempted to hurl it over the hedge.

Next to the car, Morgan collapsed.

\* \* \* \* \*

Dialling a number, after a few rings, it was picked up.

"He's safe for now, at least." Bob said down the phone. "But I want him over here as soon as possible."

"Does he know what's going on?"

"Not a clue." Bob replied, giving his head a quick shake. "Poor bastard."

\* \* \* \* \*

In the car, having just left Elizabeth's after Harry had returned, Jack and Seth stared in amazement at a black van which shot past them at high speed before screeching to a halt outside Elizabeth house. Wide-eyed, they watched as three men in dark suits hurried up Elizabeths garden path.

"Who the hell are they?" Jack gasped.

"You think they're the ones who are after Carter?"

"Maybe."

"We need to call the police." Seth gasped.

"No." Jack replied, shaking his head. "You know what Harry said – we're not to discuss any of this with anyone."

"I know but we've got to do *something!*"

\* \* \* \* \*

*"Who the hell are you?"* Elizabeth gasped, staring at the men as they burst in. *"Get out of my house!"*

Seeing the guns in their hands however, she fell silent, staring at them in shock. At the sight of them, Harry's heart sunk. Waving a gun at him, one of the men indicated the back door. *"You, out!"*

On her feet, Bess barked loudly, her teeth bared.

Resignedly Harry picked his stick up and limped towards it.

"You too." The other said to Elizabeth.

*"No!"* Harry gasped, spinning. *"Leave her out of this – this is nothing to do with her!"*

*"Out!"* The man said jamming the gun against his ribs. Behind a hedge a few doors down, Jack and Seth watched them cross the drive before getting in the van and speeding away.

*"They've taken them!"* Seth gasped, his eyes wide. Hurrying round the back Jack opened the door. Beneath the table, Bess growled.

"She's scared stiff."

"I'm not surprised." Seth said, stroking her silky head. "Her owner's just been kidnapped at gunpoint."

Narrowing his eyes, Jack stared at him askance. *"She doesn't know what a gun is does she?"*

"What are we going to do?"

"We need to get hold of that chap in New York, the one that helped Carter." Jack replied, going out into the hall. "She said he called him earlier so it might be on last number redial."

Stiffly, Seth stood in the doorway, watching him.

Clutching the phone to his ear with both hands, Jack waited expectantly.

"Harry?" A voice asked.

"No." Jack said quickly. "My names Jack Solomon – I'm Harry's friend." Quickly he told Bob how three men had just taken Elizabeth and Harry at gunpoint before driving off with them.

*"No!"* Bob gasped loudly down the phone, horrified.

"Me and Seth – my other friend – we don't know what to do."

"You did the right thing calling me. Stay where you are so I can get hold of you."

"Will do." Jack nodded. "What's going to happen to them?"

"They probably just want to find out where Carter's gone. I'm going to try and get hold of someone who might be able to help. In the meantime, just sit tight, okay?"

"Okay."

Hanging up Bob cursed, before quickly punching in another number, filled with fear.

* * * * *

Waking up, Carter blinked, his eyes feeling sore and grainy. Downstairs he could hear the sound of a television, it's volume low.

When they'd arrived at the cottage, after eating a hearty breakfast – the first thing he'd eaten since God-knows-when – Therese had shown him to a bedroom and, judging by the light beyond the window, he must've slept all day. Reluctant to relinquish what might very well turn out to be a mere pit stop of peace and tranquillity on the white-knuckled roller coaster his life had become, he decided to stay where he was for the moment.

# *XLI*

After recovering from the shock of being taken from her own house at gun point, cold, hungry and tired, Elizabeth was in no mood to be messed with.

After being bundled into the car they'd had black hoods put over their heads and after driving for what had seemed an eternity, eventually it had drawn to a halt. Hearing a barrier being raised they'd moved forward before stopping again a few moments later. After being helped out they'd been frog-marched into a building, their footsteps echoing hollowly along a passageway. At last, her hood had been whipped off and blinking, she'd found herself in a drab, grey room with no window, nothing in it but a table and two chairs. After being invited to sit, the soldier had left the room, locking the door behind him. At last, a man in a grey slate suit joined her.

"Where's Harry?" She demanded hotly jumping to her feet, her eyes sparkling with anger. "Who are you and what do you want?"

Without answering, the man took a seat before staring back at her coolly, his light brown eyes almost the same colour as his hair, his skin yellow and sickly-looking in the light from the fluorescent tube suspended from the ceiling above them. In his mid-thirties, tall and slim with wide shoulders and a chiselled jaw he was undeniably handsome, however, all she wanted to do in that moment was slap him. "I'll ask the questions if you don't mind." He replied with an American accent.

"Are we under arrest?"

"No."

"So why are we here then? What do you want?"

"We want to ask you some questions, that's all."

*"Go to hell!"*

"We can do this the easy way or the hard way."

"What does that mean?" she gasped. "What are you going to do, torture us?"

Annoyingly the man rolled his eyes at her. "We've come a long way since those days. We have more up to date methods of extracting the truth now."

"Meaning?"

"Meaning we no longer have to beat the hell out of you." he ground out, leaning forward, his eyes narrowed. "Just a quick jab and you'll tell us everything we need to know."

"Was that what made me sick?" she demanded.

"I'm sorry." The man replied, spreading his hands. "I don't know what you're talking about…"

*"Liar!"* she gasped. "Where's Harry? I want to see him."

"I'm afraid that's not possible right now."

*"I want to see him right now!"*

"If anything happens to him…"

"Ma'am, if you don't mind…"

*"Don't ma'am me!"* she spat angrily, poking her head towards him. *"Who the hell do you think you are?"*

Rolling his eyes, the man took a deep breath.

It was going to be a long day.

* * * * *

In Carter's flat, two men were systematically searching it, opening every cupboard and drawer, taking

343

everything apart, leaving nothing to chance. After every notebook, file and notepad had been boxed up, they were taken down to the unmarked van outside. Back inside, a man went from room to room with a blacklight, checking the floor, walls and ceilings for hidden codes or writings. In the bedroom he shone it at the wall behind the bed.

Wide-eyed he stiffened.

Holding the blacklight closer, the image sharpened, the purple light revealing an elongated handprint on the headboard. And one on the wall above it, higher up. Putting the light on the bed, he took a small camera from his pocket and took a few shots before lowering it again, his heart racing, filled with the usual heady mix of fear and excitement at the sight of them.

*Alien handprints.*

Meanwhile, in the house he'd grown up in, a woman made her way up the stairs to the second floor, before diligently searching the main bedroom, torch in hand. After finding nothing she went through another door into a smaller one, her heart leaping into her mouth at the sight of the three creatures on the wall staring back at her. Chilled, she raised a small camera to her eyes and took a few shots. After searching the room and finding nothing, she shivered as she passed them on her way out, and hurried down the stairs, the image of the creatures behind her, startlingly vivid in her mind.

\* \* \* \* \*

In another part of the building, handcuffed to a chair, keeping his eyes on the floor, Harry refused to look at the man in rolled-up shirtsleeves pacing back and forth in front of him.

"Again – where did you take him Harry? Who did you meet?"

*"Go to hell."*

Stopping, with his hands on his hips the man glared at him. "You're not doing yourself any favours, you know that, right?" he said in an American accent. "Nor your lady-friend. Your co-operation could go a long way to making sure her stay here is a pleasant one. On the other hand, if you don't…"

Raising his eyes, Harry's eyes narrowed. *"If anything happens to her…"*

"I don't think you realise how much shit you're in, old man!" The man spat, his face only inches from Harry's now. "You discharged an illegal firearm in a public place at a governmental car putting a man in the hospital, allowing the subject of an ongoing investigation to escape." Straightening, he stared down at him, his eyes glittering with anger. "Where is he Harry? Where did he go?"

"I to you, I don't know what you're talking about. I don't know anything."

"Really?" the man asked coming forward, his fists clenched. "Let's see about that, shall we?"

\* \* \* \* \*

After dinner, Carter joined Therese and Karl in the lounge.

"I've always had a thing about aliens so I became an alien abduction researcher, interviewing people, making

345

reports and such." Therese said. "I met Bob at a UFO convention a few years ago. We kept in touch and became good friends. I often ring him if I need advice about something. When he called me, we were only too pleased to help."

"I still can't believe what we saw up there on that hill." Karl said, shaking his head. "I just can't get my head around it."

"Karl's more, let's say, 'down to earth' than I am." Therese explained. "He's not sure about the whole UFO, alien thing. Or at least, he wasn't."

"Believe me, I know what you're going through." Carter said quietly looking at him. "The first time I saw them, I couldn't believe what I was seeing; I couldn't believe they exist, still can't in fact. Since then, I've hardly slept and when I do, I'm right back there and it's all happening over and over again."

"They helped you escape, them and that man."

"I know."

"Why?"

"I don't know."

"Do you know who he was?"

"Yeah, he's the barman in a pub in the village."

"Why was he with them?"

"I have no idea." Carter sighed, running a hand over his face. "Nothing makes sense anymore."

Taking a deep breath, he told them about his encounter in the woods followed by Harry's revelations about seeing him on the UFO standing among the aliens.

"How are you coping?" Therese asked, Karl looking horrified.

"I'm not sure. One minute I'm ok, the next…"

"It takes awhile." She nodded. "But at least once you're in the States, Bob will be able to help you through it."

"What?" Carter asked, confused.

Looking at each other, Karl and Therese exchanged glances. "We thought you knew." Karl said. "Bob's having you smuggled out of the country to the U.S!"

"You've got to be joking!" Carter gasped down the phone to Bob a few minutes later. "I'm not going to the U.S on a forged passport – *I'll end up in prison...*"

"Ending up in prison is the least of your problems right now, believe me." Bob said. "Look Carter, I know a lot's happened and you're scared and confused, but you have no idea how much danger you're in. I'll explain everything once you're here, I promise."

"Why can't you tell me now?" Carter asked.

"Now is not the time, believe me." Bob said quietly. "You've just got to trust me – I'm the only one that can help you, right now."

\* \* \* \* \*

"We have to let them go."

"What?" McCarthy gasped. "Why?"

"We're being blackmailed."

*"Blackmailed?"* McCarthy squawked, hardly able to believe what he was hearing. "With what?"

"Full disclosure."

\* \* \* \* \*

347

*"Jesus Christ!"* Seth gasped staring at Harry sporting a split lip and a vividly colourful black eye. "They've made a right mess of you!"

"I've had worse." Harry replied quietly, his hand on Bess's head. Since Jack and Seth had brought her back, she hadn't left his side, not for a minute.

*"Who the hell do they think they are threating old people like that?"* Jack ejaculated angrily.

"Less of the old." Elizabeth said, shooting him a look.

"Okay so what now?" Seth asked, looking from one to the other in turn. "You're going to *have* to tell the police now, aren't you?"

"No."

*"What in God's name are you talking about?"* Jack gasped his eyes wide with disbelief. *"Why not?"*

"For what I did, they could've thrown the book at me – I'm can't believe they haven't. All I know is, I've had a lucky escape."

"But what about what they've put you through, Liz?" Jack gasped, staring at her. "They can't just get away with it…"

"They said if we went to the police, we'd be compromising Millie's safety." She said quietly, hugging herself.

*"Christ!"*

"What, so we just forget any of it happened?" Jack gasped, spreading his hands, his eyes bright with anger.

"That's *exactly* what we're going to do." Harry replied, fixing them with his eyes. *"All of us."*

\* \* \* \* \*

348

The next evening, just after dinner, the phone rang. Hurrying into the hallway, after a few moments Therese came back into the kitchen, her yes bright with excitement. "We've got to be at Pilton airfield in an hour."

In his chair, Carter froze. "Already?"

"Yeah." She nodded, tossing the car keys to Karl. "We'd better get a move on!"

Five minutes later minutes later, they sped through the countryside, Carter on the back seat with his stomach churning, staring at the darkness beyond the window, gain wondering how any of this could actually be happening. At last, they arrived at a small, private airport, the buildings nothing more than dark, misty shapes in the fine rain. As they approached, a car flashed its lights and, pulling to a stop Karl got out and went over to it before returning a few moments later, a large envelope in his hand. "Your documentation." he said handing it to Carter.

After thanking them for everything they'd done, still unable to believe he was actually going to do this, reluctantly he went toward the plane, glancing back at them one last time as he did so, his stomach a tight knot of fear. As it took off, filled with a sense of unescapable destiny, Carter's fingers tightened on the armrest, the plane buffeted by the oncoming storm as it headed into the night, it's precious cargo, for now, safe.